RISE

of the

ARCANE FIRE

ALSO BY KRISTIN BAILEY

The Secret Order · Book One
Legacy of the Clockwork Key

RISE

✧ of the ✧

ARCANE FIRE

Kristin Bailey

Simon Pulse

New York   London   Toronto   Sydney   New Delhi

SIMON PULSE

An imprint of Simon & Schuster Children's Publishing Division

1230 Avenue of the Americas, New York, NY 10020

First Simon Pulse hardcover edition February 2014

Text copyright © 2014 by Kristin Welker

Jacket tentacle sculpture and photograph copyright © 2014 by Matthew Lentini

Jacket photographs of Scotland copyright © 2014 by Chris Clor/Getty Images

Jacket design by Regina Flath

All rights reserved, including the right of reproduction in whole or in part in any form.

SIMON PULSE and colophon are registered trademarks of Simon & Schuster, Inc.

For information about special discounts for bulk purchases, please contact

Simon & Schuster Special Sales at 1-866-506-1949 or business@simonandschuster.com.

The Simon & Schuster Speakers Bureau can bring authors to your live event.

For more information or to book an event contact the Simon & Schuster Speakers

Bureau at 1-866-248-3049 or visit our website at www.simonspeakers.com.

Interior design by Angela Goddard

The text of this book was set in Granjon.

Manufactured in the United States of America

10 9 8 7 6 5 4 3 2 1

Library of Congress Cataloging-in-Publication Data

Bailey, Kristin, author.

Rise of the arcane fire / Kristin Bailey. — First Simon Pulse hardcover edition.

p. cm. — (The Secret Order ; book 2)

Summary: As the first female member of the Amusementists, an elite secret society in Victorian England dedicated to discovery, Margaret Whitlock is determined to prove her worth—but someone is trying to sabotage the society by altering their inventions to make them dangerous, and it is up to Meg to expose the plot.

ISBN 978-1-4424-6802-3 (alk. paper)

[1. Secret societies—Juvenile fiction. 2. Conspiracies—Juvenile fiction. 3. Sabotage—Juvenile fiction. 4. Inventions—Juvenile fiction. 5. London (England)—History—19th century—Juvenile fiction. 6. Great Britain—History—Victoria, 1837–1901—Juvenile fiction.] I. Title.

PZ7.B15256Ri 2014 [Fic]—dc23 2013033791

ISBN 978-1-4424-6804-7 (eBook)

To my husband, Troy,
for all the times we've been apart and I've only loved you more

CHAPTER ONE

"HOP, DAMMIT," I MUTTERED AS I PUSHED BACK FROM the table and rubbed my burning eyes. The lantern flickered, nearly out of oil, and my entire body ached from hunching over the absurd little contraption before me.

It was hardly elegant. Or even whimsical.

The oddly shaped mechanical frog stared up at me with enormous eyes that I had fashioned from inky black marbles. It trembled, as if terrified of what I might do should it fail to obey. Eventually the cog in its back wound down without the frog budging so much as an inch.

Sighing, I blinked back my exhaustion, then glanced at the notes from one of a dozen books lying open on the table.

Finally I made one last attempt to adjust the spring in the left leg.

It was hopeless. I couldn't do this.

When I had become the shopkeeper for Pricket's Toys and Amusements, I'd known it was a very special place. While it may have seemed outwardly like a normal, if somewhat curious, shop in the heart of Mayfair, I knew it held a secret.

The former owner had been part of a reclusive society, the Secret Order of Modern Amusementists. The Order boasted a membership that included some of the finest minds in all of Europe, perhaps even the world. They would gather and challenge one another to great feats of invention, purely for whimsy—and also to line their pockets with a wager or two on the outcome.

I had seen some of the wonders the Order had created. They were haunting, often terrifying, but always beautiful. My own family had been part of the Order for generations. Both of my grandfathers had been high-ranking members. My father as well. But they had kept it all from me.

I supposed I couldn't blame them, considering that their involvement with the Order had led to their ruin.

If my adventures in the spring had taught me anything, it

was that genius often comes hand in hand with madness, and some secrets could kill.

There had been a string of murders within the Order about five years earlier. During that time, my grandfather had disappeared. His carriage had been found in the river, and by all accounts he was presumed dead. But that had hardly been the last tragedy to befall my family. A year ago I lost my parents as well, which forced me into destitution.

I had known nothing of my family's secrets when Lord Rathford took me into his household as a maid, claiming to be a benefactor. It turned out he'd only wished to use the master key my grandfather had left me, to unlock a horrible invention that had had the potential to destroy the entire world as we knew it.

It was fear of that invention that had driven Rathford's nemesis, Strompton, to murder. He would have stopped at nothing to keep the terrible invention from ever seeing the light of day.

The entire ordeal had been both terrifying and illuminating.

Now, even knowing the worst of the Order, I couldn't help myself. I wanted so badly to be a part of it. I took the frog in my hands and stroked my finger over the cool metal plate that formed the top of his head.

Perhaps that is why I'd taken over management of Pricket's Toys and Amusements.

Simon Pricket had been a gifted young Amusementist and a protégé of my father's. Tragically, he had also been a victim of the murderer. Before Simon's death, he had accumulated an entire library of prolific notes from his time as an apprentice, and then as historian and inventor for the Order. Reading them had been a revelation. Unfortunately, the elaborate texts only encouraged me to fancy myself an Amusementist.

It was an admirable, if futile, pursuit. After all, I had seen firsthand the wondrous machines my own family had built. During my adventures I had discovered a dome of stars hidden deep in the earth beneath an iron replica of Stonehenge, a labyrinth complete with a mechanical Minotaur, a set of gilded wings, and a clockwork ship set to do battle with a monstrous leviathan. Within the Order anything was possible, even tearing apart the fabric of time.

All this potential hung like tantalizing fruit before me, just out of my reach. Honestly, I didn't see the good of being born into a secret society of inventors if I couldn't make a measly toy frog hop.

I placed the frog back on the desk and rubbed the soreness from my neck. It wasn't as if dreaming about becoming an Amusementist would accomplish anything. I'd been born a girl, so I could never be part of the Order.

I could rail against the unfairness of it all, but it would be little use. I couldn't change what was. But no one and nothing could stop me from reading and tinkering in my own shop—except, it seemed, my own inability to create an insipid frog. I slammed my hand down on the desk, and the blasted frog bounced up into the air.

Wonderful.

A substantial lust for invention couldn't imbue me with comprehension of the finer points of compressing springs.

I slumped face-first onto one of Simon's journals, the mathematical scribblings turning into blurry patches of gray just beyond my nose. Simon had written that through mathematics, all the secrets of God's creation could be unraveled. If only those secrets could seep into my skull as I rested. I wanted to invent a machine that could accomplish *that*.

My eyes burned and I couldn't keep them open any longer, but of course I couldn't sleep. I could fall over from exhaustion, but I couldn't sleep. I hadn't been able to sleep for a week. Every time I let go and began to drift off, I saw the flames, heard the ticking clocks and shattering crystal.

I jolted upright out of habit.

The knot in my shoulder grew worse, and I tried to soothe the ache there. My body was wound tighter than the troublesome spring. I didn't feel I could eat, because, in spite of my appetite, everything I attempted turned sour and made me feel ill.

This was no sort of life for a sixteen-year-old girl. All the other girls my age fretted about dresses, and gossip, who invited whom to tea, and the latest society ball. Instead I spent every waking moment thinking about death—my own and the deaths of the ones I had loved.

My eyes pained me the worst of all. If I cried, perhaps they would burn less, but I couldn't bring myself to do it.

One year ago exactly I had fallen asleep in my father's clock shop on a night as unassuming as the one currently surrounding me. I tried, but I couldn't remember the book I'd been reading that night. I did recall that it had been the farthest thing possible from advanced mathematics but nearly as boring. It had been a frothy story, and I remember feeling the girl at the heart of it had been a mindless ninny. I don't know why I'd stayed up to read, other than the fact that, no matter how terrible a story is, I always must know how it will end. So much ended that night.

I couldn't recall falling asleep, but I did remember distinctly the moment I had woken.

It had been a crash that had startled me. I'd opened my eyes, then fallen out of my chair. Smoke like a heavy fog pushed down. I couldn't see the ceiling as I pressed my face to the Turkish rug and coughed until I feared blood would pour from my lungs. My eyes burned, tearing so badly, I could hardly see. The heat seared my skin like the fires of hell itself. I saw the flames flickering in the gallery and licking up the walls, turning the drapes to ash as they burned.

Like a horse, panicked and seeking safety in a burning stable, I crawled toward the stairs. Smoke poured up them and away from me, like a murky river flowing topsy-turvy along the ceiling, spilling up into our home above the shop.

I screamed for my parents. There was no answer.

The crystals of the clocks in the gallery shattered one by one with loud pops that sounded like gunfire.

I had to get out.

I dragged myself along the floor until I managed to escape out into the small courtyard in the back of the house. The windows from the upper floors burst from the heat, raining glass down on me as the flames roared out of them. I heard the clanging bell of the fire wagon as I searched the courtyard for my parents, then fervently prayed they had escaped out the front.

They had not.

The disaster left me alone and destitute in Lord Rathford's house of madness.

It wasn't until I uncovered Lord Rathford's dangerous plot to alter the fabric of time that I discovered the true culprit behind the fire.

Rathford's time machine allowed me a glimpse into the past, and in it I witnessed a man with a clockwork mask that covered half his face. He was in the gallery of my father's shop at the moment it burst into flames.

I stopped Lord Rathford and his terrible machine and also exposed Lord Strompton as the real murderer of Simon Pricket and several other Amusementists. But it was all for naught, because the man who had killed my parents was still at large. He had hunted me across the English countryside trying to capture my grandfather's master key.

He was still hunting me.

I didn't think I would ever sleep again.

Something rattled in the front of Pricket's shop, a distant tapping, like a wooden bead dropped onto the floor. It brought my thoughts back to the present moment.

I twisted in my chair, immediately alert. Holding deathly still, I listened for any sound at all besides the frantic thumping of my heart. I slid my hand beneath the table and withdrew my pistol from the compartment hidden there.

It felt heavy in my hand as I stood from the table and stepped toward the secret door that led from my workshop to the toy shop out front. The sound could have been nothing, only a rat most likely. I heard something thump.

That was no rat.

With my heart in my throat, I readied the pistol, feeling the strain in my pinched shoulder and praying I didn't have to use the weapon. My insides twisted into knots as I stepped into the toy shop.

The door to the workshop closed behind me with a soft *snick* and appeared once more as a high shelf of picture books and tins of toy soldiers to the left of the counting desk.

"I'm armed, and I will fire," I warned the silent shop. Dawn was beginning to break, the first dim light casting the room in eerie shadows. My hand shook, but my resolve did not.

The marionettes hung from the ceiling, their faces staring down on me like macabre grimaces of contorted men at the gallows.

I drew my gaze away from them as I searched for a single thing out of place.

The bell hanging from the front door swung like the slow pendulum of a clock. I even thought I heard a soft ticking.

"Miss Margaret!"

I wheeled toward the door to the living quarters behind the toy shop, my heart leaping into my throat. I brandished my pistol at the tiny old woman before me.

Mrs. Brindle, the housekeeper, screamed and dropped a tray laden with a pair of teacups and a plate of cheese. It crashed to the floor.

I immediately laid the pistol on a shelf and rushed to her side. She had her hand clutched to her chest.

"Mrs. Brindle, oh my goodness. I'm so sorry." I propped her up. Her wrinkled face had gone ashen. Dear Lord, I hoped I hadn't just sent the eighty-year-old woman into an apoplectic fit. She was the favorite nursemaid of Simon Pricket's widow. I had met Lucinda Pricket while on the trail of the murderer, and she had become my best friend. Mrs. Brindle's death would probably not be received well.

"For love and mercy, child," Mrs. Brindle scolded. Her arthritic hands shook as she carefully righted her nightcap. "What are you doing with that horrible thing?"

"I thought I heard a burglar," I said, though that seemed to pale in comparison to the truth of the matter. I feared murder. *My own murder.*

I helped poor Mrs. Brindle up, her thin white hair standing out at odds from beneath her cap. For as much as we both pretended she was there to look out for me, I knew the opposite to be true. After losing her usefulness as a nursemaid, she had been destitute. She needed both a home and a salary in her dotage, so Lucinda had hired her on as the housekeeper and an informal chaperone for me. I didn't mind in the least, and was simply glad for her company.

"Well, dear, if it was a burglar, best let him have what he's after. A fine young girl such as you should never take on something so base as a pistol." Showing the resiliency that had served her well through eight decades of life, she began cleaning up the fallen tray as if nothing had happened.

I couldn't quite grasp her logic. I was to become a victim of burglary, or worse, so as not to debase myself by holding the weapon? My recent brushes with death had changed my outlook on many things, especially propriety. I had discovered a newfound sense of practicality when it came to saving my life.

Thankfully, Will understood. In fact, he'd been the one

who'd taught me to use the pistol. He didn't like leaving me alone with only Mrs. Brindle, and occasionally her son Bob, for protection. My hands shook as I helped Mrs. Brindle with the tray.

Will had been the groom for Lord Rathford while I had been a maid serving in his house. I had conscripted poor Will as an often unwilling partner in my quest to discover the truth of what had happened to my family. During that time he had proven himself a brave, devoted, and clever companion. I touched my lips. Not to mention an amorous one.

It didn't hurt that he was handsome as the Devil, with dark hair, and eyes as still and fathomless as a moonless night.

Will had accompanied me to my parents' graves the first Sunday of every month since our return to London. Though my fear at the thought of an intruder in the toy shop still stuck in my throat, anticipating Will's arms around me filled me with warmth. When he held me, the world felt right and no danger could touch me.

Once again I thought I heard the soft *tick, tick, tick* of a clock.

It must have been a trick of my mind, the old memory of the clocks amid the flames. I was slowly losing my sanity.

Mrs. Brindle touched my arm, pulling my attention back

to the task at hand. "Have you slept at all?" she asked, her faded eyes too perceptive.

"Of course," I lied.

Mrs. Brindle shook her head slowly. "Don't fuss with this mess. I'll set it right. Kate will be in later to help straighten things upstairs. Go wash your face and share a cup of tea with me."

"Thank you." In spite of her words I found myself bending to gather the ruined tea. Mrs. Brindle was lively for her remarkable age, but I always felt inclined to care for her, much like a dutiful granddaughter would. I had few memories of my own grandmothers, and in my own simple way it made me feel as if I had a family again.

As I lifted the tray to the counting desk in the corner, I glanced at the small picture frame I kept next to the ledger. Frozen in time, my grandfather laughed as he demonstrated a floating top to a young boy and girl. He looked so alive. I felt as if I could touch his image and set it in motion, bringing him back. He was the only true family I had left.

I had seen proof that he'd faked his death to escape being murdered. He was out there somewhere. For the past several weeks I'd been waiting for word from him. I had thought that once I'd unraveled the conspiracy to kill anyone who'd aided in the construction of Rathford's time machine, he would return. Yet the days continued to pass, and there was no sign of him.

I closed my eyes and prayed that no misfortune had befallen my dear Papa, and yet I knew. The man with the clockwork mask had had something to do with his disappearance. I had to find my grandfather. Wherever he was, I had to somehow reach him and bring him home.

Mrs. Brindle took the frame from my hand. She touched the curls of the little girl in the picture, as if she remembered brushing them the morning the picture had been taken. "Lady Lucinda was a lovely child."

"And Oliver's hair still doesn't sit right," I added.

Mrs. Brindle's eyes sparkled. "He was a scamp then, and he's a scamp now, but that doesn't mean a mere shopkeeper like you has a right to call a duke by his given name."

I grinned. It was an Amusementist tradition to call all members of the Order by their Christian names. I had grown so used to calling the Duke of Chadwick "Oliver" that I'd forgotten the company I kept. "I beg your pardon. That should be His Grace, the Duke of Scamps." I placed the picture back on its perch. "The wedding will be breathtaking. I can hardly wait."

"If you manage to stay awake during the ceremony."

Mrs. Brindle took the tray. "Go clean up. I'll have the tea waiting when you return."

I readied myself for the day, trying to shake off my exhaustion as I donned my full mourning dress for the last time. My year in mourning was over, but the sadness remained. I intended to go to the cemetery to tend my parents' graves. Every time I did, my guilt overwhelmed me. I felt responsible for their loss, and I felt it deeply. I'd had a chance to use Rathford's time machine to return to the night of the fire. I could have warned them to escape. I'd had the choice to save them, but I couldn't do it and risk the consequences of playing God. Instead I'd shattered the heart of the machine that could have brought them back to life.

I knew it was no use wallowing in my guilt, but I couldn't help it. To let go of the guilt, I'd have to forgive myself.

Throughout the morning, memories of my parents plagued me. I thought about how if my father were alive, he'd tease me for putting too much sugar in my tea, and I wondered what my mother would have worn to church. It would have all been so normal, a quiet life, without frogs or fear.

But it wasn't the life I was meant to have. For better or worse I chose to live in a world where I knew the truth, even if knowing that truth meant knowing the danger I faced. In spite of my parents' efforts to keep me away from the Order, living in this world was better than living blindly.

Bob, one of Mrs. Brindle's middle sons, which put him at a burly and youthful sixty, poked his bald head into the parlor through the door that led in from the kitchen.

"Beg your pardon, Miss Whitlock, Mother," he said, his kindly face wrinkling around his deep-set eyes. Lucinda had hired him to care for the mews out back and act as a driver for Mrs. Brindle and me. But I knew about the pistol Bob kept in his pocket. He was here for protection, and I was glad for it, but he tended to stay to the back of the house, leaving the front vulnerable.

"Bob, did you hear anything strange during the night?" I asked.

"No, miss. Not a thing. A caller has arrived for you." He tipped his hat, then left the way he'd come.

A caller?

Will.

I smoothed the knot of braids at the back of my neck even as a deep twisting sensation pulled at my middle.

My composure completely abandoned me as soon as he entered the parlor.

"Will," I breathed.

He stood in the doorway with the light from the kitchen touching the dark waves of his hair. His skin had been kissed with gold from the country sun, and the low sweep of his lashes gave his shadowed eyes a sinful depth. He held a fistful of wildflowers he must have picked on his way to London from Chadwick Hall. He held them out to me as the corner of his lips turned up in a smile.

He looked stunning, like a changeling prince stolen away from this world to be raised in a realm of mystery and illusion.

I threw myself into his arms, and he held me, dropping the flowers to the floor. I smiled as I gained my senses and tried to put at least a modicum of respectable distance between us.

Mrs. Brindle cleared her throat.

I ducked my head as she skewered me with a single look. Will walked straight to her and flashed a charming smile, then kissed her hand. "Mrs. Brindle, you are looking as lovely as ever."

"And you are a scalawag. Best mind yourself, boy. In my day, less than that earned you a trip to the altar." For all her apparent disapproval, she gathered the tea tray with a wry smile.

"I should be so lucky," he said, the hunger in his gaze heating my cheeks.

Even Mrs. Brindle blushed. "I know what you're about, young man. Just remember I've got my eye on you." And abandoning her chaperone duties altogether, she turned for the stairs.

I giggled. "I think she wishes to see me compromised."

"It's so good to see you," Will said, stooping to gather the flowers by the door. "I brought these for your parents."

I sighed and helped him gather them. "Thank you. How long are you in London?" Every moment he had been away had felt like a lifetime to me. Will held my heart, but he was working for Oliver, and the duke kept him busy. Will acted as a personal messenger for the Chadwick affairs in London while Oliver settled his estate in the country and planned his wedding. It meant Will was often traveling for days on end between London and Birmingham.

"I'm only in town for the week. Oliver and Lucinda send their regards," Will said. "I was also told to inform you there will be a Gathering."

I looked toward him in shock. "A full Gathering of the Order?" If word reached my grandfather, he would have to return for that. A Gathering meant that as many Amusementists as could muster were to meet in London at the appointed time to discuss Order business and plan the next Amusement.

Will placed the flowers on the table. "Oliver has asked for your attendance. He figures you should address the assembly about your grandfather. One of them must know something."

"I do hope so," I murmured.

Will took my hand. "Oliver has asked for me to be there as well."

I felt my heart skip as I met his eyes. "He's going to nominate you for an apprenticeship," I said. Excitement poured through me. "Oh, Will. How wonderful."

He glanced back at the door and then down. "Aye. It would be a start."

My heart felt hopeful, and I found myself alight with giddy energy. I knew Will was concerned about making a name for himself. He had started life as a poor tinker in Scotland, then worked most of his life as a stable boy. This was his chance at a real opportunity. I knew he wasn't satisfied with his current position. He felt it was charity on the part of Oliver to employ him.

Now he had his chance. He could be an Amusementist.

Will was driven beyond the aspirations of most men to make a way for himself. He needed desperately to belong to something. Once he felt secure in his fortunes, we could be married and manage the toy shop together. We could finally begin our life.

He shifted.

Unease set upon me once again. "Will? What's troubling you?"

He shook his head. "It's nothing." His eyes narrowed as he studied my face. He lifted a hand to my cheek and let his thumb slide near the corner of my eye. "You seem tired."

"I'm fine." I turned my face toward his hand as he gently brushed his fingers over the hair by my ear. "I've been working too hard."

It was the truth. The shop had suffered from more than four years of terrible neglect. It was once again a shining gem in the bustling storefronts of Mayfair. I had worked myself to the bone to restore the shop to its former glory.

Will led us into the front of the shop. "This looks wonderful." With the morning sun shining through the sparkling glass windows, light danced over the bright colors of the shop. The dolls, games, toys, and puzzles seemed pleasant and cheery in the new light.

Then I heard it again.

Tick, tick, tick.

I shook my head.

"What is it?" Will asked, turning to me. "The shop is beautiful. Simon Pricket would be proud."

Tick, tick, tick.

"It's nothing," I said, taking a step to retreat back toward the parlor. "I can't stop thinking about my parents today. I fear it is making me a little mad."

He took my hand. I turned and stared at my palm folded in his. "You, mad? Never."

I smiled before I could help myself. "Honestly, mad. I keep hearing the ticking clocks. But that's impossible. There are no clocks here in the shop."

The teasing light in Will's eyes hardened as his smile faded to a grim line.

"Will?" His sudden change of expression sent a pang of fear through me.

"Shhh." He put his finger to his lip.

I waited.

A heartbeat.

Two.

Tick, tick, tick.

Will's gaze locked with mine. He heard it too.

Will set on the piles of toys, knocking things to the side as he overturned half the shop.

I helped him, throwing myself into the muddle. It would take forever to set it all right, but I didn't care. I wasn't losing my sanity. Whatever was making the sound was real.

Suddenly Will stilled. The skin over the back of my neck tightened and tingled. I stepped through the scattered toys to stare down at an odd contraption. It was a metal cube, not much larger than a hatbox, with windows cut out on every side. At the center was a heavy-looking orb that reminded me of a cannonball.

Gears twitched on the framework surrounding the orb as a long screw twisted within a metal filigree tube that connected the ball to the solid top of the box. With each ominous *tick* a ghastly little device that reminded me of a spider on a twisting strand of web moved closer to the ball. With each notch downward a spider leg struck a bit of flint on the spider's back, setting off a spark.

I leaned closer and detected a terrifying chemical scent.

Dear Lord, it was a bomb.

CHAPTER TWO

"TAKE MRS. BRINDLE AND GET OUT OF HERE, NOW!" Will commanded, pulling the bomb in front of the shop windows, bathing it in light.

In my mind I could see the explosion. I knew what his burned body would look like, the blackened flesh, his face torn away from the bone. I had seen it before. I could not lose someone I loved like that again. "I'm not leaving you."

He turned to me. "Now, Meg!"

I stumbled backward, then rushed through the door into the parlor. Mrs. Brindle came in from the kitchen just as Bob returned from the mews.

"Bob," I shouted. "Get your mother away from the shop. Take her as far as you can down the street."

"What is it?" he asked even as he put a protective arm around his mother.

"Just go. Alert the neighbors to a fire, then head toward the firehouse. If you hear an explosion, bring the brigade." I shifted on my heel, ready to return to Will. I didn't care what he said. I wasn't leaving him to face a bomb alone.

"Meg?" Mrs. Brindle looked fragile in her son's arms, and scared as she reached for me.

"Hurry!" I cried, backing away from them as Bob pulled Mrs. Brindle out the back door. I took a hasty breath and quickly darted into the shop and through the door to Simon's workshop. I collected a box of his tools, then returned to Will's side.

"Damn it, Meg," Will growled. He hadn't said that to me in a very long time. I supposed it had been at least a couple of months since I'd last willfully put my life in danger.

"Let me guess. My life isn't worth it?" I handed him the tools. "I won't leave you. Now let's stop this thing."

I grasped the heavy pendant hanging on a chain around my neck. It was the most precious thing I owned. Though it looked like a silver pocket watch, it was a key, my grandfather's master key, and it could unlock any invention the Amusementists had created. On the bomb I looked for a three-petal flower embossed on a circular medallion. It was the symbol of the Amusementists, and it often covered an invention's locking mechanism. "Where is the lock?"

Will gingerly tipped the contraption to the side, but the sparking wick continued down its path. "It's here."

I stared at the gear wheel on the bottom of the cube. Feeling dread in the pit of my stomach, I opened the cover of my key and watched as a structure that looked like a mechanical flower emerged from the center of the casing. I tried to fit it into the gear wheel, but it wouldn't set right. I pressed the button on the back of the key that should have turned the gear wheel and played a song I could use to unlock the machine. Instead a single note clanged out, accompanied by a sharp snap. I pulled the key back, afraid it would break. "It's not working."

Will's eyes darted over every part of the machine. I studied it as well, but the gears were protected behind riveted casings. There was no way to crack the machine open and reach the trigger. "Will, we should leave it."

He shook his head. "We still have time."

With every notch that the spider-like creature descended,

time was running out. When we first found the bomb, the spider had had about two inches to go before it would touch the orb. We'd lost a quarter of an inch already. The shop wasn't worth our lives, but if the explosion started a fire, others would be at risk. If the bomb was big enough, half of Mayfair could burn.

Time seemed to slow, each ominous *tick* drawing out and lingering in the air. Without the key I didn't know what to do. We had to stop the spider's descent. I threw open the toolbox and rifled through the tools. Something had to be able to cut through the filigree casing around the trigger. It would be difficult. The openings in the sides of the cube didn't leave much room for a person's hands, even ones so small as mine.

Will continued to study the bomb, his brow knit in deep concentration. I didn't have time for him to uncover the inner workings of the ghastly thing. I just needed to stop that spider, and if I had to pry the damn thing open with my bare hands to do it, I would.

I reached for a hammer.

"Don't," Will said, as if he could read my mind. "There's a glass pane at the top of the screw. If it cracks, the spider drops. We can't damage it."

My heart faltered. Will may not have had much school-
ing, but he had a remarkable talent for understanding how
things fit together. I believed him. "Then how do we stop it?"

"Give me a moment." He turned it again.

"We don't have a moment!" I watched as the spider clicked
closer to the central ball. It only had about an inch to go.

Closer.

"Will?" I grasped his sleeve.

Closer.

I pulled him as hard as I could toward the door.

"Meg, here. We have to stop this wheel." He pointed to
one of the cogs on the outer casing.

I fumbled with my hair, finally jabbing my finger on a
pin. I ripped it from my scalp. Will took the long, hooked
metal and drove it through a thin crack in the casing, catching
the spoke of a gear just beneath.

The spider twitched but could not flick the flint on its
back.

"Get a spool of wire," Will ordered, holding the pin in
place.

I rushed into Simon's workshop. Panicked, I swept all my
work off the table, and the papers flew like dried leaves.

There! The spool of sturdy wire I had used to coil springs

for my frog. I grabbed it, and half-stumbled back out of the workshop.

"It's here." I thrust the wire into his hands, then dug through the tools looking for shears. Will carefully threaded the wire through the filigree tube. I helped him cut six lengths, and we created a wire net just below the spider, tied securely to the casing. The hairpin snapped, but the spider remained trapped, unable to descend past the wires woven just below him. The *tick* became louder, angry.

"Now what do we do?" I asked.

Will pushed back from the thing and scrambled to his feet. "Pray."

"What?" We had to get out of there. A high-pitched whine emanated from the casing. Dear God, the thing was going to explode.

I grabbed Will and clung to his sleeve, because suddenly I felt as if my legs couldn't move. I couldn't run. No matter how I tried to push my body, I felt as if I were slipping through mud.

Suddenly I felt Will's strong arms circle my back and sweep beneath my knees. He swooped me up, cradling me against his chest as I buried my face against his neck and clung to him. He threw himself forward, carrying both of us toward the back of the shop.

I could hear his heartbeat.

Thump.

The screech from the bomb grew louder.

Thump.

It turned to a fevered whistle.

Thump.

We crashed down together behind the counting desk. Will sheltered me with his body, holding me so tightly, I couldn't breathe. His knuckles blanched as he gripped my arm.

"I love you," he whispered as the whistle turned to a frantic scream and the bomb casing clattered against the floor. "By God, Meg, I'll love you always."

No. I refused to say such a goodbye. I loved him with my whole heart in so many ways I could never tell him. We didn't have the time.

I tucked my head deeper into the shelter of his body. I didn't want to die. Not yet. It wasn't fair. There were so many things I still wanted to do. So many things I still needed to do. I bunched the fabric of Will's coat tighter in my fist, as if holding on to it could somehow hold him to me even if we were thrown into the hereafter.

A loud *snap* echoed through the shop.

I let out a yelp as Will flinched.

We waited, clinging to one another, breathing hard. I could feel the pulse of his neck against my brow. Our hearts pounded as one.

Nothing.

Tipping my chin up, I looked Will in the eyes, daring to hope we had really averted disaster. I gave him a hesitant smile as a rush of relief, joy, and exhilaration overcame me.

He took my face in his hands and kissed me, a burning, hungry, wicked kiss. It was a kiss that could possibly land me in the fires of hell for my sinful thoughts alone, but at the moment I didn't care. I wanted to burn this way. I let myself be swept away by it. As his lips slid over mine and our breath mingled, I knew we were truly alive.

The heady rush ebbed, and I regained my senses. We were tangled together, legs, arms, my thick petticoats spilling over both of us like a cascading brook. Will glanced at my exposed calf and the buttons along the seam of my boot. I pulled back, trembling, trying to right my skirt. "We should see if it's safe," I said.

Will let out a shaking breath and took another quick one, as if his mind had forgotten the process of breathing and he had to concentrate on so instinctive a task. He closed his eyes and nodded, his skin flushed.

He looked overcome, and it nearly undid me. The intimacy of it frightened me, though I didn't know why it should. I extracted myself from him due to an unfamiliar sense of self-preservation and inched toward the vile thing sitting at the front of my beautiful shop.

The spider had snapped nearly in half in its effort to push through the wires. A coiled spring hung from its cracked back like tiny mechanical innards spilling from a squished bug. Good riddance. "It seems properly broken." I breathed a sigh of relief.

Will nodded, but his jaw had tightened, and the black look of vengeance had seeped into his eyes.

"Will?" I could see the pressure building in him. I held a hand out to him. "Will, everything is fine. No one was harmed."

"Someone is trying to bloody kill you!" he shouted. I took a step back. In the time I had known him, he'd been like a rock in a stormy tide. Nothing moved him, not when he'd faced a man brandishing a pistol, and not even when he'd faced a giant mechanical sea monster.

I touched him on the arm. It shook beneath my fingertips. "We know someone is trying to kill me. Someone has been trying to kill me for a year now. Nothing has changed." I had meant my words to reassure him, but my own casual acceptance of my impending doom disturbed me. "Except now we have proof."

Will glared at the bomb and crossed his arms. "That is hardly a comfort."

"We'll bring it with us when the Amusementists gather. They cannot deny that it came from one of them. The unlocking mechanism is on the bottom of the beastly thing. Finally we'll get to the heart of this."

His gaze dropped to the floor as he covered my hand with his. "I thought it was over," he whispered. "I thought we would finally be free of all this."

I nodded, but something about his words troubled me. I didn't want to feel hunted at every turn, but I wondered what he meant by "free." Did he mean free to wed? I had to admit a large part of me desperately wanted to be Will's wife, but there was another part of me. It was like a secret hunger I couldn't seem to fill. I didn't wish to be free of the Amusementists.

Not yet.

I had too much I needed to know. I longed to find my

grandfather. I wanted to know more about the legacy of my family and the things they had helped create. I wanted to be swept away by the wonder and amazement of visions come to life through the skill and craftsmanship of Europe's most brilliant minds. I felt stuck in a strange dream, one that tended to become a nightmare, but I didn't want to wake.

CHAPTER THREE

AND SO, ONLY TWO DAYS LATER, I FOUND MYSELF ON THE single most unnerving carriage ride of my life. Which was saying quite a lot, considering some of my past experiences in a coach.

When Will told me that Oliver had invited me to attend the Gathering of the Order, I had assumed that the duke would accompany me. Instead he had sent around his coach with a note saying that he and Will had special business to attend to prior to the meeting, and that I should meet them there.

There were only three problems with this arrangement. The first was that I had absolutely no inkling where I was going. As the neat and affluent streets of Mayfair gave way to the crowded lanes of the heart of London, my apprehension grew. Wide lanes turned into narrow twisting streets as the buildings somehow crowded even closer, their shadowed windows like leering eyes. With the heavy smoke of coal fires, and the stench of human filth, this was not the London I knew. It was another world entirely.

The second problem had everything to do with the lessons taught me by my Swiss mother. Punctuality was paramount, as she liked to say. An overturned cabbage cart had caught Oliver's driver in a crush of traffic, which meant I was late. It was not the first impression that I had wished to present to the Order. I needed the Amusementists to listen to me, not discount me as an irresponsible young girl.

The third reason for my discomfiture was obvious. The bomb was on the seat directly across from me.

I crossed my ankles beneath the crisp, dark blue fabric of my new dress. Wishing to look mature and respectable in front of the Order, I had tightly braided my hair and knotted it at my nape. My head ached from my severe hairstyle, and the fabric of my dress swallowed my arms. The lace around the collar itched where it touched my skin, and I tried not to wriggle as I stared at the ominous cube on the bench opposite.

The triggering mechanism still hung limply from the net of wire Will and I had used to trap it, but the incendiary orb remained intact. I had no idea how stable or—more important—unstable the powder was, nor what sort of impact could potentially set it off.

The carriage wheel bumped, nearly throwing me from my seat. I gasped as I caught the bomb and held it steady on the plush bench. The cold frame cut into my shaking palms.

I pushed the bomb against the padded back of the seat, then quickly returned to my position, stiffly holding my hands in my lap to keep from gripping my skirts and putting creases in them. Only then did I dare to breathe.

With each passing moment my nerves grew worse. The carriage ride was either lasting half my life or taking half my life as my fear slowly killed me. Finally the wheels slowed and the footman opened the door. I lifted the bomb, struggling to find a way to hold the thing that would prevent me from dropping it and still give me a hand to hold my skirts so I didn't trip and throw myself and the blasted thing out onto the street. A fine mess that would make. Tucking the bomb under my arm like a simple parcel, I allowed the footman to help me down.

I found myself on the worn stone steps of an old monastery. It rose up in the dark before me, its heavy stone walls towering into the sky. Torches burned along the walls, leaving trails of black soot over the weathered stone.

The foul smell of the Thames mingled with the scent of torches and old stone. We had to be close to the docks, perhaps in the vicinity of the Tower. For a moment I wondered how long the monastery had stood, through fire, through war, as the city of London had grown up around it. Now it only had its formidable walls to keep out a world that, thankfully, seemed content to ignore it completely.

I ascended the steps, feeling as if I were entering the Tower itself. The heavy wooden doors were closed. I wondered if I was even in the right place. The driver could have been mistaken.

I struggled to lift the heavy iron knocker with my free hand. It was easily the size of my head and was set in a fearsome lion's jaws.

Shifting the bomb, I waited. I had spent hours thinking on what I should say once I was here. My thoughts had turned in my head, as intricate and guarded as the gears in the casing of the bomb. Now that I was here, my thoughts jammed, leaving my mind a blank canvas for the insidious whispers of my own doubt. That's when I noticed a small spiraling motif etched into the casing of the bomb near the corner. It looked a bit like a ram's horn, or perhaps a snail's shell.

The door to the monastery opened only a crack. "What is your business here?"

I had been so engrossed in the etching that I startled, then stumbled over my words. "I'm Margaret Anne Whitlock," I managed to say, though I must have sounded as if I'd had half a bottle of sherry.

The crack widened, but only enough to allow me to see the appraising look of a man with an impressively cut mustache that swept down along the sides of his heavy mouth and met with his sideburns. He peered at me through a monocle. "It has been a lovely summer in the garden," he said. I would have dismissed his words as nonsense, but Oliver had already given me the password.

"Only when the sun shines behind the iris," I replied.

He seemed uncertain, as if he were considering turning me away, even though I knew I had uttered the right phrase. I had no recourse should he choose to refuse me entrance. Finally he announced, "Come in, Miss Whitlock." The door opened and I stepped inside.

With my eyes downcast, partially due to the embarrassment of arriving late and partially to watch my step on the old stone, the first thing I noticed was light. Hundreds of patches of colored light swirled on the polished marble floor. They moved as if they were in a kaleidoscope, constantly changing patterns and shapes.

I took a hesitant step forward into the colors, as though they were a pool of water and I didn't dare disturb the surface. A glint of bright light drew my attention upward.

I nearly dropped the bomb in my awe.

Towering before me was a golden figure, as brilliant and terrible as an angel of heaven. Seamless joints formed the feminine body in golden armor. She held a shining silver sword aloft. Black glass eyes watched me from her serene face, and I knew without a doubt those eyes could see me.

On her forearm perched an owl. It turned its head to stare at me with a second set of enormous black eyes. Gears shone through its feathers, glittering as it clacked its brass beak.

Two towering panels of stained glass on either side of the statue seemed to break apart as the glass twisted and moved along a web of brass tracks, only to re-form into a new image. Lanterns shone behind the glass, bathing the floor and walls in ever-shifting light.

Above the head of the figure, the Amusementist seal glittered. The symbol was now so familiar to me, sometimes I could see it even as I closed my eyes. A strange flower with three teardrop petals nestled in a perfect circle, with three sharp spires radiating out from the junctures. In the center a tiny gear marked the heart of the flower. Beneath scrolled three words: *Ex scientia pulchritudo*.

If only I had paid more attention to my Latin.

The man who had let me in stepped past me and addressed the owl. "Miss Whitlock has arrived. She had the password."

"Very well." I nearly jumped out of my skin when a voice came from the beak of the bird. "The Gathering is in progress. Escort her to the main hall."

"This way," the man said, and I fell into step behind him. I couldn't seem to tear my gaze from the statue or the stained glass. The owl twisted his head to watch me, and blinked. I quickly snapped my attention to the man I was supposed to follow, as we passed through a narrow corridor.

We climbed a set of stairs, and out of a narrow window I caught a glimpse of a wide courtyard surrounded by a high wall. For a moment I wondered how large and complex the monastery was, or what might be hidden within it.

The man with the monocle opened a door, and we entered at the back corner of a large assembly chamber. In front of us was a straight walkway that ended with a door on the far side. To the left the room dropped down at least twenty feet. Staircases divided tiers of seats down to the floor of the hall.

On the opposite side of the large chamber, an identical rise of seats led up to a second walkway along the far wall. It created a dramatic gallery, where everyone's focus seemed to be riveted to the floor below.

The benches were filled with men in black coats with dark red waistcoats. They murmured among themselves as my escort motioned for me to take an empty seat high in the back corner. He continued down the steps and sat by the rail partitioning the gallery of seats from the floor of the hall.

I scanned the unfamiliar faces of the men. There were easily more than one hundred, some with dark skin and foreign features. There were even two or three who wore headdresses.

It was as if the entire world had gathered here, and yet my grandfather was nowhere to be found. I did glimpse Oliver sitting in the second row of seats on the other side of the chamber. He spoke to Will, who was sitting next to him.

Relieved to spy some familiar faces, I focused on them as a hunched man with thin silver hair and a gaunt face stretched by age stepped up behind a large podium on the floor of the hall. His bushy eyebrows twitched as he clanged a metal baton against an oddly shaped bell.

The room quieted.

When he spoke, his voice was thin and reedy. I had to strain to hear him, until he moved closer to the contraption on the podium. Suddenly his voice filled the chamber, coming from all corners, much louder than a single man could speak.

"It is settled, then. We shall no longer condone collaborative experimentation without approval of the council. Furthermore, rogue invention of any device that has purpose or function beyond what has been previously approved by the council shall be forbidden," he announced.

A thin man stood. He had a sharp-looking beard and dark blond hair slicked back. It gave him an air of slight superiority that matched the aloof expression on his face. "I must protest once again. Such an action taken out of fear will greatly diminish the potential for innovation from our Order."

"If an idea has worth, then such worth will be determined by the council," the man at the podium said. "The matter has been voted upon and is settled. Now, if we are agreed that the next sanctioned Amusement shall be an automaton ball, we may open the floor. All in favor of an automaton ball to celebrate the rebirth of our Order?"

The room erupted in "Aye."

"All opposed."

There was no response. The leader clanged the bell again. "So be it. Anton and Vladimir will arrange the teams. The floor is now open for new business."

At that point I tried not to fidget in my seat. I watched Will, who looked as stoic as ever, but I could tell he was nervous too. He was gripping the arms of his chair and didn't look up as five different men stood to nominate their sons for apprenticeships. Immediately, as if it were an expected formality, another would second the nomination and the man would be seated.

Finally Oliver stood. My pride in Will mingled with anticipation as Oliver announced in a clear voice, "I wish to nominate my man, Guild member William MacDonald, for an apprenticeship. He already proved his loyalty and worth during the ordeal this spring and would honor the Order. Will anyone second him?"

Low murmurs rumbled through the room. I held my breath, squeezing my hands tighter on the cold metal frame in my lap. I suddenly remembered that the cube in my lap was a bomb, and flinched. I patted it as if it were a dog, and realized I had lost all sense completely.

Someone had to second Will. It would ruin everything if they didn't.

The voices gave way to an uncomfortable silence.

Finally another man stood, a big, burly man with an unshaven face and shaggy black hair that seemed to have grown from lack of grooming instead of intent. He wore a red-and-blue kilt, and a black tam with a white rosette slanted over his thick hair. "MacDonald, eh?"

Will looked up at him. They seemed to appraise one another.

"He seems a stout young lad. I'd like to offer him a position at the Foundry." The Scot continued to stand. Several of the old men nodded as if that were the sensible thing to do. It wasn't sensible at all. Will hadn't been to Scotland since he was six! He didn't belong there.

My heart thundered to life as I felt burning heat rush into my face. The Foundry was the ironworks and smithy for the entire Order. Every part, every gear the Amusementists needed for their inventions came from the Foundry. It was filled with a horde of half-wild ex-Jacobite descendants who needed employment instead of persecution after the defeat at Culloden. In exchange for secrecy the Amusementists had given the Scots freedom to keep their clans and wear their plaid, and a strange but effective partnership had been born.

In any other regard I found the idea of the Foundry fascinating, but it was located in the Highlands. If no one else spoke to second the apprenticeship to the Order, Will would leave London. What would that do to us? He couldn't possibly leave. Not now. We were so close to having a future together.

It wasn't right to have every hope and dream of my heart smashed to pieces because these damn old Englishmen heard the name MacDonald and figured they could put one more bloody Scot back in his place at the Foundry, instead of nominating him to become an equal here in London.

I closed my eyes and prayed fervently for someone else, anyone else, to see Will's potential. I wanted to stand and protest on Will's behalf. Hell, I wanted Will to stand and protest on his own behalf. Our future was at stake. I opened my eyes and stared at the men, but no one was willing to stand.

"I'll second him," a ginger-haired man stated. He couldn't have been much older than Oliver. My relief made me dizzy as I watched the man give a friendly nod to Oliver.

"Then it is settled. All future apprentices have three days to commit to the Academy. Is there anyone who has further business?"

I waited for Oliver to speak, but he was saying something to Will. The man at the podium lifted his bar, and I panicked. I stood.

"I have," I said. Somehow my voice carried over the entire assembly.

The room fell silent, and hundreds of eyes turned to me.

Oliver looked at me in shock, then stood quickly. "May I present Miss Margaret Whitlock. She wishes to address the Order concerning the disappearance of her grandfather Henry."

I held my chin high and descended the steps until I found myself on the assembly floor, not thirty feet from the podium.

A bald old man with overly large ears stood, his face turning a blotchy red.

"This is entirely improper!" he blustered, his heavy jowls flapping. "What business could a little girl possibly have that is worth casting off almost three hundred years of dignity and tradition? If she has a concern, she should bring it to your mother, Oliver, or any of the other Society matrons. She does not belong here."

My grip on the bomb tightened as I stiffened and forced myself to look straight ahead at the podium. I would not acknowledge him. If I looked at him, I feared my humiliation and rage would overtake my good sense and I'd say something his floppy ears would not soon forget.

Oliver shouted, "Now see here. Miss Whitlock is the last of the Whitlock and Reichlin lines, and out of respect for what her family has done for this Order, we should allow her to speak."

The voices grew like a great tide, though I heard a call of "Hear, hear!" from the back of the assembly.

I advanced, feeling like a soldier under fire. With my head held high I tried to keep my face serene, though everything within me was in turmoil. The bomb felt heavy and awkward in my hands, but I reached the podium.

The leader of the assembly stared at me quizzically as I set the bomb down. The boom of the casing hitting the podium echoed through the voice projection machine.

The Amusementists quieted.

"This is a bomb," I declared as loudly and as clearly as I could while looking the leader of the Order in the eye. "It is also the second attempt on my life." I turned from the podium to face the stunned assembly. "I have proof that my grandfather is still alive. The fact that he has not returned leads me to believe he is in some sort of danger. If anyone knows where he may have gone, whom he may have trusted, or the identity of one who would do him harm, I would greatly appreciate speaking with you."

Once again the voices rose, but I slid my gaze over the assembly in spite of them. My knees trembled beneath my skirts, and I had to clench my hands in front of me to keep from wringing them. "Please help me find my grandfather. He is one of you, and he needs your aid."

The Amusementists leaned heads together, fervently speaking to one another. I looked over at Will, and he gave me an encouraging nod.

The leader inspected the bomb. "This is most disturbing. It is against the laws of our Order to create a weapon such as this. Do you have any suspicion of who may have created it?"

I turned to him. "I believe it was a man with a clockwork mask embedded into his face."

This time, amid the rumbling voices, I caught hints of patronizing laughter. It made me want to scream. This was not some game, and I was not a child having foolish nightmares. This was real. My life was at stake, and clearly they wished for me to go and discuss it with a bunch of Society women over tea.

"There is no such man within or associated with our Order," someone insisted. "A man with a clockwork face is impossible. To integrate a mechanical structure with living tissue is beyond the scope of any invention by an Amusementist. It must have been your imagination."

I felt as if my cheeks were on fire.

"While my imagination might be remarkable, I doubt it is capable of conjuring this," I said, pointing at the bomb.

The voices swelled, and the bell clanged. "Order, order!" the leader shouted. "This is all very unsettling. Lawrence, if you would take this abomination to the archives, we will study it at length once the Academy is in session. I'll leave you in charge of the investigation. Thank you for bringing it to our attention, Miss Whitlock. Please return to your seat."

That was all? They intended to study it at a later time? I let my mouth hang agape for only a moment before I caught myself. Yet another man stood in the front row and placed his hand on the rail. This one had large front teeth and a twitchy, rabbity look about him. "Miss Whitlock should be escorted out immediately. No one who is not a sworn member of the Order or a nominated apprentice with a family legacy is allowed within these walls, much less a woman. She should not remain here, in spite of her ill tidings."

I turned to the man, but he lifted his weak chin, keeping

his narrow-set eyes on the leader and refusing to acknowledge my existence.

"Furthermore," he continued, "we should punish Oliver for giving her the password only to bring us this news, which he could have easily delivered himself without defying our traditions."

I turned to Oliver, feeling suddenly ill. He was my friend. He had done nothing that deserved punishment. The young duke stood. I expected him to be angry. Instead he looked as if he were about to laugh at a secret joke. He placed a hand on his waistcoat and smiled. "I didn't bring her here to give us news," he said. He looked me in the eye and gave me a mischievous wink. "I brought her here to nominate her as an apprentice."

The room exploded in angry shouts as if the bomb had just gone off.

CHAPTER FOUR

ME, AN APPRENTICE? ME? THIS IS WHAT I'D THOUGHT I wanted. I had spent months diligently studying the equations and theorems Simon Pricket had explained in painstaking detail in his journals. I had tortured myself with them all day, every day, until my head had swum with equations. Even so, I couldn't manage to properly compress a spring. If I became an apprentice, every effort I made would be scrutinized. The pressure would be unbearable.

But I could learn. With the right instruction, I knew I could learn.

"Preposterous!" The fat one with the jowls chose to speak again. "It is a proven fact that the female brain is simply incapable of reasoning on a high enough level to comprehend the mechanics of what we create, let alone actually *invent* something."

I furrowed my brow. Who exactly had proven that as fact? I might not have known what my potential was, but I wasn't about to let some fat old codger decide it for me. A chorus of "hear, hear" echoed around the room, only I couldn't hear anymore through the furious rushing sound in my ears. They weren't even going to give me a chance.

I opened my mouth to speak.

"Miss Whitlock has a very gifted mind," Oliver cut in before I could say a word, looking unshaken by the turmoil. "I'm sure she will prove herself well, given the opportunity."

Clenching my teeth, I decided to hold my tongue, lest it grow sharp. I needed to keep control of myself, but they all acted as if I weren't even in the room, let alone standing right before them.

"It isn't simply a matter of having a gifted mind," another man retorted. "It is a matter of education as well. She will have to compete with peers who have been highly trained in mathematics and science, where she has had what? The limited knowledge of some governess trained to teach her how to properly pour her tea? I wouldn't want to see the poor girl humiliated. It's not fair to her."

This was the argument against me? I could show him where to pour his tea.

Another man stood. I squinted in the dim light, sure that I recognized him. He had round spectacles and a long patrician nose. He had been a close friend of my father's, and had often visited the shop. "The sons of the merchants often don't have the privilege of a boarding school education, and yet they manage well enough. Lest we forget, this girl is the grandchild of two of the best minds the Order has ever seen. I know for a fact that George used to teach her regularly."

"Yes, Ezra, but if you second her nomination, it would surely ruin her." I turned around to another man, about my father's age, with a predominant bald spot that made him look a bit like a monk. I could only assume the enormous sideburns clinging to his cheeks were meant to make up for his lack of hair elsewhere.

He stood in the middle of the rise and gave me a patronizing look. "How is the girl supposed to find a respectable husband if she pursues this course of action? We've all been through the Academy. It's not possible for her to be chaperoned at every moment. We cannot guarantee her safety, and her reputation will be in shambles. The Whitlock and Reichlin lines are too important to tarnish in such a manner.

Let her attend the Society balls, find a good match, and allow her husband to take his place among us. That is only proper. It's what her father would have chosen for her, and we must do right by him."

At this point I felt the anger inside me about to boil over. I supposed he thought I should be grateful for his concern for my future marital status. Frankly, I found it unbelievable that any woman would marry him, with two rangy squirrels clinging to his cheeks.

I didn't even bother to look as another man shouted, "What of the boys? We must think of them and their education. How can they possibly learn the intricate nature of design with a young lady in their midst? It would be too much of a distraction and unfair to them."

Enough! This was my life. They had no right.

"I accept," I announced. My voice projected through the entire assembly, without the aid of the machine on the podium. The men's voices quieted as I once again felt the weight of all their stares.

"I accept the nomination." I stood as tall and straight as I could. It confounded me that here in England, an empire that had given rise to our glorious Queen Victoria, and the great Elizabeth before her, men could be so thick. Without this chance I could not prove my worth to the Order. But I would be damned before I let the lot of them cow me.

The old man at the podium gave me a condescending grin. "I'm afraid no one will second the nomination." He lifted the baton to strike the bell. "If there is no further business, I motion to adjourn."

The gallery remained silent. The leader shrugged. "Nigel, please escort Miss Whitlock from the premises."

No. My heart raced as I looked toward Oliver. He spoke frantically with the man beside him. This was my only opportunity to become a true Amusementist. I wanted this. It was what I was meant to be. I knew it with all my heart.

"Wait," I shouted. "Please!"

The man with the monocle who had escorted me in laid a viselike grip on my arm and pulled me from the podium. I stood fast against his hold. I didn't wish to be brushed aside. I felt it would crush me.

I looked around the room, but it was just a sea of faces, blurring through the beginnings of stinging tears. I would not let them fall. Not here. I wouldn't assure their victory in such a way.

A tall man stood. He was the one with the slick blond hair and sharp-looking beard that had protested whatever the

Amusementists had decided as I had come in. I turned to him. If he seconded the motion to adjourn, it was over. Silently I pleaded that those words would not come from him.

"I second," he announced, and the weight of his words fell like the blade of the guillotine.

The old goat at the podium nearly bleated his approval. "Good. Motion to adjourn is final." He lifted his hand to strike the bell.

"No." The man tucked his thumb into the pocket of his waistcoat in a casual way. My heart pounded like an executioner's drum. He cleared his throat, then rocked back on his heels as he said with a ringing voice, "I second the nomination of Miss Margaret Whitlock as an apprentice."

I froze, as did Nigel, though he did not let go of my arm. My shock mingled with newfound hope that was slowly turning to joy.

The voices erupted again, reminding me of a pack of barking dogs. I ignored them and watched the man who had just seconded my nomination. He didn't bother to look at me, but instead remained nonchalant as he waited for the furor to die down. At one point he pulled out his pocket watch and inspected the time, then tucked it back into his waistcoat with a smug grin.

"What do you mean by this, Lawrence?" the old man at the podium snapped. "You of all people should realize the integrity of the Academy and seek to protect it."

"Indeed. As headmaster, the Academy is my responsibility," he answered in a cool voice. "And if I choose to give Miss Whitlock a position there, then I am the one who will handle the matter."

Headmaster? I grinned before I could help it. Surely no one could protest if the headmaster himself wished for me to attend the Academy.

"Why would you do such a thing?" someone shouted.

The headmaster turned, his long face scowling. "Perhaps I see it as a challenge," he answered with a hint of irritation in his voice. "Isn't that what this Order takes pride in?"

I didn't know what to think. I only felt the swelling of gratitude that at least one man embodied what the Amusementists stood for. Other than him, and Oliver, the lot of them could rot, in my opinion.

"It is unfair to ruin the child's future in such a way," another protested.

The headmaster tilted his head. "Whatever happens here will not be spoken of in proper society. Or am I mistaken, and this is *not*, in fact, a secret order?"

"But would that be enough to protect her?" someone shouted.

"It would if she were my ward," Oliver proclaimed. "It's the least I can do for the memory of George and Elsa. She would be part of my family, and any who dishonor her would answer to me."

Lawrence grinned and gave Oliver a nod. "It is settled, then."

My elation felt full to bursting at his words. I would not disappoint Lawrence's faith in me. None of the others mattered. He was willing to see me as a person with potential. I owed my loyalty and my dedication to the headmaster.

"Settled!" The blustery old fool with the flappy jowls stood with his face as red as a baby's smacked bottom. "I propose the removal of Lawrence as headmaster of the Academy at once!"

The headmaster arched a brow and looked down his long nose at the man. All the men around the older man with the jowls seemed to wither. They shifted uncomfortably in their seats just like errant schoolboys, leaving the old man standing alone and flustered.

"It has been six years since the Academy has convened," the headmaster said. "This will be the largest class in history, from five different countries, no less. I will gladly turn over my duty to any here who wish to dedicate every moment of their lives to the education of twenty-five young men"—he glanced at me and grinned—"and one young lady."

All talk died down immediately. I almost laughed as all the rest of the Amusementists cast their eyes to the floor. Clearly, no one wished to be saddled with such a responsibility. I couldn't hide my smile as my gaze met Oliver's. He gave me a sly grin and a nod.

The headmaster held his hands out in mocking disbelief. "No one? Well, then, in the interest of preserving the Academy, I shall gladly serve as headmaster, and I second the motion to adjourn."

The man behind the podium clanged the bell. It rang out with a defeated tone, and I fought the urge to dance. The Amusementists began congregating and shuffling up the stairs, huddled in conversation about everything that had transpired.

Yes! The battle had been won.

Oliver leaned over and said something to Will. Will nodded, then spared me a glance. I smiled at him, but he didn't return it. He seemed lost in thought and concerned about something.

The elation I had been feeling cooled somewhat as I

wondered what was wrong. Will slipped out the door in the back of the chamber as Oliver climbed down the steps to the floor and met me there.

"Leave her to me, Nigel," he said, taking my arm.

I had completely forgotten about the old man with the monocle. He seemed at a loss for what to do with me as well, and he shook as if coming awake, then nodded.

"Yes, yes, of course." He hurried off after the other Amusementists, leaving me alone with Oliver.

Oliver took a step toward the stairs, and all my strength rushed away from my body as soon as I tried to move.

"You did well, Meg." He patted my arm, and I felt my strength returning. When I had first met him, he had been living in the servants' quarters of his own abandoned estate, and his choice in clothing had been eccentric to say the least. Now he was the very image of a dashing young duke in the finest of style. If I had been any other girl in London, I might have swooned. But I never held to such nonsense. Oliver was like a protective older brother. Perhaps "protective" wasn't quite the word, but a brother nonetheless, and now he had declared me a part of his family.

"You could have warned me," I said as we ascended the stairs.

He just chuckled. "You are always at your best when facing the unexpected. You will do well."

Would I? I really had no other option. I had just proclaimed in front of a room full of Amusementists that I was more than worthy to be an apprentice. These men were capable of bending the fabric of reality, and I couldn't invent a simple frog. "I'm not so certain, but thank you."

Oliver stopped at the top of the stair and turned to face me. "Listen, Meg. That doubt has no place here. Maybe others can afford it, but not you. I wouldn't have nominated you if I didn't have complete faith that you will make fools of the lot of them. Prove me right."

I nodded. His faith in me bolstered my spirits, but it didn't quash the niggling doubt that lingered in my mind. "I'm just glad Will was nominated as well. Thank you for that."

Oliver paused. "He's a good lad."

"We'll be able to help each other, as always." I clung to the thought as Oliver led me through the crowded hall, back down the stairs, and out into the courtyard I'd noticed through the window earlier. At least I wouldn't be alone. Several Amusementists were standing on a ramp that led down below the courtyard to an alcove beneath the ground.

I could hear the clatter of hooves and carriage wheels echoing out of the pit. Curious, I craned my neck to get a better look.

It seemed to be an underground bay where the carriages were lined up to take all the men home.

Clouds darkened the sky overhead, and I thought I felt a drop of rain against my cheek.

Will came up from the ramp with his jaw clenched, and walked straight toward us with hurried strides. "It leaves tonight," he said to Oliver.

"What's this?" I asked, puzzled. Will looked solemn. I brushed my curiosity away. They were probably just speaking about Oliver's business dealings.

"Very well." Oliver handed my arm over to Will. "I can't say I'm not disappointed. I have some business with Victor here in town. Meg, when you are ready, my carriage is waiting below to take you home." He nodded to me, then clapped his hand on Will's shoulder. "Do what you must."

I didn't like the sinking feeling that accompanied his words, but I tried to convince myself they were trivial. Will's job was to inform Oliver of comings and goings.

"Will?" I turned to him. He wouldn't look me in the eye.

That's when I knew for certain something was amiss. "Will, what is going on?"

"Come with me," he insisted.

"Not until you tell me what has you so troubled." My voice rose, and the group of men closest to us paused their conversation and turned.

Heat rose in my cheeks, and I grabbed my skirts as Will led me across the courtyard to what used to be an old shrine set into a rounded alcove in the wall. At some point the Amusementists had decided to convert it into an aviary of sorts. They'd built a gilded cage that had now tarnished. The bars came out from the inlet, forming an aviary with brass vines and leaves growing over and through it.

Mechanical birds perched throughout the vines and bars of the cage. Old and rusting, they waited lifelessly in the dim light.

I let out a breath and put a hand on Will's arm. I was being unfair. If he needed to speak, I should listen. I gave him a reassuring squeeze. "I know this is all overwhelming. I'm frightened too," I offered. He had to be as nervous about the apprenticeship as I was, perhaps more so. He had only just learned to read and write, but he had picked it up quickly. His mind was as keen as any I had known.

"The apprenticeship will be difficult, but together we can help—"

"I'm not going to be an apprentice." He squared his shoulders and looked me in the eye. "I've decided to join the Foundry."

CHAPTER FIVE

"WHAT?" MY BREATH CAUGHT IN MY THROAT. HE DIDN'T need to go. His nomination had been seconded. This had to be a mistake.

Chills ran up and down my arms and legs, turning them numb.

Will had a fixed and determined look on his face, as if he were bracing for a fight. "I'm going to the Foundry, Meg." He reached out to take my hands, but I yanked them away. My face was on fire and my pulse turned heavy, pushing my heated blood at a furious pace.

"Don't touch me." I turned from him, unable to form any

more words than that. He wanted to leave for Scotland. It might as well have been the moon. I'd never see him.

"Please listen to me." He reached out again, taking my arm.

I stiffened, pulling against his grip. "You've said your piece."

He drew me closer, keeping his grip firm. "No, I haven't."

I wrenched my arm away and took a step back. "I'm not one of your horses. You can't lead me around."

He paced toward the mechanical aviary and back, like a caged lion.

I watched him, keeping my fists clenched. My fingernails stung as they dug into my palms. He wasn't thinking. Leaving made little sense. Everything we were building together was here in London. "How are we to have a future if you are in Scotland?"

He stopped and splayed his arms out in a flash of indignation. "I'm trying to build our future." His hands shook as he said it.

No, he wasn't. He was trying to leave me. He was trying to run just when we were on the verge of everything we had dreamed of.

"Then accept the apprenticeship." I tried to sound reasonable, but my words snapped out. Anger twisted my thoughts until even I couldn't comprehend them. Words—dangerous, vile words—lingered on the back of my tongue. I needed to be civil, but fighting the impulse to spout all the horrible curses in my head took effort.

For all the distasteful thoughts forming in my mind, they didn't compare to the sharp pain beginning to slice through my heart. Will had walked away before. He had always come to his senses and returned to me. This time would be no different. We needed one another. "You must stay here in London."

"I can't." His voice cracked. He took a breath and raked his hands through his hair, then met my gaze. I could see the torment in his furrowed brow. "I don't belong here, Meg. I don't belong anywhere. That's the problem."

"Don't be ridiculous." Will was always the practical one. I waved his doubt off with a flip of my hand.

He looked up at me with such heartbreak in his gaze. "It's the truth."

Truth? The only truth that would come to pass is that the whole of the British Isles would stand between us. "I know you're worried about the studies, but I'll help—"

"We both know it wouldn't be enough." He hung his

head. "I don't want you to have to do everything for me because I can barely manage to read."

"You read fine!" He might have been a bit slow, but there was hardly anything he couldn't sound out, and his vocabulary was growing.

"And my writing? What of my figures?" He counted off his perceived scholarly failings on his fingers as if to make a point.

"You can learn." I gripped his hand and held on. "I know you, Will. You can do anything you put your mind to."

"You are the one who is good with your mind." He pulled his hand from mine and turned to lean on the framework of the aviary. He looked at his palms. "I'm good with my hands. I don't want to live my life studying and drawing out ideas. I want to make things. I want to fit them together and see them work. You're the dreamer, Meg, not me. When Oliver asked me if I wanted to be an Amusementist, I said yes because I just wanted to be *something*. But now that MacTavish has made his offer . . ."

"To be an ironworker? That's not what you are, Will."

"What am I, then?" He sighed. He looked so lost. "A gypsy, a filthy tinker, a bloody Scot, an orphan beggar. It wasn't that long ago that even being in my presence would have earned you a trip to the gallows."

I felt tears gathering as my heart broke for him. He was none of those things to me. He was my Will, my heart, and he was good. Everything about him was good. "Will, you can't believe—"

He met my gaze. "I need this."

"I'm sure Oliver would—"

"Oliver has done enough!" Will shouted. I took a step back in shock at his sudden change in demeanor.

He let out a heavy breath. "You *never* listen. I will not live on the good grace of others anymore. Not from charity and not from pity. I have to find my way. My own way." He looked away and his voice turned soft as he said his piece, but it was no less determined. "I can't do that here."

All the words swimming in my head faded down to just one. *No.* Over and over it echoed in my mind, bringing with it a ripping and tearing pain. It started in my heart, but then it encompassed all of me in relentless waves. The pain was so acute, I felt I would be sick. The words he had left unsaid lingered between us.

I can't do that with you.

I fought my tears as my throat closed around my words. "Don't you still love me?"

Will looked back to me, and the stoic expression on his

face broke. He looked as heartbroken and shocked as I felt. I had to look away as he approached and gathered my hand in his. He kissed the back of it, the way he always had.

My fingers suddenly felt so cold. His warm breath shook as it caressed me. One of his hot tears fell onto the back of my hand, and slowly trailed over my skin before it fell to the ground. "I love you with everything I am." He swallowed, then pressed my hand to his heart. "I just want to deserve you."

"You do." I felt my own tears slide down my cheeks.

He looked me in the eyes, and the pain receded, washed away by the tide of love I felt for him. "Then marry me," he said.

I felt as if he'd just scooped me up and pitched me over a cliff. I pulled my hand from his and took a step back to regain my balance. I still felt as if I were falling. "I beg your pardon?"

He dropped to his knee. "Marry me. Come away with me to Scotland. We can start a new life in the Highlands, away from bombs and murder, just the two of us. We'll make our own home. A place that is just ours. Say you'll be my wife."

I blinked in shock. For a moment elation flitted through me.

His wife?

In the briefest of moments that seemed to last twenty lifetimes, I pictured us living in a little cottage in a village near Inverness. Will would come through the door while I kneaded the dough for the bread and a shaggy dog snored by the fire. Will would sweep me up in his arms and kiss me until we both succumbed to laughter.

But the vision fell dark around the edges. There was an emptiness surrounding our little world, a terrible void that turned the joy that had come from my thoughts into panic.

The chill of it poured through my blood.

My legs shook as I looked down on Will, his eyes imploring me not to break his heart.

I wanted to say yes. I wanted to scream it and leap into his arms, but I couldn't move. It was all so terribly wrong.

"I can't," I whispered, unable to say anything more.

His gaze fell to the hem of my skirt. We remained there, silent, with Will kneeling like a knight before the queen. He was a good man, strong and loyal. I loved him, and yet I couldn't say yes. Will rose much like Atlas carrying the weight of the world.

"You can. You just won't." He wouldn't look up.

"That's unfair." I cast my eyes to the worn stone beneath

my feet. A scraggly weed had pushed up in a crack, trying valiantly to grow in a place where it oughtn't.

"Is it?" He touched my face, bringing my gaze to his. I'd never seen him so confused, or possibly frightened.

"I'm not the one leaving," I protested, throwing my hand back toward the underground carriage bay.

Will's expression turned cold. "I'm trying to give you a home where I can provide for you and protect you." He took a step toward me, trampling on the weed.

"You don't want to marry me. You want to keep me." I tilted my chin so I could look him in the eye.

He threw his arms out in exasperation. "Isn't that what a husband does?"

His words felt like a blow. I turned from him, because I couldn't stand the pain of it, or the horrible ill feeling that had gripped my middle. He didn't understand. He didn't understand at all.

"I can't give this up." I had to be reasonable. Reason and logic would win the day. We'd both do better with him here. We could both have what we wanted. If we traveled to Scotland, he would become something, and I would sit at home, as was expected of me. I couldn't stand it. "I've already accepted my nomination."

"And it will destroy us." He paused, as if he couldn't bring himself to say what he was thinking. Finally the words came, softly, so softly. "There's a greatness in you. It's a part of the reason I love you, but I fear that greatness will take you from me. Our love would be like tying a bird to a stone."

I glanced back at the aviary and the mechanical birds that had become so neglected that they had rusted. They perched still and quiet, diminished from what they could be. "If I don't take this chance, it will crush me."

"What would happen should you fail? You heard them in there." He waved toward the hall. "Those men have no intention of allowing you to succeed. They will wear you down, and they'll humiliate you . . ."

Yes, it was going to be a challenge. Of course I knew it would be difficult. I didn't need anyone to tell me that it was impossible or that I would fail. I had no room for such doubts. That's when it struck me.

I looked at him in disbelief. "You don't believe I can do it, do you?" I took a long breath to try to steady my heart. The pain returned, the crushing pressure. My head and heart ached in a way they never had before.

"Of course I do."

I shook my head. "No, you don't. Or you wouldn't say such things."

"You don't owe them your life." He reached out and twisted a leaf off the aviary with a snap. He dropped it. The leaf clanged against the stone, and the sound echoed off the walls. I looked around and for the first time noticed that the courtyard was empty.

"I owe it to myself to try." I touched the key hanging from the chain around my neck. "I want to be an Amusementist."

He gripped the cage so tightly, his knuckles turned white. "Do you love me, Meg?" he whispered.

"Of course I do." I answered quickly, but not tenderly. He flinched. I paused, wanting to say something more, but I didn't know what to say that could make this right.

His hair hung in his eyes as he stared at the hard stone beneath our feet. His shoulders rose, then fell. "It's not enough, is it?"

Once, he had claimed that love alone was not enough to feed us. At the time I'd thought our love was more powerful than anything. Now I wasn't so sure. I didn't answer.

"Well," he said, his voice resigned. "I suppose love can't help us, then." He kept his eyes downcast, focused on the ground just before his feet as he straightened his coat and turned away.

I panicked, reaching for him and catching his sleeve. "Will?" My voice didn't sound my own. It sounded as broken as my heart. I clung to him and he turned back to me. "Please don't say goodbye."

Will blinked, his dark lashes sweeping over his glittering eyes. He swallowed; then his lips parted.

I leaned toward him, hoping he would close the distance between us. His lips touched mine. It was a ghost of a caress against my tender skin, but I felt it in my soul.

"Farewell, then." He gently pulled my fingers from his coat, then took a step toward the ramp. His eyes burned with longing as he watched me. I didn't know if he hoped I would follow, but I couldn't. "Good luck, Meg."

He was leaving. He was leaving me.

With a final wave of his hand, he turned and disappeared down the ramp.

No.

I followed for one step, two, then balked. Bringing my hand to my mouth, I gasped as I turned and retreated back toward the aviary. He'd come back. Any second, he'd realize this was foolish and come rushing up the ramp.

Holding my breath, I glanced back to the ramp, drawn once again toward it. I had to force my feet to be still as I gripped my skirts so tightly that my knuckles ached. I prayed fervently in my mind. I swore to the good Lord above that I would give up on all wickedness if he would just make Will return. A cold drop of rain landed on my cheek, and a hot tear washed it away.

Please. Please come back.

My shoulders and arms shook as I shifted from foot to foot, craning my neck at the ramp. It fell away beneath a vault-like arch. Torches glowed from somewhere below, and the flickering light up the tunnel seemed ghostly. Any moment I would see his face rising from the ground as he ran back to me. He couldn't leave.

I love him.

A crushing agony pressed down on me, and I thought I would die of it. He wasn't coming back.

He was gone. I clasped my hands together as I sat in shock on a cold stone bench beneath the silent bower. The beady eyes of the mechanical birds stared at me, corroded and still. A light rain began to fall.

I pressed my lips to my knuckles.

My shoulders shook. How was I supposed to do this

alone? I needed him. He was the one person I could depend on. The tears streamed down my face, hot and stinging. Will had always been there for me. In the darkest of times, even when he'd wanted nothing to do with me, he'd always returned. I trusted him.

Now I had to face everything on my own. Somehow I had to find the courage and intelligence to prove myself. He'd left. He'd left me so he could become a laborer instead of something more. Why didn't he see in himself what I could see in him?

He had all the potential in the world. I didn't understand why he didn't wish to use it.

I clenched my jaw. It ached, and I bit down harder. The cold rain beat against my neck. I couldn't stay here like this. While it seemed certain my heart had been torn and would never again feel whole, the rain would not soothe such an ache.

Nothing would, and so there was nothing for it.

I rose to my feet. I had to move forward. The first step was to find my way home.

I followed Will's path across the courtyard, still silently hoping he'd realize his mistake. I kept picturing him running back to me, apologizing for his lack of faith in himself and us, and sweeping me around the courtyard as he kissed me.

My steps faltered. Lamplight shimmered on the rain-slicked stones. The entrance to the ramp jutted out from the thick monastery wall. It made the archway adorning the barrel-vaulted tunnel seem like the entrance to an ancient catacomb.

If I left this place, there would be no chance for Will to come back to me. It really would be over. My wet hair clung to my face, and I had to wipe it away from my eyes. The courtyard was dark, cold, and empty. I had no choice. The torchlight beckoned as I descended the ramp to the underground passage.

A great tunnel lit by torches stretched out to either side, rising and then turning beyond a bend in each direction. The tunnel was easily as large as one of the streets just beyond the monastery's walls, yet completely beneath the ground. On the far side of the wide tunnel was another archway and a similar ramp leading farther down into the darkness.

No light flickered within it. A heaviness settled over me as I turned away.

Oliver's fine coach waited for me. The only person remaining in the long tunnel was Oliver's coachman. He jumped to attention, then immediately offered me a blanket.

"Are you well, miss?" he asked, opening the door and giving me a hand up. The young man seemed genuinely concerned, but I couldn't bring myself to even look him in the eye as I settled into the dark corner of the carriage.

"I will be." I had to believe it was true.

"I'll get you home. A hot cup of tea will set you right." He closed the door. It creaked like the lid of a coffin as it shut, and I was surrounded by darkness.

Nothing would be right again.

CHAPTER SIX

THE NEXT WEEK PASSED BY IN A DRUDGING MISERY. EVEN with Mrs. Brindle doing her best to cheer me with fresh biscuits and cream, I found I had little appetite for either her treats or her conversation. The only thing I did seem to have an appetite for was creating a new lock and hidden bells that would ring loudly should anyone come into the shop.

Once both the front and the back were secure, I hid in Simon's workshop, spending hours upon hours on the spring in the frog's leg. No matter what I tried, I still couldn't get it to compress correctly. For some reason the tiny room tucked away behind the secret door gave me a sense of comfort. My world became very small, and so I felt I could manage it.

I didn't wish to go out and face my life. I don't know how long I concealed myself there. Mrs. Brindle knew about the workshop and kindly would leave me food on my counting desk just beyond the toy-laden shelves that masked the door, but she never dared intrude upon me.

I tried one more time to set the tension in the spring, then wound the frog. One leg kicked out, followed by the other a second later. As a consequence the poor thing looked like it had just suffered a sudden and painful death.

It lay on the table, twitching.

Lovely.

The door to the workshop creaked open behind me. I stiffened and whipped around, grasping the pistol as I did so.

"Leave it where it is." The voice was as feminine as it was gentle.

Lucinda.

She stood against the open shelves on the door and straightened one of the hand puppets that had fallen askew. The young widow looked a bit resigned, as if she had once been used to dragging her late husband out of the depths of the workshop as well.

I leapt from my seat and rushed toward my friend's open arms. As beautiful as sunlight on a clear spring morning,

Lucinda radiated warmth and compassion from her red-gold hair to her dainty toes. She held me tight as I fought tears of relief. I hadn't let myself feel anything for days. Being with Lucinda brought all the pain rushing back, but at least I didn't feel so terribly alone.

She offered me her handkerchief. "Oliver told me what happened."

I took the lacy little bit of silk gladly and dried my eyes. Lucinda led me out of the workshop and fixed the door so that it once again became a seamless part of the row of shelves filled with toys in the shop. Then she led me into the parlor. Mrs. Brindle set out tea. It shocked me that so much time had passed. I hadn't eaten yet that day.

Lucinda and I sat together, and she immediately fixed a plate.

"I can't believe he's gone," I said, knowing it was a silly thing to utter aloud. But then, I could hardly express how it felt to have my heart cut out with a hot knife.

"He's not gone." Lucinda took a sip of tea. "He's in Scotland." She handed me the plate as if nothing were the matter, and I immediately felt my chagrin as I took a bite from a cucumber sandwich.

It was a gentle reprimand, as such things go, but I heard the message all the same.

Quit your fuss. At least he's not dead and buried.

It wasn't as if I had forgotten that Lucinda's husband had been murdered. I lived in Simon's shop and studied his writings every single day.

Granted, it had been a bit of a shock to discover it had been her own father, Lord Strompton, who had committed the murders, in an insane attempt to prevent anyone from discovering or unlocking Rathford's time machine. At least that's what I believed motivated him. It all seemed so insane to me.

But truthfully, if having your father murder your husband was the threshold for allowable personal misery, I wouldn't ever be able to express my own sorrow.

My stomach twisted, and I put down the sandwich. If anything ever did happen to Will, I would beg for someone to gut me with a hot knife. It would be far less painful. Still, nothing could change the fact that I had been wholly abandoned and it felt miserable.

"If Will ever really loved me, he wouldn't have left," I muttered into my tea.

"Margaret Anne Whitlock, you stop this at once," Lucinda demanded. She snapped a serviette with a sharp *crack*, then laid it daintily over the frothy green skirt of her afternoon dress. "Will is trying to make something of himself. I, for one, support him. As should you, if you care for him at all."

I gaped at her in shock. "I thought you would side with me in this matter."

"I do." She placed a hand on my knee. "Which is why I'm here. You have the chance to do something great, something I have only ever dreamed of. I'll not have you throw that away for a broken heart. You're made of far greater mettle than that."

I tucked my head in chagrin and sipped my tea. My heart warmed at her faith in me in spite of my ill mood. It was only then that I fully became aware of her dress.

A rare blue-tinted green, or perhaps it was a green-tinted blue, the shade nearly matched her eyes, and complemented her honey-colored hair. "You're not in mourning for your father."

She scowled. "I refuse to mourn Simon's murderer."

Well, that would hardly go over well, considering the only people who knew of Lucinda's father's murderous tendencies were me, Oliver, Lucinda, and Will. The rest of society would be in a dither over her blatant affront to the dearly departed earl. "I can't blame you, but isn't your mother livid?"

Lucinda rolled her eyes. "She's half in the grave with it,

but I don't care. I just wish there were some way I could avoid her barbed insults at every single tea."

"There's room here if you'd like to return," I offered. It would be grand to live with my friend, and I wouldn't feel so alone. I only felt a modicum of guilt at my selfish intentions, if I felt any at all.

Lucinda gave me one of her warmest smiles. "I'd love to, but I really should go. Oh, that reminds me." She produced a neatly addressed envelope.

"What's this?" I took it and broke the wax seal. Lucinda didn't answer. Instead she allowed me to read the elegant and very precise script.

It was an announcement for an Amusementist wake for the late Earl of Strompton.

I met her gaze as she arched a brow at me. "Your father's funeral?" I asked.

Lucinda looked far too serious. "More like a summons to battle. Be warned."

I glanced back down at the neat handwriting. "It can't possibly be worse than battling a sea monster."

"Trust me, it will be." Lucinda sipped her tea, then placed the cup back on the tray.

She stood and pulled me to standing as well.

"Chin up." She held me out by both shoulders and gave me a regal nod. "You're going to be fine."

I certainly wished for that to be true. While her visit had done much to lift my spirits, it couldn't take away the aching sadness completely. I feared nothing ever would. Lucinda kissed me on the cheek, then breezed into the kitchen, where she spoke with Mrs. Brindle.

I knew they were talking about me, and I didn't want to hear it, so I retreated back into the workshop to straighten it up. One of the open journals caught my attention. It held a list of names, members of the Order. I had a habit of ignoring most of Simon's random scribblings in margins, as he'd had a tendency to draw whimsical things, I suppose to amuse himself.

This time they drew me in—at least one image did. It was a spiral, like the ram's horn, exactly like the mark on the bomb. Beside it a name had been hastily blacked out.

That was unusual. The rest of the page looked like a list of personal marks, with symbols followed by names, yet this was the only name that had been struck from the record. Holding the page up to the light, I tried to see what had been written before it had been blacked out, but it had been too thoroughly erased.

Deciding to leave it for a moment when I could delve into it deeper, I retreated from the workshop, closing the shelf that hid the secret door. A tin soldier fell over.

I picked him up and turned him over in my hand.

He was handsomely painted, a Highland fighter with a red kilt. I wondered if Will felt half as terrible as I did.

Lucinda approached my left. She plucked the little soldier from my hand and put him back on the shelf. "I'll see you soon." She tucked her gloved knuckle under my chin and tipped it up. "Until then."

I waved her out the door.

I had a new mystery to ponder.

CHAPTER SEVEN

I HONESTLY COULDN'T FATHOM HOW QUICKLY TIME could pass, until I felt I needed more of it and it simply wasn't there. While the constant ache of Will's absence filled me every day, I had too much to do to allow myself to steep in such thoughts. Instead I invested myself in my studies with greater vigor, hoping that the knowledge Simon Pricket had left in his journals was enough to keep me from making a fool of myself at the Academy.

The summons to appear at the monastery arrived one morning in a plain envelope sealed with bloodred wax. That evening, as I stood in an alley behind the mews, I felt as if someone had released a bucketful of mice down the back of my deep red afternoon dress. I tugged on the tight sleeves of my fitted black jacket. The dressmaker had accused me of having a frightful sense of fashion, but I had insisted that the dress be practical. The last thing I needed was yards of fabric hanging over my hands and wrists. The skirts were bad enough.

Fighting the urge to fidget, I waited as Bob adjusted the harness on his old gray gelding. Then he helped me up into the cart. "Good luck tonight." The old man smiled as if he were proud of me. For the first time in weeks, I felt I could breathe. Bob gave me a nod. "I'll be there for you when it's over. Don't be too late, or Mother will worry."

I smiled at him as he snapped the reins, and then the old cart clattered down the streets of Mayfair under the fading sun. It took a frightfully long time to cross London, and Bob's gelding wasn't a sprightly horse, to say the least. I looked around to pass the time.

Old London in the light of day didn't seem as bad as it had when I had first made this journey. Even the scent of the Thames wasn't quite so overpowering. I listened to the call of the birds on the docks. The streets were crowded, full of the hustle and bustle of London.

A deep and unmistakable sense of foreboding overcame

me, and I touched Bob on the arm. "Is that cab following us?" I whispered. It seemed to have been behind us an unnatural amount of time.

He stole a look over his shoulder and frowned. "I wouldn't worry about it, miss."

"Need I remind you that someone wants me dead?" I risked another quick glance, but from that distance the driver looked like a heap of dark clothing behind an equally dark horse. I strained to see if a clockwork mask covered his face, but it was no use.

"We'll see if he follows on the next corner." Bob urged the poor old horse faster as we turned down some of the narrow lanes. The evening sun grew darker and the shadows of the buildings loomed, while the clatter of the cart wheels rang in my ears.

I kept looking behind me, but the cab was gone.

Taking a deep breath, I tried to calm the worst of my fears. As soon as I reached the Academy, I'd be safe.

Finally we arrived at the old monastery. In the light the building seemed less ominous than the last time I had visited, but to my surprise Bob drove right past it. He turned down a narrow alley that ended at a large brick wall about twenty feet in front of us. Facing the dead end caused a sudden flash of panic. I felt trapped, and I looked back over my shoulder, expecting to see the man with the clockwork mask standing behind me with his pistol.

But there was nothing.

I was being a ninny.

"Why would you drive us here?" I asked him.

He winked at me. "It's not just inventors who are sworn members of the Order. We servants have a Guild of our own."

Using an old cane, Bob tapped a hanging lamp to his left. A voice emerged from it.

"Is it market day?" It sounded squeaky, like a rabbit speaking into a tin cup.

"Oi, carry the fat cabbage back to the house," Bob replied. I tried not to giggle nervously at the ridiculous password as the phantom mice seemed to run up and down my back. I should have realized certain servants would have had to be sworn to secrecy as well.

Suddenly what had been the solid brick street split before us, dropping down and sliding beneath the piles of old crates on either side of the narrow alley with surprisingly little noise. Beneath the false street a long ramp descended, leading to the underground carriage bay I had seen before.

Thank God, Bob's old gelding was nearly as old as

Mrs. Brindle and half-blind. The sweet old horse plodded down the ramp as if nothing unusual had just happened. When we reached the bottom of the ramp leading up to the courtyard, Bob helped me down and then tipped his hat before driving off.

In the dim light of the carriage bay, I took one deep breath, then headed up the ramp to the courtyard to meet my fate as an apprentice.

About ten boys stood in small groups laughing and taunting one another. Some were older, nearing nineteen years or so, and some looked closer to my age, not much more than sixteen.

All the conversation stopped as I walked forward from the carriage bay. Frankly, having conversations cease as soon as I entered was becoming quite tiresome. I searched the boys for any familiar face. In the far corner of the courtyard, near the aviary where Will had proposed to me, an older boy with dark skin and a strange cloth turban knotted at the top of his head stood in the shadows, watching.

I averted my eyes, not wishing to stare, and recognized someone at once. His name was Noah, and his father had often brought him into my family's shop. My father used to instruct me to entertain him as the adults talked. He was as lanky as ever, with long arms and wide hands. He had tamed his thick curling hair with a balm and stood proudly and stiffly. As the twisting feeling in my center tightened, I hurried to Noah's side.

"Hello, Noah," I greeted.

"You know the girl?" one of his friends exclaimed with a gleeful look on his face, as if he'd just won a round of cards. He laughed then, and I felt my face flush hot. Noah glared at me.

"Quiet, Jorgen." Noah didn't look at me, nor did it seem he would address me at all. "We knew each other as children."

I steeled myself, determined to find a place in one of the circles so I wouldn't have to hide in the shadows like the boy in the turban.

The towheaded boy named Jorgen held his sides as he laughed, and Noah grabbed me by the arm. He forced me a step back, then said in a furious tone, "See here, Meg. I promised my father I'd try to help protect your reputation, but we are not friends. Understand? I'm not going to help you, and I'm not going to let you hold me back."

Stunned, I retreated toward the ramp, not knowing where to turn, or where to take shelter. Noah was supposed to be a friend. I had become like a strange creature in a menagerie as the boys turned furtive glances at me. It felt as if every word they spoke were about me. I just wanted to wither away, to become something insignificant.

I found myself in a corner by the entrance to the monastery, watching the boys and imagining the worst as more and more of them strode confidently up the ramp from the hidden carriage drive.

I had never felt so alone in all my life.

"Don't worry about them," someone said near my left. I gasped and turned to see a boy with a round face. He unfortunately seemed the type who would always hold on to a vestige of youth. He had soft-looking brown hair near in shade to mine that fell over his brow in a careless way. "We're not here for them."

"That's true," I said, thankful that I had someone to talk with. My heart still hadn't settled. I wasn't sure if it ever would. "I don't believe we've met. I'm Meg Whitlock."

He smiled shyly. "I think we all know who you are. I'm Peter."

"It's a pleasure to meet you, Peter." Some of the strain I had felt began to ease, though I wondered why Peter had separated himself out from the rest of the groups as well. At least he was polite.

Just then a large pack of young men ascended the ramp, laughing and joking with one another. The crowd parted, and a tall and handsome young man with a smart red waist-coat and a neat black coat adjusted his lapels and beamed at the group. He had golden-blond hair and the air of a boy who felt he had no limits and expected attention as a matter of course.

I frowned as I watched the others in the courtyard. Like a magnet he attracted them. They couldn't help but turn and pay attention as he walked past. In his wake a small group followed like altar boys at the hem of the bishop. I couldn't figure what he could have done to deserve such adulation, and I found myself quite vexed, though I didn't know precisely why.

"Who is he?" I asked, not really intending the question to be answered. I wasn't sure why I cared, other than something about the way he only grinned out of one side of his mouth bothered me. That, and he looked familiar.

"You mean you don't know?" Peter looked appalled. "How can you be female and not know?"

"Should I be insulted?" I turned to Peter, and his shyness overcame him.

"That's David." Peter let out what sounded like a sigh.

Perfect, as if David's type needed a fatter head. Of course he was named David, the glorious young king of the Bible, chosen by God himself. How fitting. I gave Peter a wary glance, suspicious there was more to this story. "David who?"

"David Archibald Harrington, Earl of Strompton."

Oh, dear Lord. He was Lucinda's brother.

He looked just like his father. No wonder I didn't like him. I seemed to be in the minority. Even Noah followed in his wake, though the Earl of Strompton didn't seem to notice him.

Unfortunately, he did notice me.

His pale eyes met mine, and I felt trapped for a moment as he carefully considered me. Then he came forward.

I tried to appear interested in something else, anything, as he approached. Peter looked as if he were trying to become part of the wall. David sauntered up to us as though he were cock of the walk.

"Miss Whitlock," the young earl greeted me. "I've heard so much about you."

If there was one phrase I wished never to hear again, that was it. "I'm sorry I can't say the same. You are?" I tried for my sweetest smile as Peter raised a fist to his mouth and coughed.

To David's credit he replied, "David Harrington." He eyed me warily. "I'm hurt my sister Lucinda hasn't mentioned me."

I gave a casual shrug, doing my best to mask my sudden nervousness. "I'm afraid the subject never presented itself."

We had now gathered a large crowd. Indeed, now that our meeting time approached, the entire class of apprentices seemed to be huddled around David and me.

The crowd made me uneasy, and I feared I was doing myself no favors by needling the one boy in the group who had some semblance of power among the others.

A large and bulky boy with thick black hair and close-set eyes let out a low laugh that sounded more like a warning. "So this is the illustrious Miss Whitlock." His lip curled as he looked me up and down as though I were some broodmare at market. "I don't see what the fuss is about."

My heart pounded harder. While David might have irritated me out of principle, this boy scared me.

"She has a certain potential," David countered with that half-mouth grin that I supposed he felt was rakish or charming. I glanced around, but there was no escape. They literally had me with my back to a wall.

"Leave her alone," Peter said, moving closer beside me. I felt grateful for him. I hardly knew him, but he was the only boy so far who had extended me any sort of courtesy.

The dark-haired boy laughed. "Are you her nanny, Peter?" A low rumble of chuckles answered from the crowd. "At least her reputation is safe with you, eh?"

More laughter broke out, and Peter flushed.

"Sam." David crossed his arms.

"What? What can a girl possibly learn? Nothing." He laughed again, though it reminded me of a dog growling. My anger tightened my throat, and I fought to regain the power to speak. He sneered at me again. "Unless she wants to learn how to please her future husband. In that case, I'm sure we'd all be glad to tutor her."

The laughter frightened me now. I searched for a way to regain my sense of self as all the boys around me stared at me like a pack of dogs.

"Samuel, enough," David said, but he didn't bother to look at me. "You'll invite trouble from the headmaster."

"Honestly!" Samuel shouted to the crowd. "I bet the only pi she knows is in the kitchen!"

I took a step forward with my head held high. Righteous fury burned through me, and I did my best to imitate the daunting presence of the queen herself. In a sweet voice I said, "You're right, I do keep pies in the kitchen." The laughter died down as everyone looked to me. "Exactly three and one, four, one, five, nine, two, six, five, three, two, four, nine, seven, one . . ." His eyes widened, and I knew I had him. "Four, eight, five, one, three, seven, nine, two, four, two . . ."

The laughter now turned in my favor as the crowd of boys began making taunting sounds toward the brute and whistling their encouragement. I must confess, I had only memorized the first eight digits of pi, thanks to Simon's writings. After that I was just making things up. Apparently, I was quite convincing. "Shall I go on?"

Even David shook his head in amusement as he slapped his friend Samuel on the shoulder. The burly young man had turned as red as a radish, and was probably just as sour. David gave me an assessing gaze that made me uncomfortable. "Never enter a duel without knowing your opponent," he said to Samuel, though he didn't break his gaze from mine.

I couldn't determine what it was about him that made me want to kick him soundly, but my toe twitched to do it.

Just then the large doors that led into the monastery opened. Five men stood in the doorway wearing dark scarlet robes with hoods, like old monks.

The one in the middle lifted his head, and I recognized his monocle. He had been the one to lead me into the main hall of the Order during the Gathering.

He lifted a long black staff.

"Welcome to the Secret Order of Modern Amusementists!" He let the staff fall to the stone with a loud crack.

CHAPTER EIGHT

THE BOYS FELL SILENT, AND I FELT AN UNWANTED shiver race over my shoulders and arms as I lifted my chin and tried not to appear nervous.

"You are about to enter hallowed halls of science and imagination," the man with the monocle announced. I vaguely recalled someone referring to him as Nigel at the Gathering. "Within this sanctuary of the mind, we expect the impossible, and we demand perfection. We will hone the best and brightest among you and lead you to your rightful place within the Order. Only then will you know what it means to bear the honor of calling yourself an Amusementist. As for the rest, should you fail, you will always be no more than a child within the Order and a scourge upon your family name."

One of the boys coughed. I spared a glance, and judging by the wan faces on the others, I was not the only apprentice who suddenly felt pressure. Peter's face had turned a rare shade, and he looked as if he might take ill and loose the contents of his stomach upon the ground.

"Follow me," the Amusementist announced, and turned away from us with a sweep of his dark red robes. The boys pushed forward, falling into a neat queue, and I found myself between Peter and a stocky young man with chestnut hair.

My throat felt dry and my palms damp as we ascended the steps, snaked through the dark corridors, and passed the statue by the front entryway of the old monastery. Several of the boys gasped as the light swirled around us, glinting off the goddess's shining sword.

One of the men in the dark red robes fell back until he walked alongside me. "Don't worry, Meg. She's been here for centuries. You're not really the first woman to set foot in these halls," a familiar voice whispered.

"Oliver!" My voice squeaked as I tried to contain my relief. At least one person I could trust was here with me.

He put a finger to his lips beneath his red hood. "I just

wanted to wish you luck." He gave me a parting smile, then lengthened his steps to return to the front of the line. I now recognized where we were as we followed the same path I had the day of the Gathering.

We filed into the assembly chamber and descended the stairs between the gallery of seats to the floor where I had stood before the podium. A stream of men in dark red robes flooded into the chamber to stand just behind the top rows of benches along the high walkways. Each carried a torch, their faces obscured by the heavy hoods.

It all gave a rather dramatic impression, like a ritual sacrifice. For the briefest moment I wondered what I would have to lay upon the proverbial altar. I already felt I had sacrificed too much.

A loud *boom* echoed through the chamber from the ceiling above us. I gripped the silver key hanging by a chain around my neck and looked up with the rest of the apprentices.

The clicking of moving gears and the rattling of chains filled the room.

Like with the deus ex machina of ancient times, a platform slowly lowered from the ceiling. A man in a black robe with deep-red-and-gold trim stood amid four columns of fire that seemed to twist along coils around him.

For a moment I wondered if all this was necessary, but in truth the spectacle was so magnificent, I felt a deep desire to prove myself worthy of it.

Headmaster Lawrence pushed back his hood, looking very dramatic with his sharply angled face and pointed beard. He stepped off the platform and made his way to the podium before us. At once the contraption he had descended upon retreated, and the ceiling righted itself.

"He certainly has my attention," Peter murmured, and I bit back a laugh, doing my best to look somber and serious.

"My dear students," Headmaster Lawrence greeted. "It is my great honor to be the one to lead your instruction and initiation into the Secret Order of Modern Amusementists. As the majority of you already know, our Order is based on a foundation of absolute secrecy and trust. Betray the Order at your peril, for here you will find inspiration and fortune, but never fame. We create because it brings us closer to the divine."

His words boomed through the chamber, aided by the machine at the podium.

"It is time to pledge your fealty."

He waited as we each raised our hands and swore the oath I had already carefully memorized. At first all our voices were jumbled as we each said our name, but as a group we fell into rhythm, the words coming from us as one. "We swear by the arcane fire to guard the secret of the Order with our lives, to be true to the lineage that has made us great, and to aid one another when the need arises. . . . "

My mind wandered a bit as I recited the rest of the oath. During my initial adventures with Oliver and Lucinda, I'd found that the oath held little weight at all. It didn't stop a terrible string of murders, and sometimes the Order's secrecy was its greatest weakness. Too many dark intentions could hide behind the veil.

"And should I betray that trust, I forfeit my life."

The last word rang in the silence as we each felt the weight of it. I glanced around, wondering if the others felt the same heaviness that seemed to press on my shoulders. Peter looked at his shoes, clearly deep in thought about something. Only David looked confident. Surely he wouldn't have looked so righteous if he'd known the truth about the atrocities his father had committed. It was a horrible thought.

Secrets were a heavy burden to bear.

"Congratulations!" Headmaster Lawrence proclaimed. A round of applause and cheers erupted from the men in robes standing above us. They began to take down their hoods, beaming. Some, most likely proud fathers, waved to the boys.

Headmaster Lawrence continued. "You are now sworn apprentices of the Order. We are all equals here, and no title should set you above your peers. The honor and the prestige of your family name now rest upon you. Do well, and your family will gain greater power and fortune within the Order. Do poorly, and your family's fortunes will pay the price. From this point on you shall only refer to one another by your given, Christian names." At this point the boys around me seemed to breathe a sigh of relief as they started to mingle and introduce themselves. "Except!" Headmaster Lawrence's voice rose even as I felt my heart fall. His gaze locked on me. "Due to propriety, the young lady in our midst shall only be called by her proper name, Miss Whitlock. For the duration of your time as apprentices, she is to be treated with special care."

Oh, hell!

I opened my mouth to protest. I didn't wish to be the only one forced to use my family name. Propriety could be damned. I had worked as a housemaid, for heaven's sake. My name was Meg! And frankly, while I understood the need, I didn't wish to feel the burden of such scrutiny, either.

"With that, we shall adjourn until instruction begins. Welcome, apprentices, and best of luck."

"Wait!" I called out, holding my hand up toward the dais, but Headmaster Lawrence had already disappeared into the crush of men descending the stairs.

Men pressed in all around me as fathers congratulated sons. I felt adrift in the sea of bloodred robes. Everyone seemed to know everyone—they were smiling and patting backs—but I was lost and very much alone.

I tried to imagine what my father's face would have looked like as he stood among his peers welcoming me to the Order, but he was dead. My dear grandfather wasn't here to see me either.

The worst of it was, if they had been here, I wouldn't have been. They never would have allowed me to become an apprentice. Only Oliver was enough of a rebel to suggest it. Suddenly the crowd of bodies was too much. The overlapping scents of torches, sweat, and imitation cologne nearly choked me.

A hearty laugh rang out over the crowd, but it sounded as harsh and jarring as breaking glass. I looked up to see David with his head thrown back, regaling a large group. His ice-like gaze met mine, and he cocked his head, watching.

I felt my eyes sting. I couldn't show weakness here. Not in front of any of them. Lifting my chin, I climbed the steps and found my way into the cool, dark hall that led outside.

My breath caught in my throat as I stepped down into the empty courtyard. The warm summer air didn't give me much relief, and the smell of the Thames was hardly more appealing than the air in the hall.

Glancing around, I noticed a light glinting off the mechanical aviary.

Oh, how I wished Will were with me. I depended on him too much. Perhaps that was the problem.

I didn't wish to linger in the courtyard, either. It was only making me feel worse. With no other place to go, I descended the ramp to the carriage bay and sat near the bottom, waiting for Bob to return with the cart. If I had to wait an hour, at least I'd be alone.

Propping my hands under my chin, I sighed and listened to the dark and empty tunnels before me. Only then did my exhaustion begin to take hold. My eyelids felt heavy, and I rested them for only a moment.

Something clattered from beyond the second ramp that led down into the darkness on the other side of the carriage bay. I bolted up, my heart suddenly in my throat.

My mind raced as I fought the urge to call out, "Who's there?" My silence was my only advantage. I pressed myself against the smooth brick and listened. If I had any sense, I'd return to the hall at once.

It was dark, and I was alone.

If the man in the clockwork mask came upon me now, it would be all too easy for him to carry me off into the catacombs beyond the second ramp. He could murder me in the dark, and no one would hear me scream.

As I grabbed my skirts to retreat to the courtyard, I thought I heard footsteps.

They seemed to be coming from the catacombs. If I tried to run up the ramp to the courtyard, a person climbing up from the catacombs would see me. I didn't have a weapon, which was foolish.

There was only one thing to do. Keeping myself pressed to the brick, I slid deeper into the long dark tunnel of the carriage bay until the inky blackness completely shrouded me.

Footsteps echoed, coming closer . . . closer. Someone was down there.

I held my breath and tried to make my body as still as possible. Whoever it was, they would hear me. Somehow they would see me.

I felt a bead of sweat trickle close to my ear as I stared,

transfixed by the patch of evening light pouring down through the ramp's archway that led to the courtyard.

A distant rumble of hooves sounded, and suddenly the entire corridor brightened as the whirring flint-wheels fixed above the lights spun against strikers and rained sparks down on the braziers beneath them. In the glow of the sparks, I could have sworn I caught a glimpse of a dark cloak caught in the air as a man turned and disappeared quickly into the darkness of the catacombs.

The braziers blazed to life, and I winced, closing my eyes. I held my breath as I blinked, trying to adjust to the light. When I could open my eyes once more, the dark apparition I thought I had glimpsed was gone.

I feared he was all too real.

The plodding gray horse and old cart ambled toward me with Bob at the reins.

"I'm here!" I called.

"Hullo, miss!" he greeted as he waved. "Did you have a good time?"

I rushed to the cart. "I have never been so glad to see you." Or the pistol he carried.

"As my mother likes to say, if you're early, you're on time." He gave me a cheerful grin as I climbed into the cart, and then I looked down the ramp toward where I had heard the footsteps. I wasn't sure if it was the man in the clockwork mask, but I didn't wish to linger to find out.

"Your timing is impeccable," I responded. I wanted to believe the Academy was safe. Now I had my doubts.

CHAPTER NINE

I RECEIVED MY FIRST SUMMONS TO THE ACADEMY FOR lessons the very next morning. It was a simple card marked with the symbol of the Order and a date and time. I would likely see several more of the notes before the summer was through. The majority of our instruction needed to take place while my fellow apprentices were home from their other schools.

The following day I had prepared to arrive well before the appointed time at the Academy, but the horse threw a shoe on the way there. I could see the tower of the old monastery peeking above the roof of a trodden-down apothecary, but I couldn't get there. Bob had to check the poor beast for lameness, and I was forced to wait patiently while he unhitched the old horse and then led him up and down an alley, watching his feet.

The horse had a slow and awkward gait on a good day. I couldn't see anything amiss, but Bob insisted on walking him up and down five times before he was satisfied the situation wouldn't get worse. I could swear my insides were crawling with frustration as I watched Bob's knotty hands slowly buckle the harness once more. It was a nightmare, and the panic I'd felt at being late for the Gathering was nothing compared to this.

Finally we reached the monastery, but I was so late, the person managing the hidden ramp had left his post, and I was forced to enter through the front. After I gave the password, the doors pulled open. I could sense disapproval from the statue of Athena in the entry. She peered down at me with a scowl as if she were thinking the very thing I was.

You're tardy.

I had only ever been in the Gathering hall and did not know my way around the stone corridors. A man with a pronounced widow's peak and an equally impressive glower led me to a room on the second level. Our footsteps echoed down the long, empty corridors. I winced with each step. He opened the heavy door to a large room. It creaked almost as if it were laughing at my predicament.

The large room had tiers of heavy wooden desks, with a stone stair leading down to a large table at the front of the room. Weak light filtered in through mullioned windows, but it did little to augment the light burning in glowing lamps suspended from the ceiling with thick iron chains.

I tried to slip quietly into a seat at the back, stowing my basket beneath the bench, but it was of no use. The room was filled with young men in smart red waistcoats and trim black jackets. All their eyes were on me.

"Good of you to join us, Miss Whitlock," stated the old man standing behind the long table at the front of the room. He squinted at me through his spectacles, and his heavy jowls twitched. Dear Lord, it was the same man who had so vehemently protested my nomination at the Gathering.

I felt hot through the tips of my ears as I kept my eyes down. I didn't even know his name, or what the rest of the apprentices had been discussing. A large arrangement of parts and gears had been spread out over the head table, but I didn't know what to make of it.

"As I was saying." He sounded quite perturbed. "First

and foremost our work is about precision." His wrinkled brow creased. "Miss Whitlock!"

I stood while keeping my hand pressed against the desk to steady myself. I waited, knowing he was only calling on me to humiliate me. The quiet huffs of suppressed laughter from the boys in the room weren't muffled enough for me to ignore.

"Could you please tell me what the gear ratio for an epicyclic gear configuration should be and describe the difference between the ratio from the sun gear to the planet gears versus the annulus?" He clasped his hands behind his back and rocked on his heels so that his rounded belly swung forward and back.

Epicyclic gear trains. I knew I had read about them, but I couldn't recall the exact formulae regarding them. I needed to see it written down. I attempted to picture the complex gears from the drawings in Simon's notes, but the pages of his journals remained blank in my mind. My palm began to feel slick on the smooth wood of the desk.

"Is the sun gear to remain stationary?" I asked, horrified that I didn't know the correct answer. I needed more time. The hushed whispers among the boys grew louder. My cheeks felt as if they had caught on fire.

"Sit down, Miss Whitlock." There was no ignoring the disgust in his voice. I didn't just sit; I tried to melt into the floor. I wanted to disappear. I felt as if every boy in the room were staring at me as though I were an imbecile.

The instructor continued on for two hours, and his voice sounded as if he were speaking through mud. I tried to write down all the things he said. Simon's notes were so fluid and clear. Mine looked like bits of words here and there. When I looked back on them, they seemed to have no real meaning at all.

Finally the instructor announced a break between lectures, and instead of feeling elated I felt completely defeated. I just wanted to escape, but as I tried to leave the room, the boy named Samuel blocked my path. David stood beside him.

"Feeling overwrought?" Samuel asked, his voice pitched high with fake concern, like a violin bow scratched discordantly against a string. "You know there are places dedicated to the care of women suffering from such maladies."

David arched a perfect eyebrow. One of the other boys knocked into my shoulder, throwing me off balance.

Horrified at the suggestion that I belonged locked up in

an asylum, I tried to think of a witty retort. In the end all I could say was "I've done nothing to you."

Samuel scowled as if he'd just swallowed something distasteful. "You're insane if you think you belong here."

"Leave her," David said, and pulled Samuel away. "She's not worth the trouble."

Samuel shook off his grasp and glared at him. "You're the one who finds her so interesting."

"This isn't about her, and you know it." David placed his hand on Samuel's shoulder again and turned him toward the door. The young earl glanced back at me over his shoulder with an inscrutable expression.

I felt as if I'd just been gutted as the room quickly emptied. Finally I stood alone and tried to calm the sick feeling in my middle.

It had taken all of one day for the Academy to reduce me to a flayed piece of meat hanging, cold and exposed, on a hook. I just wanted to get away from the classroom. The air inside was choking me.

I wandered through the halls without really looking at where I was going, until I found a small storage room. Thankfully it was empty, so I tucked myself inside and sat on a lopsided bench near the narrow stained-glass window. I attempted to regain my composure. My hunger growled at me. In my distraction I had forgotten my basket with the luncheon Mrs. Brindle had prepared for me.

A light rapping sounded at the partially open door. "May I enter?"

I lifted my face from my hands to see Peter leaning against the door. His heavy-lidded eyes considered me carefully. I smoothed a wrinkle from my skirt and sat straighter under his scrutiny.

"Do you wish to taunt me too?" I asked.

"That was unfair of Instructor Barnabus," he said without even acknowledging my question. Peter entered the room and took a seat on the low end of the bench. He rested his elbows on his knees and laced his fingers together.

I turned and traced the edge of a curving piece of dark green glass in the window. "It wasn't unfair. That's the problem. I was late, and ill prepared." I had known this wasn't going to be easy, but I felt horrid all the same.

"I couldn't have answered," Peter confessed. "I doubt anyone could have. We've only been here half a day, and he had barely explained what planetary gear trains were before you walked in. I wouldn't concern yourself with being the worst in the class, because I'm certain that title will fall to me."

That made me smile. "No, it won't. You were raised to be an Amusementist."

He gave me a strange look, and I realized that I had absolutely no basis for my assumption. "Weren't you?" I added.

Peter shook his head. "I was studying to become a man of the church."

"No." It burst out of me, and I smiled. Actually, he had the sort of demeanor that would have suited a man well in such a profession.

"Truth." He placed one hand on his heart and the other in the air to testify to his oath. "Life was blessedly unremarkable. I was the son of a country physician. Now we have inherited the estate of a cousin I knew nothing about, and everything has changed." He twisted his hands, then clenched them into fists. "This is just one more thing that is expected of me as the only heir to our new fortune. I don't even like London. When I fail, all this bother will be for naught."

"Don't say that." I didn't want him to fail. He was the only other apprentice who was willing to speak with me. "You won't fail," I said, and his shoulders eased ever so slightly. "I'm sure you'll be brilliant."

"Clearly, you don't know me well." He smiled shyly, then my middle gave a horrible rumble.

"I have some cheese and bread here. You're welcome to a bit if you'd like." He pulled a small bundle from inside his coat and unwrapped the cloth.

I gratefully took what he offered.

He leaned back against the wall and stared at the ceiling as he tore a piece of bread and chewed it thoughtfully. "I'd offer you more, but the new cook is a bit odd. She has certain well-tried specialties, but for some reason she absolutely refuses to make them. Says she's bored with them. Instead she keeps experimenting, and I'm afraid my palate can't afford her broadening her horizons."

I laughed out loud, and it lifted my spirits considerably. "I'm fairly certain my housekeeper was a nursemaid to Caesar, but she puts her experience to good use, so long as you keep her from the pepper."

It was his turn to laugh.

"You're good company, Miss Whitlock."

I was the one who was grateful for him. It was nice to have someone I could consider a friend. "Please, call me Meg."

We ate in companionable silence, and by the time our

small meal was finished, I was in a far better mood, even if I had not regained my confidence.

All too soon our brief reprieve was over, and we had to wander back to our lectures. Thankfully, Peter knew the way.

Whatever spirits I had bolstered during our luncheon were swiftly quashed. The sheer amount of information— gear ratios, compression limits, calculations for potential energy, and calculations for steam pressure in a closed vessel—pummeled me. My head felt numb as I tried furiously to comprehend what was being taught.

The equations might well have been in Greek. In truth, they looked as if they were in Greek, considering they seemed to utilize more than half of the Greek alphabet and yet managed to contain no numbers.

Having pi memorized helped considerably, but I still felt as if I were swimming in water too murky and deep for me to make it back to shore. Thankfully, Peter had chosen to sit beside me. When Instructor Barnabus prattled on about how material affected the compression of springs, Peter was quick to offer me a roll of his eyes. And when the subject turned to pistons, he shared a bewildered shake of his head.

Instructor Barnabus seemed intent on proving I had no mind for numbers at all. He singled me out four more times, and I wasn't once able to give him an answer to his satisfaction.

"Miss Whitlock!"

I sighed as I stood yet again.

"Yes, Instructor Barnabus?" This was really becoming quite tedious.

"How would one determine the correct radius for a gear needed to increase the speed of the turning axle by a factor of two?"

I blinked. Finally! Something I knew. I'd had to calculate something very similar while working with my mechanical frog. "Begin by—"

"That's enough, Miss Whitlock," he said, dismissing me. I stared, slack jawed. Enough! I had hardly begun. He didn't want to hear what I had to say. He didn't want me to show him I could answer him and answer him well. Enough indeed. I had had enough.

"David!" he called. The young earl rose at the front of the class. To my endless humiliation he proceeded to say exactly what I had intended to say.

"Very good, David," Barnabus praised. "Clearly, you have a capable mind."

I clenched my fists, and Peter had to gently take my wrist

and pull me back to my seat. "Ignore it," he whispered as David beamed at the class, then perched on his chair like it was the royal throne.

By the end of the day, I felt as if I had been run over by a locomotive. I wanted to follow the boys out to the court-yard and down the ramp to the carriages, but I had promised myself I would do one thing first.

At the entrance hall I stood amidst the shifting colored light on the floor, wondering if I shouldn't just go home to lick my wounds. The day hadn't gone in my favor, and my luck was unlikely to turn. But I couldn't leave what I felt unsaid. I turned to the owl and looked directly into its large glass eyes while the tiny gear wheels just above the beak turned. "I'd like to speak with Headmaster Lawrence, please."

There was no answer. I shifted from foot to foot, wait-ing for something, some sort of acknowledgment that I even existed at all. I could trace the path of one blue triangle of light on the floor from memory before the headmaster finally entered the hall.

"Come with me," he said. Subdued and concerned about my interview with him, I followed, watching the edge of my skirt as I did so. He led me to one of the upper floors and to his office.

It was clear immediately that he had held this position for some time. The room was well lived-in. Bits and pieces of half-built machines each had a space, from the body of a carefully crafted mechanical peacock, to abstract brass and silver contraptions with unknown purpose. His tools and papers were well organized.

I watched the headmaster carefully as he arranged himself in an ornate high-backed chair that dominated the desk. It fit in well with the oppressive bare walls and narrow windows. He smoothed his sharp beard and steepled his fingers.

"You wished to speak with me?" He seemed unconcerned.

I looked down to the smooth polished wood of the old desk. I had practiced in my mind what to say, for hours on end the night before, but now I struggled to find the strength to say it.

It was best to say it outright. "I wish to be called Meg by the other students, Headmaster."

He pursed his lips and folded his hands on the desk. "I see. I'm afraid that is not possible."

Of course it was possible. My name was Meg. Three letters. *M-E-G*. It wasn't even difficult to say. I looked him in the eye as I swept my hand out. "Insisting upon calling me by my family name singles me out from the others."

He seemed unimpressed as he leaned back as far as the stiff-backed chair would allow him to go. "You are already singled out." He tilted his head ever so slightly. "Whether you wish to be or not."

I looked down at my hands and fell silent. I couldn't deny that.

He let out a heavy sigh. "Perhaps it was unfair of me to nominate you—"

"No," I protested, looking back to him.

He raised his hand to silence me. "No matter what you are called, the fact remains you will never be the same as your peers. You have to be something more, and when you are, any acknowledgment of your success will be grudging. Your name is inconsequential."

"My apologies, Headmaster, but I believe you are mistaken." I placed my hand on the desk. Indeed there was no changing my gender, but my name would be a constant reminder of that division. "If the others are to see me as an equal member of this Academy, my name should not stand between us. How am I to be treated as an apprentice if every student here must address me as if they were paying call. I cannot be both things at once."

"But you can be quite bold, which is part of the reason

I nominated you. You will remain a part of this Academy so long as it is on my terms." The corner of his thin mouth turned up in a smile. "However, you have no room for error, my dear. If you have to leave your home on Wednesday to be here on Sunday, I expect you to do it. Am I clear?"

"Yes, Headmaster."

"I do not wish to be made a fool. I greatly admired your father, and I expect you to honor his legacy." He stood, towering over me.

I felt suddenly guilty. "Yes, Headmaster."

"Go now. I have much to prepare before the next meeting." He casually waved a hand toward the door.

"But my name—"

"Shall remain as it is. Call it a concession to propriety. I do not wish for the young men to forget themselves. As long as you are here, I am responsible for your welfare. Good day, Miss Whitlock."

He sat back down, and I had no other option but to leave the room. In one day I had run the gauntlet, and in the end my reward was a curt dismissal.

It was my name, and yet somehow my name was prisoner to the need to make sure the young men didn't behave boorishly. I just wanted to learn. That's all I'd ever wanted, and yet today I had learned several things, and none of them had anything to do with inventions.

Something woke in me. I didn't know what it was, only that it felt raw and powerful. I would prove myself. I would show them all.

And I would start with the headmaster.

CHAPTER TEN

OVER THE COURSE OF THE NEXT WEEK, THE WEATHER grew hot, and I grew hotter. I harnessed the power of my anger, and I used it to forge myself armor and weapons to use against my fellow apprentices and, unfortunately, my instructors. Every morning when I woke, the first thought I allowed in my mind was a single statement.

If knowledge exists, then there is nothing preventing me from learning, and learning well.

And learn I did.

Gear train configurations, common joint couplings, output potential for different rotor configurations, calculations for determining the center of gravity, numbers upon numbers upon even more numbers.

And then there were the drawings. The Amusementists had a very specific annotation technique that was almost an art form.

Everything else in my life fell away. I hardly noticed dust on the shelves of the toy shop, and if I did, I forced myself to leave it be. I had more important work to do.

Mrs. Brindle did her best to keep shop, but she became very concerned for me. Several times she implied that it simply wasn't natural for a young girl to think of nothing but figures and calculations. On one occasion her advice pushed me over the edge, and I snapped at her that while well-meaning, she knew nothing about what I could or could not think.

I was determined, but it hurt. I ached with exhaustion. My eyes would burn with fatigue, and my body grew stiff as I studied for hours before the dying light of the lantern in my workshop. I was living two separate lives stacked atop one another. My sleep paid the price.

I didn't feel like myself. Instead I was becoming a machine. My mind worked through problems the way pins and wheels seamlessly fit together, but there was no emotion in it, just the drive of never-ending pressure.

One evening I returned from my lessons with my mind spinning like a web of intricate gears. I couldn't make it stop. Visions of joints, pins, bolts, and springs arranged themselves over and over in my imagination. I could hear the endless drone of my instructors prattling off a ceaseless string of numbers. I didn't see the toys as I passed through the shop. It was a blur of shadows and color. Instead I stumbled into the parlor and fell into the chair by the fire. I didn't even bother to say hello.

Mrs. Brindle came in carrying tea. She placed it on the table, but I still couldn't bring myself to speak. The instructor for the day had been from Belgium. He had been fair, but every time he'd asked a question, David had stood and said, "I believe Miss Whitlock knows the answer, sir."

Bastard.

I found myself repeating the same responses over and over as the instructor struggled to comprehend me. Eventually I forced David to quit his game by giving my responses in French. While my versatile language skills had put David in his place, it had been taxing.

Mrs. Brindle gave me a concerned smile and placed an envelope on the tray beside the teapot. "This came for you, dear." She folded her hands and left the room.

I glanced down at the battered envelope, then blinked. It

took me a moment to find the courage to reach out and grasp it. I turned it over and recognized the writing at once.

Will.

My heart nearly burst with everything I was feeling at once. Elation that he had written, fear of what he had said, deep and terrible grief that he was not with me, and more than anything else, I felt relief that he thought of me at all.

With fumbling fingers I tried to open the envelope gently, but it was no use. I tore it as I revealed the single page of neat, blocked writing.

Dear Meg,

I hope you are well. I am happy here in Scotland. The others at the Foundry took me in at once, and it is good to feel I am part of a clan. Our last conversation didn't end well. I want you to know, I think of you often.

In spite of all I have discovered here, my life is not the same as it was in the spring. I am doing my best to make my name one you can be proud of. I hope your fortunes are as favorable.

Until we meet again. I hope it will be soon.

With love,

Will

I read the note over and over, my eyes tracing each careful stroke of ink on the paper. It must have taken him hours to write the letter. On the one hand, I wished for more. I wished that he'd filled the page with declarations of love and remorse at leaving me. On the other, the note was genuine Will, through and through. He was never one to waste words.

Tracing my finger over the sentence "I think of you often," I felt something in me break. Like a spring that had been pushed too far, my thin control snapped, and every other thought in my head fell apart. All my worries, all the pressure, fell away and was replaced by a new image of Will in my mind, happy and surrounded by friends.

A tear splashed onto the page, and I cried. Pressing the letter to my chest, I cried until sleep claimed me by the fire.

As I arrived in the carriage bay for my next set of instruction, my spirit felt lighter than it had in months. I could feel the crinkle of Will's letter tucked into the pocket I had sewn into the folds of my skirts. Usually the pocket held small springs, gears, writing utensils, and other sundry things I tended to need on hand. Today it held my heart. As I caressed the corner of the paper, I could think of nothing else I wished to have so near.

It felt freeing to think of something other than formulae and mechanics for a change. Will thought of me often. I was determined to do the same.

I actually found myself smiling as I ascended the ramp into the courtyard. Unfortunately, David was there with Samuel by his side as always.

Still, the pair of them couldn't dampen my mood. "Good day," I greeted with an even brighter grin.

"What's come over you?" Samuel asked with his usual scowl. David just watched me closely with his disconcerting light eyes, like a Siamese cat, intent and curious.

"Am I not allowed to smile?" I grabbed the side of my skirt and gave it a playful swish. The letter crinkled softly, as if laughing with me. Samuel took a step closer to me, leaning forward to force me to back down with his bulk.

I sidestepped and nodded to the boy with the knotted turban, standing on the steps that led inside. He kept his eyes trained on Samuel.

"You wouldn't smile if you knew how poorly you were doing," Samuel taunted.

I tilted my head in a saucy manner. "I know I scored twice as well as you did on our last exam."

A ginger-haired boy who had just reached the top of the

ramp guffawed. Samuel lunged, but David grabbed him and held him back. "Don't," he warned.

I started up the steps to put distance between us, even as the boy with the turban took a step down toward the courtyard.

"What are you looking at, Punjab!" Samuel shouted. Then he straightened his waistcoat with a stiff jerk. I turned away and entered the safety of the halls.

Peter met me there and walked with me to the lecture room. He gripped his handful of books tightly. "You shouldn't provoke him," he warned.

"He's like a dog barking from the other side of a gate," I said. David was irksome, but at least I could grudgingly acknowledge that he was intelligent and had a mind for numbers. But he was arrogant, privileged, and a general thorn in my side. Samuel was worse, insulting others from the safety of David's coattails.

"He's also the headmaster's son." Peter opened the door, and we found our place in the back of the hall.

"Is he really?" I'd had no idea. They didn't resemble one another much. While the headmaster was slight with light hair, Samuel was dark and burly. He probably took after his mother.

"Talk of the Devil," Peter whispered as Samuel entered the room, his eyes still burning with fury.

"Hey, see here," Samuel called to the class. "Both ladies are in the back tittering like old hens."

Peter flushed and looked down at the desk.

"Why don't you sit in the front so no one can see you moving your lips while you write," I suggested to Samuel.

Again a couple of boys punctuated the insult with a low ooh and a laugh.

Samuel could have spit fire at me.

I crossed my arms. "Care for another go, or is it too taxing?"

"I wouldn't mind doing battle," David interjected as he came through the doorway.

I swung my gaze to his, and my confidence dropped, along with half of my innards. Thankfully, I didn't have a chance to retort.

"Take your seats, everyone," a familiar voice called.

Oliver!

My smile stretched across my face as I watched Oliver enter through a narrow door at the corner of the room behind the large table. His wild hair was as messy as ever, but his face glowed with good humor as he tucked his thumbs into the pockets of his waistcoat and looked over the class. I pressed a hand to the letter in my pocket. For a moment it felt as if the sun had broken through the endless fog of winter.

"David, to your seat," Oliver said with casual warning in his voice. David marched down the stair, brought to heel by his older, richer, and higher-ranking future brother-in-law.

I could have done a jig.

Peter opened his books and prepared his inkwell, but before he could dip his pen, Oliver held out a hand and said, "Books away, if you please. Today will be a practical lesson. Bring only a small notebook and a drawing stick."

Everyone in the room spoke in hushed voices at once, and the excitement in the air was palpable. We could actually *do* something, instead of listening to a lecture and writing notes.

"Very good," Oliver announced as we scrambled to collect our things. "Follow me, if you will."

We arranged ourselves into file as Oliver led us back down the hall and out to the courtyard. Once we had grouped together in the large space, he led the way to the aviary of mechanical birds standing silently in the corner.

He clapped his hands together once, then addressed us.

"So far you have been learning theory and mathematics, which are all well and good." Oliver placed one hand behind his back and gestured with the other. "But being an Amusementist is not simply about numbers. We find solutions to problems." He paused and gave us a playful shrug. "Or we create problems and force another to fix them. It's a long-standing tradition, I'm afraid."

I edged around the back of the crowd, unable to see over the tall boys in front of me.

Oliver continued. "As you can see, this Amusement has been corroded by age. When it was first invented, the birds could sound a whistle using steam channeled through the pipes. We used them to call those in the courtyard to meetings. The birds haven't worked in more than twenty years. Your assignment is to inspect the birds and before our next meeting come up with a design that can either repair the aviary as it stands or create something even more spectacular." The light caught on Oliver's spectacles and he grinned. "You have three days. We'll implement the best design, and together hear the birds call once more. Good luck!"

I surged forward, ready to pull the entire aviary apart if I had to. This was what I had been waiting for. I embraced the challenge as I caught a glimpse of Headmaster Lawrence watching us from the top of the steps.

I had to be the one to come up with the very best solution. This would be my chance to shine.

CHAPTER ELEVEN

UNFORTUNATELY, I WAS NOT THE ONLY ONE EAGER TO
inspect the birds. The other boys crushed forward, and
I feared they would knock the entire Amusement over in
their haste.

Realizing it was a futile effort, I took a step back and
sketched what I could of the upper portions of the cage of
pipes. I needed a closer look. I couldn't force my way in, and I
couldn't see anything useful if I did. Sometimes being a head
shorter than all the others was a real hindrance.

I looked away in frustration, and noticed a small portion
of dark pipe running along the base of the high stone wall.
Curious, I stepped over to it and kicked the dirt. The pipe

continued along the entire length of the wall. It disappeared into a small hole along the portion of the wall that stood above the sunken carriage bay. The skin on my arms tingled.

There was more to the aviary than it appeared. I needed to find the rest of it. Holding my sketchbook close to my chest, I made for the ramp and hurried down.

"Miss Whitlock, giving in already?" David called out. I didn't bother to look back at him. Fools could follow their own folly. I was on the path of discovery. I only hoped it wouldn't lead to a dead end.

As I glided down the ramp, only the light from the archway behind me lit the long corridor beneath the ground. I took a step to the right and inspected one of the braziers that illuminated the passage when the carriages came through.

It had a flint-wheel above it. I had seen similar torches before. The mechanism was fairly simple: When a line was pulled, the wheel above the torch spun. The outer edge of the wheel was lined with flint. As it spun it rubbed against the striker and showered the torch with sparks, allowing it to light.

I just had to find the line. Following a thin pipe that linked the torches together, I traced the connections to a small lever near the bottom of the ramp. It stuck a bit, but I managed to pull the lever. There was a popping sound, and then the flint-wheels spun in a rain of sparks. The torches caught fire, lighting the passage.

I peered up and down the passage, not forgetting the strange footsteps I had heard the last time I had wandered down the ramp alone. I couldn't be certain that the man with the mask had been lurking in the darkness, but I had to be careful. I took a turn to the right and walked along the carriage bay, until I found a large metal panel easily six feet tall affixed to the wall, with two doors bolted to it.

I reached out to open the door.

"What are you doing down here?"

I jumped and spun around, bringing my hand to my throat. "Peter!" I gasped, suddenly dizzy from my shock. "Don't ever do that again."

He held his hands up. "My apologies. I didn't mean to frighten you."

I motioned for him to come closer. "I think I found the engine."

Peter's round face went slack with relief. "Brilliant!" He hurried to my side, and together we swung open the doors.

A rat scurried out, squeaking as it did so. I squealed, jumping behind Peter. He laughed at me so forcefully, he nearly doubled over. I shoved him hard on the shoulder, and he stumbled to the side.

"It was just a rat," I grumbled.

"I'm not the one who leapt to the ceiling." He wiped his eyes, then stepped closer for a better look. A large boiler took up most of the chamber, but there was little extraordinary about it, just a firebox steam chamber and pipes. "What a mess."

"There's your problem," I said, pointing at a large crack in the pipe leading from the old boiler.

"Well, you certainly saved me a lot of work." Peter closed the door. "This should be simple to repair."

I nodded, but already I was thinking far beyond repairing a cracked pipe.

Back in my workshop I hastily pulled journal after journal from the shelf above my desk. I flipped through the pages with a driven urgency, searching for something I had read months before.

This was the one time Simon's prodigious volume of notes became a terrible hindrance.

One of the leather-bound books fell to the floor with a soft thud. I stooped to retrieve it, then thumbed through the pages. Finally I found it.

Simon Pricket had taken elaborate notes on the inner workings of several Amusements that had been created by the Order. Sure enough, within the journal he had created a detailed map of the flow of steam through the pipes of the gilded aviary at the Academy, as well as the inner schematics for the birds.

A rudimentary whistle was embedded in the body of each bird. Simon had noted which tone each bird in the aviary emitted. He had also noted that as the pressure built, it opened various valves and the chorus of birds would chirp at random.

I could do better than that.

If I could find a way to time the release of steam into the body of each bird, I could make them sing not at random but in chorus.

It would be brilliant.

But I only had three days.

If I had intended to draw a sketch of a replacement for the cracked pipe, it would have taken me all of an hour at most. What I was proposing would either make my idea stand out from the rest of the apprentices for its creative genius, or it would make me look like an overambitious fool.

If I wished my idea to be a success, I needed time. Time was the one thing I never seemed to have enough of.

I pulled out a large sheet of clean paper, took my drawing stick in hand, and set to work.

I worked all day and night. Even when I was trying to eat or help customers in the shop, I found my thoughts wandering back to my great plan. It became my obsession, but in a way that made me feel alive and powerful. I could only imagine how it would feel to put my plan in place and have it work.

While the idea was simple, the application of it would not be. I had to create a large music-box tumbler with raised bumps to signal the note from each bird. As a spring lifted over each bump, it would pull open a valve, allowing steam to enter the correct bird and sound a note through the whistle.

I chose a simplified version of the fourth movement of Beethoven's Ninth Symphony. The rhythm and progression of tones of the famous *Ode to Joy* were easily recognizable and fit the tones I'd be able to produce through the birds.

I became so fixated, I found myself humming the tune constantly and making up words to fit the song, about whatever I was doing at the moment. One morning I began singing in a loud, boisterous voice, "I need butter for my crumpet, and perhaps some jam and tea. If I'm hungry, I'll have biscuits, and eat them with revelry." Obsession had turned me into a poet.

After figuring out how the maze of valves and triggers could tie back to my springs, I worked on the pattern of notes as they would have to appear as bumps on the tumbler. I nearly drove myself mad with the details.

By the end of the third day, thank heaven, I had something of worth. I looked at the sheet of paper with my careful drawings and detailed notes. Pride that I could not begin to describe welled up in me. It was beautiful.

I gingerly rolled the large sheet and tied it with a rose-colored ribbon before meeting Bob behind the mews so he could take me to the next lecture. I could hardly contain my excitement.

The trip to the monastery took little time. It was early, and London had barely opened its eyes to greet the sun by the time we reached the secret carriage bay.

I flew up the ramp, feeling a bit like a bird myself. I wasn't watching and accidentally ran right into David.

He caught me before I stumbled, his grip firm on my arm as he waited for me to find my feet. My drawing had fallen to the ground.

"Good morning, Miss Whitlock," he greeted me as I reached for the drawing, but he picked it up before I could. "What's this?"

"Give it back, David." My heart pounded with both fear and anger as he slipped the ribbon off and unrolled it. He had no right to it. I kept my teeth clenched tight as I held out my hand.

"Just taking a look." He flashed me a smile filled with arrogant swagger, and I lunged for my drawing. He pivoted on his heel in a graceful turn he had learned either in his fine dance lessons or perhaps from some expensive Italian fencing instructor. Each time I moved closer, he expertly feinted to the side. His pale eyes darted over my drawings, and the half smile I found so irritating slowly faded.

That's when Samuel and four others approached from David's other side. My fear sharpened to panic as Samuel reached David. "What have you there?" he taunted. "Did she want to decorate the birds with ribbons and lace?" Samuel picked up the discarded ribbon like a hunting trophy, then peered over David's shoulder.

As his eyes skimmed my drawing, the cruel smile disappeared from his face.

I couldn't scream or cry. I knew I couldn't lose my control in any way, or they would have gotten exactly what they wanted. Both of them would like nothing better than to reduce me to the antics of a little girl begging for her toy.

"I said, *give it back*." I don't know where I learned the

tone that came from my mouth, but it was not the voice of a frantic child. The boy from Ireland and Noah took a step back as I marched forward.

David seemed stunned. That's when Samuel grabbed the paper from him, nearly ripping it. I felt a sharp jab in my chest as I squared myself to him.

"Give it back to me, now," I demanded.

He bunched the plans in his fist and held it behind his back. "What are you going to give me for it?" There was a mad look in his eye as he pushed forward directly in front of me. "Surely it's worth a kiss."

I retreated.

"I heard you did a lot more with that gypsy mongrel you took up with," he taunted. I felt my face burn red hot.

"Leave her alone, Samuel." I turned just as Peter came marching forward. He was not nearly the size of Samuel, but something in his demeanor had changed, and he looked menacing.

"Are you going to fight me for it?" Samuel sneered, clenching his fist. "That should be good for a laugh."

To my surprise Peter stopped and leaned back, cocking his head in a jaunty way. "No, but I'll make good on your other offer."

The boys in the yard howled like dogs, some of them gripping their sides as they puffed and hollered, smacking one another on the arms.

Peter stood his ground while I tried to work through my sudden confusion. I was certain I hadn't heard what he had said quite right. I couldn't have.

"What is going on out here?" We froze as Headmaster Lawrence descended the stairs with a regal air. Nothing escaped his scrutiny as his too-intelligent gaze swept over us all. He strolled to his son and held out his hand.

Samuel scowled as he gave my plans to the headmaster. I held my breath as the headmaster snapped the paper to smooth some of the worst wrinkles, then perused it. One sharply angled eyebrow slowly rose. He didn't take his eyes from the drawing. "Whose work is this?" His voice still carried a tone of disapproval, and the crowd seemed to step away from me as if I had just contracted the plague.

My doubt pushed out every thought in my head, and I couldn't seem to speak. Just that morning I had been so proud of my design, but I was only sixteen. I had more experience embroidering pansies on silk than I had drawing designs and creating inventions. I worried it was horribly flawed and my ambition looked foolish. I should have simply drawn a plan to repair the broken pipe. I should have only attempted what I knew for certain I could accomplish.

The headmaster swept his inscrutable gaze over the crowd. "Well?"

"It's Miss Whitlock's work, sir." Noah stepped forward, and I felt I was about to die on the spot. I glared at him, but he didn't bother to look at me.

"I see." The headmaster hastily rolled the plan without bothering to look at me. He looked both disgusted and disappointed, and I felt as if someone had just trampled on my heart. "I will not tolerate a lack of discipline in these halls. At all times you are being judged, not just for your learning but for your behavior as well. A man without control has nothing." He tucked the plans beneath his arm. "Please hand your assignments to Instructor Nigel, then meet Instructor Oliver in the lecture hall. You are dismissed."

The boys fell into line, handing their rolls of papers to Instructor Nigel as we entered the dark halls and trod down the familiar path to the lecture hall.

I still found I couldn't speak. I felt ill as I sat in my usual spot in the corner. David was cruel and Samuel a brute, but their taunting seemed small compared to the reaction of

Headmaster Lawrence. He hated my work. There was no mistaking the look on his face.

"Meg, are you well?" Peter whispered as he sat beside me.

The use of my name shocked me, and I blinked, rapidly trying to fight the stinging in my eyes.

I brushed a hand over them, making it look as if I were casually smoothing the front of my hair. "I'm fine," I lied.

For the rest of the day, Oliver had us split into teams. In the lecture hall one person would attempt to draw and describe a contraption that Oliver had placed on the front table. In another room, the other person on the team would then take the drawings and try to replicate the machine.

I tried to concentrate, but my confidence was lacking. I drew the machine as best I could, but my hands were shaking, and my proportions were off. My explanations of how things fit together left much to be desired as well. I just wanted the day to be over.

One by one the boys left and the lecture hall emptied, until the only other apprentice in the room rose and walked through the door, leaving me alone. Feeling the pressure of being last, I hastily finished my last note, then snatched the drawing and followed.

Peter's eyes were wide and nervous as I entered the room

where everyone had gathered. He looked at me as if to say, *Where were you?*

I lifted one shoulder in a defeated shrug and handed him the drawing.

Thankfully, whatever skill Peter felt he lacked in comprehension of mathematics, he made up for in his ability to assemble complicated structures. His hands moved with certainty and speed as I watched the machine being born of a pile of parts.

He caught the attention of some of the others as he quickly surpassed their efforts. I watched in awe, feeling relieved and grateful to him.

Peter slowly pulled back a large spring-loaded hinge. Once he had it set in place, we would be the first team to finish.

I watched as he turned the clamp down to hold the hinge back.

It snapped, whipping a sharp edge of metal through Peter's hand before striking the engine casing with a sharp *crack* that echoed off the stone walls.

Peter cried out, cradling his hand to his middle.

"Peter!" I shouted, and ran to his side. Blood poured from his palm as he looked at me in shock and pain. I snatched his handkerchief and used it to wrap his hand as all the others seemed to crowd in around us.

Peter hissed as I tried to press hard on the wound. "Leave it. You've done enough!"

"What's going on?" Oliver pushed through the crowd. He took one look at Peter's hand, then leveled me with a stern, accusing look. "What happened here?"

"I—I . . . ," I stammered. "I must have made a mistake."

I stood numb as I watched Oliver gather Peter and lead him from the room. To my left Samuel chuckled under his breath. I gathered my things to leave, feeling helpless, worried, and defeated.

That night as I sat in bed watching the candlelight flicker against the plain white walls of my unadorned bedroom, I tried to write a letter to Will. Sheets of paper littered the floor. None of the letters seemed right. I wanted to tell him I was happy too, and that the Academy was all I'd hoped it would be. I wanted to tell him that I was managing on my own, and that I was doing well.

I wanted to tell him that I didn't regret my decision. I needed to tell him I was sorry.

Instead I placed a blank piece of paper on the bedside table and blew out the candle.

CHAPTER TWELVE

IT TOOK MORE THAN A WEEK BEFORE THE NEXT LETTER calling us back to the Academy arrived. The summer heat made London oppressive and stifling. Stale and bitter scents hung in the air and stuck to my skin, making me feel loathsome.

Even when I sat at my counting desk going over the shop ledgers, I couldn't keep my mind on the numbers at hand. Usually the task of settling the books soothed me. There was something so simple about adding and subtracting numbers in neat rows and seeing the clear result at the end.

My work at the Academy was so much more compli-cated. It didn't matter if I was balancing the accounts or making tea, my thoughts remained fixed on one thing: Where did I stand?

Not in very high regard, most likely. The headmaster's scowl upon seeing my design had been so sharp and harsh. My idea couldn't have impressed him. I had thought I had been so clever, and now I just felt foolish.

My distraction hadn't just cost me, either. Guilt still ate at me about what had happened to Peter's hand. I didn't know how deep the cut was, and I prayed it had healed without complication. I had tried to write to him, then realized I didn't even know his surname. In this instance the Amuse-mentist rule about Christian names was frustrating, to say the least. In the end I jotted a letter of apology and sent it to Oliver with a note to forward it on to Peter.

Oliver sent a note back saying he'd had it delivered, but from Peter I received no response.

Finally the day arrived for the next meeting. The ride from Mayfair to the old monastery seemed longer than it ever had before, even though there was hardly any traffic for an early Friday morning. The old horse plodded along at a brisk enough pace, and Bob whistled cheerfully as he shook the reins.

I gripped my small basket and stared at a crack in the floorboards, watching how quickly the stone street passed beneath. For once I wasn't concerned about arriving late. I dreaded arriving at all. When we finally reached the carriage bay, I gave Bob a brief wave goodbye, then took a deep breath as I looked up at the bright sky at the top of the ramp. My steps felt heavy as I ascended into the courtyard, only to find a large crowd near the aviary. I had no wish to join them, but lingering in the archway by myself would hardly do either.

Resigned to my inevitable disappointment, I walked up to the others.

"What is happening?" I asked the tall Irish boy. I believed his name was Michael, but I wasn't sure.

Michael shifted his weight over his long, gangly legs. He tucked one hand into his pocket, which made his equally spindly arm stick out like a chicken wing. "The instructors chose the best design to remake the aviary. They've spent all this time repairing it. And now they're about to reveal it."

I wondered for only a moment who might have had the best design, then decided it must have been David. Everything was always so easy for him. Surely the golden halo of perfection that constantly surrounded him would extend to this project as well.

Glancing at the young earl with his impeccably cut coat and shining silk waistcoat, I realized it must have taken his valet three days to brush it until it was flawless. I tried to imagine what it would be like to have life be so effortless, but I couldn't fathom it.

From the arrogant tilt of his head to his proud stance, outwardly he seemed so assured of himself as he crossed his arms and glanced back at me. But there was something in his eyes, an uncertainty there. Samuel said something to him, with a rare smile on his face.

Now there was a horrible thought. Samuel was the headmaster's son. Surely his father had helped him with his own design. It wasn't fair, and I couldn't stomach the thought of passing by the aviary every day knowing Samuel was the one who had designed the repair.

I balanced on my toes for a better view, but it was of little use. The aviary had been covered in a large white cloth. The boys around me all watched with anticipation as well. Any of them could have taken this honor. They were all brilliant—well, most were. Even the boys who tended to remain quiet—like the older boy from Russia and the Indian boy—never seemed to miss a calculation.

I noticed Peter was standing along the wall on the outside of the crowd, near the boy from India. His hand was still wrapped in a bandage. I moved back to the other side of the group, where he wouldn't be able to see me. I didn't know what to say to him. I felt horrid that he'd been harmed because of me.

Three loud *crack*s sounded as a staff struck the stone at the top of the stair that led into the building. By moving away from Peter, I'd unwittingly placed myself directly in front of the headmaster.

He looked at me briefly, then lifted his hand for silence.

The boys fell into a hush. Anticipation could be an effective disciplinarian.

"I'm disappointed in you," he said, looking imperious and intimidating. I glanced down at the stones at my feet. "Too many of you were blinded by what you saw before you. You made no effort to discover how the Amusement functioned. You based your designs on conjecture. Blinded by the complex, you failed to see what was simple."

I looked up as my legs went a bit wobbly. Peter and I had discovered the cracked pipe, and my plans certainly had addressed the problem, but I had also added complex elements based on conjecture, and I'd failed to keep things simple.

"Power is crucial!" Headmaster Lawrence puffed out his chest. "Without power you have nothing. Everything else is trivial."

It was my fellow apprentices' turn to look uncomfortable. Several of them looked down at their feet as they shifted uneasily. Only David had the temerity to look the headmaster in the eye.

"The winning design addressed both the problem of power and function, embracing the Amusementist motto." For the first time the headmaster smiled. "From science, beauty!"

Oliver and Nigel yanked on golden ropes on either side of the aviary. The cloth fluttered down, and the bower gleamed, gold in the sun.

It couldn't be. I pushed my way through the other apprentices, forcing them to step aside. Finally I reached the front of the crowd. I didn't dare to hope.

Behind the aviary a squat cylinder with a cap marked with the seal of the Amusementists had been tucked near the wall.

I recognized it immediately for what it was.

It was the casing for the tumbler I had so carefully planned. There it was, before me, my vision come to life.

A great excitement, like the sun on the first fair day of summer, was glowing within me and straining to burst through my skin. The headmaster descended the steps and crossed the courtyard.

"Congratulations, Miss Whitlock. Would you care to do the honors?" the headmaster offered as Oliver gave me a sly wink. Instructor Nigel scowled at him, then looked resigned to the inevitable.

I took a step forward, but when my foot hit the stone, I feared my leg wouldn't hold my weight. My knees had turned strange and weak, and I forgot to breathe.

Somehow I managed to reach the headmaster, though I must have resembled a drunkard.

"Let's see if your plan worked," he said, and I couldn't help feeling there was an ominous undertone to his words.

Pinching the inside of my lower lip between my teeth, I took hold of the lever and pushed it down.

A hiss sounded through the pipes, and the birds began to tremble. They bobbed forward and back, flexing their metal wings. Then they opened their beaks.

Just like I had envisioned, the notes poured out of the birds in a slow but recognizable tempo.

The boys gasped as they listened to the wonderful music springing forth from the birds, cheerful, joyous, and grand.

My heart swelled as I sang along in my mind.

I am clever. I have done it. Now the birds here all can sing. I will one day join the Order. This has been my vic-tor—

There was a *pop*, then a loud whistle and hiss. A jet of hot steam shot out of the beak of the small bird near Oliver.

He shouted in pain as he tucked his face into the crook of his arm and leapt away from the bower.

At once chaos broke out as everyone in the courtyard scurried to the far side, shouting and pointing.

One by one more jets of steam erupted from the beaks of the birds.

"It's going to explode!" someone called out. I jabbed at the boys beside me with my elbows, trying to create enough room that I could reach the ramp and open the release valve on the boiler.

I caught a glimpse of Peter running down the ramp into the carriage bay, just ahead of me. We turned right together and ran. I hurried to his side as he ripped open the door and turned the wheel for the emergency release. A valve opened just above where the cracked pipe had been, and steam whistled out, spilling from the small compartment and curling over the ceiling of the carriage bay. With the pressure gone the shrill whistling from the courtyard fell silent.

Peter fell back on his bum and rubbed his hands over his face. His shoulders slumped as he pulled his hands away and stared at the bandage there.

"What did you do?" Peter asked, looking at me with such horror on his face.

"I don't know what happened," I tried to explain. "I didn't change the valves, only the mechanism for opening them."

"This is your second accident." Peter shook his head the way one laments an urchin in the street. "They're going to fail you."

The large stone that had settled in my stomach felt like a boulder. As if I didn't know that. Even the thought had me in a tizzy.

Why?

I couldn't figure what I had done wrong. I could admit I'd been distracted when writing the plans for the machine that had harmed Peter, but this one was perfect. I had studied every detail over and over. Nothing in my plan could have caused the birds to fail in such a way.

Unless I was simply not intelligent enough to see the problem.

I couldn't do this.

My heart broke, the pain deep and powerful. Hearing the birds sing had been amazing. It had filled me with a sense of wonder and pride. I had never been more proud, and now this had to happen.

Peter rose to his feet and looked back to the ramp. "Best hope no one was badly injured." He fisted his injured hand around his bandage.

"Oh, Lord," I whispered as guilt added to my abject misery.

We emerged from the ramp to find my classmates speaking in low and urgent whispers.

I approached the first person I saw. "Noah," I called. He turned to me, and his eyes immediately narrowed with suspicion. "Was anyone harmed?" I asked.

Noah's jaw flexed before he let out a heavy sigh. "Instructor Oliver has burns all along the side of his face. His condition is serious."

I felt ill, more ill than even the time I'd contracted scarlet fever as a child. I wished the Lord would take me, right in that moment. "Where is he?"

"Inside."

I grabbed my skirts and ran for the stairs that led into the monastery.

"Be warned," Samuel called after me with an edge of cruel humor in his voice. "Next machine she touches will kill us all."

I tried to ignore him. Samuel was the worst sort of vile thing, but every once in a while the Devil spoke the truth.

None of the others had proven to be half the disaster I had become.

Racing through the halls, I searched for where they had taken Oliver, but there was no one around. When I reached the lecture hall, it was empty.

The main hall was also empty, as were all the rooms down the long corridor to the left. Finally I found myself at the door to Headmaster Lawrence's office.

I raised my hand to knock but just clenched my fist in the air. Forcing myself to take a steadying breath, I tried to calm the panicked beat of my heart.

Slow and cautious footsteps echoed through the long corridor. I froze. Something wasn't right. Everyone in the courtyard had been rushing, not stalking.

I turned, staring down the dim corridor, but I couldn't see anything in what little light filtered through the dingy window behind me. "Is anyone there?" I called.

There was no answer.

Wary, I took a tentative step, peering deep into the corridor.

The door to the headmaster's office slowly creaked open to my left.

A whole new fear caught hold of me.

"Come in, Miss Whitlock."

CHAPTER THIRTEEN

I ENTERED THE HEADMASTER'S OFFICE WITH MY HANDS folded neatly in front of me, and my breath coming in shallow little bursts. Headmaster Lawrence let the door fall closed, then walked solemnly to the far corner of the room. He peered into what looked like one of Lord Rathford's spying machines. It had the same structure of brass piping surrounding a large oval glass about two feet tall, with a crank to one side, and a dial just below it.

In Baron Rathford's house, turning the dial had allowed you to see out of glass eyes set into various statues around his property. I suspected the same system was at work here.

A hazy, colorless image of one of the smaller classrooms

glowed in an orb-like glass. I could see men moving around, and Oliver with a cloth pressed to the side of his face.

Dear God, I hoped he hadn't been deformed from the steam. Oliver was a handsome man, and my best friend's fiancé. How would she ever forgive me if I ruined his face just before their wedding? My insides twisted painfully, and I sat down in the hard-backed chair facing the headmaster's desk. He clicked the machine off, and the orb faded to deep black.

"Are Oliver's injuries serious?" I asked, my voice cracking.

The headmaster eased into his throne-like chair. "The burns are not superficial." The sides of his mouth pulled down into a concerned frown. "And it is 'Instructor Oliver' until you are fully part of this Order. Do not forget your place."

I felt tears stinging my eyes. How could things have gone so horribly wrong? I had been so careful, and still I had burned off half the face of a man I admired. He'd have to wear a mask to be seen in public from now on, and it was entirely my fault.

Headmaster Lawrence's bright blue eyes softened with sympathy. "They are tending to him. I'm sure they're taking the utmost care."

I had to do something for Oliver to make up for this. He had trusted the aviary to work because he had believed in me.

Now his face was wrapped in bandages. Oliver was my dear friend and mentor. I would have never forgiven myself if he had been disfigured, or killed.

He could have so easily been killed.

I swallowed a lump in my throat. "I hope he heals quickly."

Lawrence straightened, looking down his long and pointed nose at me. "So the question becomes, what to do about you?"

I had only once before felt so crushed and disappointed. My life was unraveling right before my eyes, just as it had in the courtyard not that long ago, beneath the very same cage of birds.

I despised that aviary. It had brought me nothing but misery.

"I failed you," I said, though it came out as hardly more than a whisper. I tried to keep my emotions in, to be strong in the face of such disgust with myself, but my throat closed up and my voice cracked as if I had a heavy noose around my neck. "I'll leave the Academy. My apologies that your faith in my abilities wasn't better deserved."

The headmaster looked at me with his brow furrowed. "What nonsense is this? You're certainly not leaving the Academy."

I sat back in disbelief. Surely I had not heard him correctly. "I beg your pardon?"

He leaned over, opened a drawer, and pulled out a familiar piece of paper. It was my drawing of the aviary, but it had been annotated. At least four different scripts had scrawled all over the surface. "I suppose you recognize this?"

I reached out and touched the edge of the beautiful drawing. "Of course, but my design proved dangerous. And earlier there was the accident that injured Peter. Clearly, I made mistakes."

"No." The headmaster's voice dropped to a low and very serious tone. "No, *you* did not."

I sat, flabbergasted.

Headmaster Lawrence dropped his gaze to the plan before him and ran his hand over it, tracing the various pipes. "I don't mean to imply you are without error. You tend to forget that you're merely a student, Miss Whitlock. In spite of my reputation I expect my students to learn from their mistakes. I don't expect them not to make them.

"In this case Instructor Oliver, Instructor Barnabus, Instructor Victor, and I all looked over your design, and we corrected any errors we found. In truth, there wasn't much to correct. You did remarkably good work. The birds should have played the song exactly as you had intended."

I felt a rushing in my ears and pressure in my chest. Praise. He was offering me praise. He wasn't throwing me out in the street just yet. It took a long moment for me to find my voice. "Then what happened?"

The headmaster flattened his hands on the paper and fixed me with a serious look in his pale eyes. "I believe it was sabotage."

Sabotage? On the one hand, it seemed so sinister, like a plot out of a dark and twisted novel. On the other, it made too much sense, and that was what bothered me most. "Surely that can't be true. Who would wish to sabotage me?"

Headmaster Lawrence arched one eyebrow. "At this point the question becomes, Who does *not* wish to sabotage you?" He stood from his desk and retrieved from one of his shelves the machine that Peter had attempted to assemble. "And it wouldn't be the first time. Take a close look at this."

I peered at the machine as he placed it in front of me. I couldn't see anything awry. It looked exactly like the one that I had so painstakingly described in my assignment that day. "I don't see anything amiss."

"Of course you don't," Lawrence said dismissively. "But here is the assembled machine you used to make your drawing." He retrieved a second, seemingly identical machine and placed it next to the first. "What do you see?"

They were the same. Peering closely at both machines, I tried to magically reveal with the power of my will alone whatever the headmaster was trying to show me. "I don't see the differ—"

Wait, just there. The spring, the one that had snapped. It was too thick, and there was a subtle difference to the shape. "That's not the correct spring." My words tumbled out of me even as my heart seemed to follow them, falling onto the floor.

"Indeed, but young Peter couldn't have known that. The spring on the table in front of him was the only piece that remotely resembled the one he should have used, the one that had been a part of this exercise for decades without incident. Someone replaced that spring with this one. The latch could not withhold the added pressure of this more powerful spring."

Dear God in heaven, I hadn't been the one to harm Peter. I felt a weight lift from my shoulders, only as a new burden took its place. Someone had replaced that spring intentionally. Someone had *meant* to cause harm. It could have easily been me assembling the second machine and not Peter.

"Maybe this is all a simple mistake. Perhaps the spring was replaced by accident." I was so weary of the danger and the intrigue of it all.

Lawrence shook his head slowly. "It could be, but I doubt it. We will know for certain when Instructor Victor, Instructor Nigel, and I dismantle the aviary. I suspect we'll find the valves have been altered."

"Who do you believe is behind this?" From this point on anything I touched at the Academy would be suspect. I couldn't continue on this way.

The headmaster seemed exasperated as he sat back in his chair and perched his elbows on the rests. He folded his hands across his narrow body. "My dear Miss Whitlock, if I knew that, I wouldn't be speaking with you right now."

So he was as lost as I. Wonderful. I had to narrow my list of potential saboteurs. Most of my classmates couldn't stand to have me in the same room with them, and so most of them had to be suspect. "Do you believe a student could have done this?"

Lawrence sighed. "It is possible. One of the students might have slipped the stronger spring into the pile of parts on the table while he was waiting for his partner to finish his design."

"And the aviary?" I asked.

"Very few students knew I had chosen your design," he answered. "My"—he hesitated, the fingers of his left hand closed in a loose fist—"son was caught sneaking through some of my things."

I knew it. Samuel was the one who would most wish to humiliate me. He also seemed to care little about harming others. Samuel was the only possibility that made any sense.

"And he was the only one?" I asked. Of course, if Samuel knew, then David would have known as well. Between the two of them they could have enlisted the help of any number of the sheep that liked to follow them around.

"No. Peter was called back to the Academy to settle a matter of some work I had wished for him to complete now that the use of his hand has returned. When I entered my office, he was studying your plans very intently. I shouldn't have left them out on my desk, but I didn't suspect sabotage at that point," Headmaster Lawrence said.

I couldn't believe it. Peter would never do such a thing. Why would he? "He wouldn't purposefully injure himself."

"It would be the perfect deflection from guilt, and perhaps he hadn't anticipated the spring failing as he set it. It could have easily snapped later, when an instructor attempted to dismantle it." The headmaster tested the spring, pushing it forward, before carefully easing it back.

"But he has no cause," I said. Peter was my friend.

"Doesn't he?" The headmaster looked at me as if I should know something obvious. I backed off, unsure what I was missing. No matter what, I couldn't believe Peter would betray me.

Headmaster Lawrence let the question go unanswered. "If the saboteur is a student, it would be a remarkable feat. We have to accept that it might be a higher member of the Order."

"Why would one of the instructors attempt to sabotage my efforts? If they wished to be rid of me, they could easily ensure I fail." I was no fool, and I certainly hadn't forgotten the reception I'd received during my nomination, but there was no need for deception among the adults.

"No, they cannot. I watch everything that happens in the lectures, and all marks for students are finalized through me." The headmaster rolled up the plans and tucked them back into the desk. "You will not fail, so long as you don't deserve to." He scowled, only a flash of an expression. "As for those who do deserve such a fate . . ." His voice trailed off as he returned the machines to their places on his shelf.

Certainly I was relieved that my merit alone would keep me at the Academy, but I still felt uneasy. Like I was a special oddity, a pet project for the headmaster. I didn't want to need his protection, but if I didn't have it, I knew I would never take the Amusementists' oath as a full member.

He retrieved a box and opened it, revealing a very old pipe with a fat carved-ivory bulb and a long mahogany stem. With delicate care he packed and lit it, puffing as he stared at the narrow window. "This is all far more complicated than it seems."

"It appears fairly simple to me." I sighed as the scent of sweet tobacco filled the room.

"Does it?" Lawrence removed the pipe and held it contemplatively near his chin.

"The others don't wish for there to be a woman Amusementist," I said.

The headmaster took another puff, then watched me closely. "I believe it goes much deeper than that. Whoever is sabotaging you doesn't wish to see a woman become head of the Order."

I kicked out a foot in my shock, and nearly toppled the chair. "I beg your pardon?"

"So much has changed with the recent murders." He paused. "I believe you are to attend the memorial for Lord Strompton. I'm eager to hear some of the rumors. Surely others have noticed that all those who died conveniently made it possible for the Harrington line to ascend." Headmaster Lawrence watched me very carefully, as if looking to my face to confirm what he really wished to know. "Brilliant political strategy, really. Wait for one of us to inevitably go mad, then mask your own dark intentions."

I tried to hold deathly still. Alastair Harrington, the Earl of Strompton, had been a ruthless man. I had seen firsthand the depths of his obsession and manipulation. He'd even shot his son-in-law in the back in cold blood. "I wouldn't know much about these things," I lied.

The headmaster considered me. "Indeed." He puffed his pipe. "Very few things can prevent David from becoming the head of the Order when Octavian passes, and we have to be honest. Octavian doesn't have many years left in him. I felt certain your nomination was going to make his heart give out, and yet he lives."

"So, David is to become head of the Order. What does this have to do with me?" I stared at the headmaster, though the pipe smoke was beginning to burn my eyes.

Lawrence looked briefly at the ceiling, then back at me. "You are the last of the Whitlock family. Add to that your Reichlin heritage, and you have just as much political power within the Order as David does."

My hands started to shake, so I tucked them into my lap. "I don't understand."

"I think you do," he continued. "Family ranking within the Order is critical. The higher a family ranks within the Order, the greater their portion is for the patents we release to the public."

"I thought the Order was against some arbitrary social hierarchy."

"For all our knowledge, we're not above the occasional hypocrisy. However, there is nothing arbitrary about it. The heir to a family line is the one who *earns* his family legacy through stellar work as an apprentice and later as an Amusementist, not always the firstborn. The Order tends to rely on family reputation to make our politics more predictable. The system only works so long as the family in power is seen as having intellectual merit."

"But if the Whitlock and Reichlin families have been earning greater portions of returns on patents or investments," I said, "that would mean I have some great fortune." I was a clockmaker's daughter, not an heiress. We'd lost everything in the fire. What little money had been in my father's business accounts had been used to pay our debts. I had been forced to become a housemaid out of destitution. "My family lived well, but we didn't have wealth. I was left with nothing after the fire."

"And you didn't find it suspicious that your father didn't have *any* funds to pay off his debts, when you had lived so well, far better than a clockmaker should? On the contrary. You are the sole heiress to a great fortune. The tragedy is that no one knows where it is." Headmaster Lawrence contemplated his pipe for a moment. He took another thoughtful puff. "Your grandfather had a great knack for locking things away. I suppose he is the only one who would know where the Whitlock fortune is kept. This bomb you found may have been motivated by lust for that fortune, a crude attempt to take your grandfather's master key, then claim the fortune."

I slumped in my chair. The man in the clockwork mask certainly seemed intent upon claiming the key by any means.

The headmaster shrugged and puffed on his pipe. "I do hope Henry is safe, for your sake. As it stands, should he return, he would become head of the Order as leader of the Whitlock line and a senior member to David. If he does not, the ranks of the Whitlock and Harrington lines rest entirely upon you and David. Whoever ranks higher by the end of your apprenticeship will become head of the Order eventually."

So David had the motive to sabotage me as well.

The headmaster blew out a cloud of smoke, which curled around his face. "Since it is clear you are a target, the question remains, what to do with you."

And we were back to where we had begun, though so many things had been made clear and confusing at the same time.

"Keep wary, Miss Whitlock. If you notice anything out of the ordinary, I want you to speak with me, and whatever you do, I expressly forbid you to mention any of this discussion to your peers." He rose. "It could jeopardize our chances of finding the saboteur."

I thought about the man with the clockwork mask, and the shadowy figure I had thought I'd seen at the Academy.

"Headmaster." I didn't know how to ask what I so desperately needed to ask. "Is there any way for someone outside the Order to enter the monastery?"

"No," he answered with a heavy shake of his head. "It's impossible."

That's what I was afraid of.

CHAPTER FOURTEEN

MY TROUBLES AT THE ACADEMY WERE COMPOUNDED AT the memorial for Lord Strompton. I had only had a few dealings with Lucinda's father myself. The most acute of those memories involved his pistol pointed at my chest. Needless to say, I did not bring a handkerchief to dry my eyes. I hated that I had to stay silent about his murders, but I had caused enough controversy in the Order, and telling everyone what had really happened wouldn't have brought back the dead. Knowing this didn't make attending his memorial any more comfortable, though.

As I followed the string of people walking from the country estate dressed in their finest black, I knew the saboteur was likely among them. The line reached down a hill like a monstrous snake, its body undulating through the waving grass until the head reached a rotunda of old Roman ruins on the edge of a vast, sun-soaked lake.

While we all moved forward at an appropriately somber pace, the front of the line never extended beyond the rotunda, and I wondered what awaited me within the ruins.

I didn't know where Lucinda was. The Strompton estate made the splendor of Oliver's palace look quaint. The dowager countess was managing to host most of the Amusementists, with the remainder staying at Chadwick Hall. I had only briefly seen Oliver. Having had a week to heal, the skin on the side of his face was still raw and red, though the blisters were mending. He wore a patch over one eye. I tried to speak with him, but he was too busy managing the many guests and couldn't be bothered.

His reluctance to speak to me only made me feel worse. It was just like with Peter. I couldn't explain to either of them that I was not at fault. The saboteur had hurt my friends. Now I paid the price with their silence. Unless Peter was the saboteur. . . . Oh, I didn't know what to think anymore.

I knew it was selfish, but it drove my ire to no end that the whole reason I was here was to give my support to Lucinda and she was nowhere to be found. She had specifically asked me to attend, and yet I could not find her. Though I was certain she was probably busy with the many guests, at least we could have kept one another company in this dreadful parade. It wasn't as if she were in the mood to mourn her father either.

The sun made the heavy black fabric of my dress unbearable. I felt a trickle of moisture meander down the back of my neck as I walked on.

No one spoke.

I kept glancing at the faces of the men and women around me, but they all seemed deep in thought or in memories of the departed. Meanwhile I struggled to keep my mind from wandering to mundane subjects, like whether the hair of the woman in front of me was hers in truth, or a wig.

I had mourned long enough for people who rightly deserved it, and I refused to do it any longer.

With no other choice but to go along, I kept my head down and followed the line until the shadow of a worn stone column passed over me. My breath caught as I looked around the weathered ruins. At the center of the rotunda there was a small marble building that looked to be nothing more than a crypt with a heavy iron door emblazoned with the Amusementist seal.

I watched the line of mourners slowly disappear into the building, and I pondered what might lie deep within the crypt.

Inside the crypt a servant handed each of us a lit candle. I held mine with a slightly shaking hand as we descended a narrow spiral stair deep into the cool earth.

My legs ached with the effort of climbing down the endless stairs. The air became stuffy, heated with the breath and bodies of so many people holding candles in such a stifling place.

Finally we reached the bottom, and we walked down a long, dark tunnel lined with low-burning torches. Their light flickered in the steady breeze that rushed through the tunnel.

I didn't know what caused the air to move, and couldn't discover the source, since there was very little in the tunnel other than dank stone walls and a distant, wavering light up ahead.

The queue of people seemed to move faster, drawn toward the swirling light. We passed beneath an ornate arch defined by a bronze column on either side.

What I saw as I passed through stole every thought from my head, and I realized that nothing I could've imagined could equal this.

It was magnificent.

I had entered a great room made of glass, deep within the lake. The clear ceiling arched over me, supported by curving iron beams with enormous rivets whose heads were the size of eggs. It was like standing within a shimmering bubble beneath the surface of the water, held trapped within a dark iron web.

I stared, awestruck at the beauty of the shafts of light penetrating the gloom of the lake and reaching through the glass panes. The other Amusementists continued to file into the room, but it easily held the entire assembly. The light of the candles held by the mourners flickered, reflected in the glass dome like shimmering stars within the depths.

Something moved through the murky waters, and I gasped. Others noticed it too, because they stopped and pointed. Transfixed by the sight, I watched in wonder as an automaton mermaid swam lazily past. At first I was so captivated, I simply watched it swim, but it didn't take long for me to notice that a dark chain tethered the mermaid to a track. I had seen that mechanism used before in another lake to disastrous effect.

Now my mind pieced together the various joints and connectors of the mermaid's tail and undulating body. A bit of pride filled my heart, along with a certain sadness. I felt I could see behind the magician's cloak and now knew how the trick had been done.

The watery light glinted off her corroded scales, and lake weed streamed from her wire hair, making her look both ghostly and horrifically beautiful at once. In spite of knowing the mechanics, I could still appreciate her haunting beauty.

Soon others joined her, swimming in and out of view as they moved along their preordained paths. Their glass eyes had grown foggy, and their elegant tails hitched slightly with every hypnotic sweep through the dark water.

The murmurs around me turned hushed and reverent. People spoke of the time when the mermaids had been new and shining as they'd swum in and out of the elusive light.

I tried to imagine it, but with the streaming plants and the corroded metal, to me they seemed real, alive and not at all like machines. Or perhaps the illusion of life came from their likeness to death.

"My dear friends." The voice of the dowager countess echoed in the cavernous glass room. Those around me hushed and turned to where she stood on a platform. "It is with great sorrow that I invite you here to honor the legacy of my dearly beloved husband. In our darkest hour, when the loss of so many of our finest and most well-connected members nearly drove us to despair, he in his great wisdom and bravery stood up to the evil that had tormented our Order and sacrificed his life to save us all. . . ."

Her voice trailed off as the dark mass of spectators parted for a single hooded figure. The person, draped from head to toe in a long and heavy black cloak, walked slowly to the center of the room. At first a sharp jolt of fear shook me, and I tucked myself behind a rather portly Amusementist. Then I realized the figure in the cape was too small and too slight to be the man in the clockwork mask.

Oh, dear Lord.

Realizing who it was, I jumped forward, jostling the man in front of me. What was she thinking? I had to get to her before she made a fool of—

Lucinda whipped the cape from her shoulders with a flourish, standing tall, with her chin held high, in a flaming red dress. Her hair flowed loose over her shoulders and back, wild and uninhibited. She glowed like an ember in the sea of black, her fury and defiance burning brightly beneath the water.

Several people gasped, and one woman near the back fainted.

"Yes, Mother. Let's celebrate him." Lucinda didn't look at anything but her mother's heavy veil.

The veil slowly lifted as the dowager countess pulled it back. She had sharp and striking features that might once have been considered beautiful, but the look on her face now could have turned half the assembly to stone.

"How dare you?" The countess glared at her daughter. "You have no cause to ever speak ill of such a great man."

Lucinda laughed. "How dare I? How dare *you*, Mother? We all know whom this charade of a funeral is for. You couldn't resist a chance to flaunt your wealth in front of the Order. The rest of this is nothing but a farce. There has never been love here except for money and power."

"You are in no position!"

Lucinda tossed her hair back with a fierce shake of her head. "No. I am in the perfect position to tell everyone the kind of man Alastair Harrington really was."

I couldn't move. I felt as if I were watching some horrible drama play out on a stage, and I was merely a voiceless witness in the audience. I was one of the few who knew how deep the depravity of the old earl had reached, but he was dead and gone. The only person Lucinda could hurt with the truth was her mother. And she seemed fixed on doing it.

Then David stepped forward.

I felt my heart jump to my throat as Lucinda's composure cracked for the first time. The fist she'd held before her loosened, and her eyes darted from her younger brother back to the glare of the countess, as if whatever devil had possessed her had now suddenly fled.

"Sister?" David approached her, his usual arrogance gone in the wake of the confusion painted on his face. A young and gangly girl that had to be Lucinda's younger sister took her brother's hand. The girl couldn't have been more than twelve, her visage stricken with love and worry for her sister. David tucked his younger sister behind him and turned his attention back to Lucinda. "I don't understand. What do you mean by this?"

Lucinda no longer looked up at the countess. She blinked rapidly as she pressed her lips together, then opened them as if to speak, but nothing came out. I knew what she desperately wanted to say. I knew how it must have been killing her inside that no one knew it had been her father who had murdered her beloved husband in cold blood.

I knew that every time someone blithely blamed *poor mad Rathford* for her father's murderous acts, or her mother flaunted his legacy, she died inside. She had confessed as much to me. I could see in her face how desperately she wanted to speak, but she didn't. If she did, it would ruin her brother.

Whatever she had been thinking when she'd planned this stunt, I couldn't begin to fathom. I understood her desire to chastise her mother for defending a monster, but she had clearly forgotten about the other lives at stake. Now she was caught in a trap, and I hated to see her so torn.

Oliver came up behind her, and for the first time since she'd entered the room, I felt my shoulders loosen. He pressed his face to the side of hers and whispered something into her ear. I couldn't see his expression with his eye covered by the patch, but he took her hand, and her body folded into his in a defeated way as he led her back out the way she'd come.

She had been poised to ruin the Harrington name for all time. I glanced at David. His brow had furrowed, as if deep in thought. A shadow came over him as if the specter of his father had risen. I could almost feel the presence of the old earl hanging over the lot of us.

The chamber erupted with hundreds of voices at once.

I had to escape. I knew too much, and if I weren't careful, I would ruin the entire Harrington line by blurting out the truth.

I blew out my candle and pushed through the crowd.

I needed air. Bits and pieces of conversation struck me as I passed.

"Well, she's always been that way. Impetuous to a fault and too willing to ruin the reputation of her family, for what? Love?" An older woman with a rather beakish nose and narrow eyes cackled a jarring, crow-like laugh. A younger woman with ash-blond hair and the same unfortunate nose smiled maliciously at me. "Love is for fools and never brought a woman to greatness."

I slowed my step. I had assumed they were talking about Lucinda, but as the younger girl watched me, I wondered if their words weren't meant for me.

"Wouldn't you agree, *Meg*?" the girl asked, her toothy smile widening.

That stopped me in my tracks. For as much as I wanted to insist upon my fellow apprentices calling me by my given name, the girl had said it as if she were addressing her maid. I couldn't let the insult stand.

"I don't believe we've been introduced." My tone was hardly polite. The older woman, most likely the girl's mother, noticed and turned to us. "And you are?" I asked.

The mother had the sense to feign surprise at my presence. "Why, if it isn't the little Whitlock girl," she said in greeting.

A very old matron with a face like carved granite and eyes just as hard turned to us. "Lady Thornby, if you care to spare your fragile ego, take your harpy of a daughter and be gone, before I introduce you to Miss Whitlock properly. I haven't had occasion to exercise my more colorful vocabulary lately. If you wish to increase your tediousness, please, continue to grace us with your presence."

The hook-nosed Lady Thornby gave me a simper even as she looked at the old woman with a mix of both terror and bluster. The Thornby woman bore a striking resemblance to a long-necked bird. A goose. Definitely a goose. "Lady Chadwick, I apologize. I didn't see you there. I assure you, I meant no offense. I was honestly surprised by the child, that is all. I'm quite pleased to make her acquaintance. She needs some fine associations among the other women if she wishes to purge the taint of her unfortunate education."

Of all the nerve.

Lady Chadwick leaned heavily on a cane with a brass eagle head at the top. The fires of battle burned in her eyes, and she smiled with a thin press of her lips. She tipped her head, the tall, jet-black dyed pheasant feathers on her hat twitching slightly as she considered Lady Thornby. So this was Oliver's formidable grandmother.

"Perhaps," the dowager duchess said. "But some connections are finer than others. I am sure Miss Whitlock has enough intelligence not to ruin her family's fortunes, unlike some people here."

"After this debacle I wouldn't be surprised if your grandson's future wife is never invited to another Society function again. I don't care if she is to be the Duchess of Chadwick." Lady Thornby's daughter, who had been watching the exchange, giggled behind her hand.

How dare they?

Lucinda had been a part of their "Society" for all her life. She had grown up under the pressure of their scrutiny, and now that she'd found the courage to attempt to defy the lot of them, they set their tongues wagging like a bunch of chattering hens ready to crucify her.

"Yes, strong head, fickle heart in that one. Such a temperament tends to cause difficulties in our politics, but it has never caused as much ruin as blind ambition." The duchess arched a knowing brow at me.

It seemed I was being conscripted to fight in this war. Very well. I could handle myself. Determined to tell them exactly what I thought, I answered, "If the Order bases power and influence on family connections, the vagaries of the human heart will always be a variable. The intelligent course of action would be to give up on manipulating the system through marriage entirely and distribute power equitably through merit alone."

"Rubbish." Lady Thornby screwed her face up as if she had just tasted something foul. I was pretty certain it was her own tongue. "Do not listen to her, Lady Chadwick. She is young and foolish, if her own marriage prospects and latest embarrassment with this apprentice nonsense are any indication."

Lady Chadwick grinned in a way that reminded me very much of her grandson. "I would agree with you, Lady Thornby, except Miss Whitlock's family has a long-standing tradition of following the whims of their hearts." Lady Chadwick tilted her head. The twitching feathers looked as if they were holding back laughter.

"And what has it gotten them?" Lady Thornby asked. "Nothing but tragedy and ruin, so far as I can tell."

The duchess half-closed her eyes in the way a cat does when it deems itself far too clever to even acknowledge a mere mortal. "Yet they stand poised to take control of the Order, should Henry still be living. He was the worst of the lot of them, the fickle beast. In spite of that, none of the Whitlock affairs seems to have lessened the standing of the family as a whole, unlike your carefully managed arrangements, which landed you with an imbecile."

I tried hard not to laugh. I did, truly, but I am a weak soul, and I had to look away to hide my unrepentant mirth. Lady Thornby didn't seem to notice, as she quickly excused herself without another word, her daughter following at her heel.

"Dear, dear, I think I may have offended her." Lady Chadwick tapped her cane on the floor. "I wonder what it was I said."

"The truest barbs stick deepest." I collected myself, though I felt the strain of holding back my smile.

"Indeed." She carefully looked me over. "You remind me of Henry. You have his spirit."

"Should I take that as an insult, since you claim he was the worst of our lot?" I tilted my head at her in challenge.

"Yes, well, I suppose he settled down some once married. In his youth, though, he was a man who knew little restraint. Very little. But Henry was that way, always dancing along the edge of scandal and causing controversy within the Order." She waved her hand in a flippant way as if to say she didn't wish to discuss it, so I shouldn't ask.

All the noise of conversation filling the glass chamber seemed to quiet to a murmuring hush in my mind.

If my grandfather had enemies, the man with the mask might be counted among them.

I wanted to know more, but then, on the other hand, I was too afraid to look behind the smoke and mirrors and expose the illusion of my grandfather as a good and well-respected man. The prospect of hearing about my grandfather's youthful dalliances seemed distasteful. Frankly, the thought was appalling.

I swallowed the foul taste in my mouth and continued. "I can't believe my grandfather would be involved in a scandal. He was always a gentleman and never involved in anything unsavory."

The duchess laughed.

"Oh, my dear child." She took my arm and waved her cane in front of her skirt. The crowd parted out of self-preservation. "How sweet you are. Perhaps such innocence serves you well. I shouldn't spoil it."

I certainly didn't want to hear ear-burning details about long-dead affairs, especially ones involving my *grandfather*. I only wanted to know one thing. "Would any of these scandals have caused someone to stoop to murder?"

The duchess continued to walk, swinging her cane, clearly enjoying drawing out my suspense. "Well, there was that unmentionable business with the Haddocks, but they were a bit before my time, really."

"Clearly, a woman as clever as you knows something." I continued to hold the old woman's arm gently, even though I wished I were leading her to Scotland Yard to interrogate her properly. Instead she found a bench near the edge of the glass and shooed away the occupants, then perched upon it like a proud old crow.

In the background I could hear Lucinda's mother resume her speech about her husband's great achievements, though her voice now wavered and cracked with uncertainty, after her daughter's outburst. Those around us turned to listen. The cool glass curved above us, making me feel crowded into an uncomfortable confidence.

The duchess smiled. "Richard Haddock had been your grandfather's mentor, treated Henry like the son he never had."

"What was so scandalous about that?" I felt something cold drip onto my neck, and I looked up suspiciously at the seam in the glass. I didn't like to think what would happen should those seams fail.

"I really can't mention what nasty business Haddock was up to. In fact, I shouldn't even be saying his name. He found himself afoul of the rules of the Order. I was never privy to the meetings involving his trial. But I do know that if your grandfather had testified on behalf of Haddock, things might not have ended so badly." The duchess didn't look at me. Instead she seemed riveted by the quavering eulogy. "Of course I couldn't blame Henry. The influence of the Haddock line was waning considerably, and your grandfather had great ambitions. It would have been fool-ish to tie his fate to that. None of us want the scourge of the Black Mark. Better to be the betrayer than the one who has to endure that fate."

Betrayer? My grandfather was as loyal a man as God had ever created. He would never betray anyone. It didn't make any sense. "What is the Black Mark?" I asked, feeling vaguely ill.

The duchess polished the brow of the eagle head with her handkerchief. "The family line is quite simply erased, and any fortune that has been made through the Order is returned to the coffers. If the crime is severe enough, your life is for-feit. Your grandfather on the Reichlin side was charged with enforcing the sentence against Haddock. He never believed Henry was innocent of the crimes Haddock died for."

My mind went immediately to the blacked-out name in Simon's journal. The name must have been Haddock.

"What happened to the rest of the Haddock family?" I asked. Any one of them would have just cause to wish ill upon my family, both the Whitlocks and the Reichlins.

"They were well in decline before the whole mess. The more superstitious among us would say they were cursed. Haddock's only true family was his daughter. She was a silly young girl, always far away and lost in her own head. About the time Haddock fell afoul of the Order, he shipped her off to live with her spinster aunt on the Continent. I believe he wished to spare her the pain of his trial."

"Did she ever marry?" If she had, the Haddock line would have continued through her.

"No, I don't believe she ever did."

I leaned back, my shoulders hitting the ice-like glass behind me. And that was the last of my only lead to the identity of the man with the clockwork mask. There was only one thing I knew for certain. The man behind the mask was clearly not an old woman.

"Don't fret, child. Your grandfather knows how the game is played. Henry Whitlock is one of the most intelligent men the Order has ever seen. He knew exactly what must be done to ensure the Whitlock lineage at that time. Not even your mother's broken betrothal to the dearly departed Lord Strompton put him off for long."

What? I found myself speechless, which was a blessing, since the old duchess continued as if she hadn't just shattered everything I'd ever thought to be true of my family. "He took advantage of the new ties to the Reichlin clan and still sealed his carefully planned political agreement with the Harringtons. It all tied up very neatly when he arranged for your marriage when you weren't yet a year old."

Shocked, I sat upright. "I beg your pardon?" It came out as a squeak.

"Didn't you know, dear? He had an agreement for you to marry Lord Strompton."

I had to clutch my stomach as I nearly became violently ill on the floor. "But he was old enough to be my *father*." Suddenly there wasn't enough air in the bubble. I felt trapped under the glass.

The old woman cackled, which made Lady Strompton

pause in her speech, and the assembly turned their pale faces to us. "Gracious, not that Lord Strompton," she said with a labored breath. "*That* Lord Strompton."

And with her pronouncement she pointed the head of her cane directly at David.

CHAPTER FIFTEEN

LADY CHADWICK'S UNEXPECTED REVELATION ABOUT MY betrothal consumed all my thoughts as I tried to return my life to some semblance of what it had been before Lord Strompton's memorial.

It didn't work.

Not a moment seemed to pass when I didn't tumble from a deep feeling of betrayal and disillusionment on the one hand, and sheer revulsion on the other. Secret affairs, betrothals, scandals, intrigue—I'd had my fill of them.

The only peace I found was back in my workshop, where I could focus on the Haddock mystery. However, that peace came at a high cost. I found myself burning candles well into the night, scouring Simon Pricket's writings for any information about the Haddock line, and yet I found nothing.

The Haddock name had been well and truly blacked out, or carefully not mentioned at all.

The entire affair put me in a foul mood so severe, it could not even be soothed by the promise of buttered cheese crumpets. I felt tired all the time. My muscles ached with my fatigue. It became difficult to muster the will to move at all. At times I would find myself staring at the mantel, letting my eyes trace over the swirls in the polished wood. I didn't want to think. My head swam, as if underwater, but out of some heavy sense of duty, I managed to pull myself through each day.

I feared I would never be cheerful again.

The family I had held so dear to my heart had only been wooden dolls. I had dressed them in the manner I'd wished to see them, but I knew nothing about who they really were. I could only see them from the outside.

My mother had been intended to marry Lord Strompton. My soft-spoken mother, who had always been so accommodating, had broken an engagement to an earl and eloped with the son of a man her father had believed guilty of a horrible crime.

I didn't remember such spirit in her, and now that she was gone, I felt I'd never truthfully known her. I never *would* know her. It broke my heart.

And my grandfather.

I was still trying to find a way to combine my memories of a kind and gentle man who danced with me and sang me silly songs, with the truth, unless that truth was nothing but vicious old gossip.

I clasped my hand around the clockwork key. My grandfather had used me and my childhood games to create a failsafe for his precious master key, a key that people were still trying to murder me for.

And now I had come to discover that he had been willing to bind my future, my entire life, to whatever family could gain him the most political power. Strompton must have been so eager for the arrangement. He never would have imagined that I would become an apprentice, and his son's rival. I was to be David's bride and the final nail in the political scaffolding that would give the Harrington family control over everything.

What was I to do with such knowledge? I wanted to burn it from my soul, and I couldn't.

My grandfather had betrayed me.

Perhaps it would be better if he were dead.

I hated that thought most of all.

Back at the Academy things seemed to go from bad to worse. How I found the strength to keep going was a mystery to me. Yet I managed to attend each of my lessons and performed my tasks as well as I was able, in spite of the nagging doubt that no matter what I did, it would never be good enough.

The current seating arrangements didn't help.

Now that the headmaster suspected sabotage, he kept me under extra scrutiny. I was forced to sit at the very front of the class, and I was not allowed to collaborate with anyone.

This made it difficult to even speak with Peter. I couldn't believe he was the saboteur. I had to find a way to prove he wasn't.

But that was not the worst of it.

I glanced at the ceiling as David stood next to me in his perfectly brushed coat. With all the arrogance and self-assuredness of the lord of the manor, he confidently answered Instructor Barnabus's questions one after another.

And the praise rained down on his perfect golden head.

I loathed him.

Each time he sat, his eyes would dart my way and that vexing half smile would touch his lips.

He acted as if the entire world should bow before him, without his ever doing anything in my estimation to deserve such adulation. I refused to give it to him, on principle.

He probably knew about our supposed betrothal. It was no wonder he treated me like a pathetic spaniel puppy that someone had given to him as a gift for his own amusement. He had the greatest cause to sabotage my work, considering I was the only one who could knock him from his gilded throne.

"Very good, David!" Instructor Barnabus said, clapping his hands together. "Brilliant, as always. If you would, please instruct Miss Whitlock on the finer points of compression, as she seems unable to grasp the intricacies of it."

I let out a resigned sigh.

"Of course, Instructor. It would be my pleasure."

David looked at me, something wicked and amused glinting in his pale blue eyes. And there it was, his bloody smirk as he gave a short bow to the instructor and sat.

I shifted away from him and looked out the window at the aviary. It was still covered with a thick cloth, a monument to the success of my saboteur. Then something else caught my eye.

Several men seemed busy in the courtyard. Three of them were wearing kilts.

My heart leapt. I stood, my hands shaking. "Instructor?"

The commotion outside had caught his attention as well, and he glanced out the window. "Ah! The ship has come in from the Foundry." The room came to life as the rest of the apprentices suddenly leaned toward the window for a better look. Instructor Barnabus glared at us. "Since it is clear the lot of you will be distracted for the rest of the afternoon, you might as well make yourselves useful. There is much to be done when the shipments from the Foundry arrive. Follow the lighted corridors to the underground dock. Instructor Nigel should be there."

With a clatter of moving chairs, everyone pushed for the door at once. I followed the group out into the hall and through the courtyard, finding it difficult to draw breath.

I didn't dare to hope, and yet my heart steadily picked up its pace in spite of my efforts to tamp down its enthusiasm. He couldn't possibly have come.

Could he?

I caught my skirts and followed my fellow apprentices down the ramp, across the bay, and down through what had always been a dark tunnel before.

Today it was lit with torches. We descended a second ramp into the deep heart of the catacombs beneath the city streets. The catacombs were a great maze of dark passages. Several special tunnels had been dug specifically for the Amusementists under the guise of developing the city's new sewer system, and these tunnels were still quite new, with neat bricks formed into perfect barrel ceilings.

Along the path several small storage rooms had been closed up by heavy iron gates or solid doors, the mysterious contents languishing in crates or beneath thick cloth covers. The air felt cool and damp on my cheeks as I trotted along, desperately trying not to break into a full run down the torch-lit tunnels.

Finally I heard something, voices echoing through the narrow halls. The stench of Thames water was oppressive as I came upon a great open chamber. I stared in disbelief at the enormous steamship docked in a narrow water-lock channel. It didn't seem possible to hold something so large beneath the ground, under the very feet of the people of London, and they had no inkling it was there.

I had never seen a ship like it. While it was large, there was also a powerful sleekness to it. I couldn't see a great wheel like on other steamships, though two stacks reached nearly to the ceiling of the chamber. It looked as if it were built for both power and speed, and seemed to come from another era, one we had not yet witnessed.

Several men were milling about, and my fellow apprentices melted into the crowd. The dock was filled with boys dressed in the red waistcoats and black coats of the Academy. The Foundry men were wearing kilts of several different patterns, along with uniform white shirtsleeves, black waistcoats with brass buttons, black knee-high stockings, and black tams bearing a white rosette above the left ear.

I felt pulled forward as I watched, hope flitting in my heart. The burly men carted several large gears and heavy brass plates over a wide gangplank to the men waiting near the walls.

I found myself searching their faces, looking for any sign of . . .

"Meg!"

Will stood near the rail, leaning over it as if he were about to defy the laws of physics and leap the distance to me. He seemed so different. He looked taller, and his chest and arms had filled out from the effort of his labors at the Foundry. His dark red kilt hung to his knees, giving him the air of some wild Highland warrior, and yet in his face, and in his dark eyes, he retained the vestiges of his traveler heritage. No person had ever looked so wonderful to me.

The elation and relief at simply seeing his face overwhelmed me, and I was flying. It was as if a great phoenix had possessed my soul and come to life in a blaze of wondrous glory as it freed itself of the ash of its former life.

He pushed down the gangplank, running to me, only to sweep me up into his arms. I clung to him, holding so tightly to his neck, I lost sense of anything else but the heat and strength of his body. His hair smelled like smoke, and the skin of his cheek felt like fire against mine.

Finally he placed me back on my feet, and I faintly became aware of the jovial cheers and taunts coming from the ship. I didn't care much what was said, mostly because I could not understand a word of the Foundry workers' speech.

Will touched my cheek as he looked at me with such deep longing in his eyes. "I cannot say how much I've missed you."

His own accent had thickened. It had been hardly a twinge in his speech when he had lived in London. Now it qualified as a true brogue, though he'd only been gone half the summer.

I smiled, my heart full to bursting. "That's a lovely kilt," I teased. If he stood right, I could see the skin of his knees beneath the pleats of the deep red plaid with black patterning. It felt so dangerously forbidden.

"The MacDonalds of Glencoe have taken me in." He gathered my hands in his and squeezed them tight, as if he never wanted to let go.

"Are you related to them?" I asked. It felt so good to simply talk with him again. I had missed him so much.

"Haven't the faintest," he said, and laughed.

I couldn't help laughing as well.

"William! Is this the young lass ye've told us about?" A young man with a smartly cut beard and a red-and-blue tartan asked as he strolled toward us flanked by three others from the Foundry. He had a wicked look of mischief in his eye as he crossed his arms and looked me over. "She's not exactly Fiona from the inn, but I suppose she'll do." This pronouncement was followed by a very inappropriate gesture with his hands demonstrating Fiona's *considerable* charms. I felt my cheeks burn, while simultaneously feeling a bit sorry for the weight poor Fiona must have been carrying around.

Will shot me an apologetic look as he tilted his head toward his friends. "That's MacBain."

The Scot looked offended. "What now, I don't deserve a proper introduction?" He bowed low and took my hand, only to plant a completely inappropriate kiss on the back of it.

Will kicked him in the leg. "No, you don't."

"Miss Margaret Whitlock," I said, pulling my hand away and smiling at the rugged Scot. "I'd say it's my pleasure to meet you, Mr. MacBain, but I fear it may earn you another kick."

He chuckled. "I would gladly endure for your pleasure, lass."

Will took me by the shoulders and pulled me back. "Duncan, you'd best watch yourself before I throw you in the lock."

"As if you could." He gave us a parting bow before saying, "Go find yerself a quiet corner. We'll make sure no one comes looking for you."

"Thank you," Will said as he took my hand again and led me back into the catacombs. About halfway to the carriage bay, he pulled me suddenly to the right, down a dark hall and into an alcove.

Every part of me wanted to kiss him until I had no breath left and I died of it. I wanted to forget myself for a moment in his arms. The pull of my desire met with the chains of my restraint, and every sense felt heightened as I looked at the man I had missed so much.

"How is Scotland?" I asked, partly wishing he'd say it was horrible and that he wanted to return to me.

"It's wonderful," he said, and I could feel it in his tone, much to my dismay. "The Foundry is astonishing. MacTavish has taken me under his wing, as have the other MacDonalds. Right now I've been learning to manage the blast furnace, while Duncan has been teaching me how to create forms. MacTavish says I have a true gift for working metal, a finesse some of the others lack."

I smiled weakly. His eyes were so bright and full of life, even in the dim light. "That does sound wonderful."

"Then there are the lochs, and the glens. You should see Loch Ness from atop Grant Tower. Sometimes the mist clings to the water in the early dawn . . ."

His voice trailed off, and I realized it was more than I'd heard him say in quite some time. Will was never one to use flowery speech, and this was nearly poetic.

I could feel a hot tear gathering as my nose began to burn and I fought the urge to rub it. "I'm glad you're happy."

The wistfulness in his eyes deepened into longing. "It's not the same without you. Why didn't you write to me?" There was no mistaking the hurt in his voice now as he brushed the back of his knuckle over my cheek, then smoothed the bit of hair that had come loose at my temple.

"Will, I'm sorry. I just—"

"Is there someone else?" He took a step back.

"No!" I protested quickly. "I've been so overwhelmed, I haven't been able to write to anyone. I barely managed to send a letter out to Peter when he—"

Will took another step away from me, his shoulders squaring. "Who's Peter?"

Dear Father in heaven, why couldn't I learn to think before I spoke? "He's a fellow apprentice and a friend," I said quickly. "Nothing more."

"Well, if you're writing to him . . . ," Will continued.

"Enough. Stop this right now. You have no idea how difficult things have been. At every turn I feel like I'm being punished for the choice I've made. I have exhausted myself struggling day and night to keep up with my lessons, all while being constantly taunted and sabotaged." I was on the verge of breaking. Everything I had so carefully shut away threatened to explode like a valve that had been opened too fast. "I don't have anyone I can truly count on. I didn't write to you because you sounded so happy, and I couldn't think of a single cheerful thing to say in return. Perhaps this was all a mistake. Maybe I should just give it up and return to Scotland with you. We can live in a cottage in the glen, and I could just disappear."

"Might I remind you, you chose this," he said.

A tear slipped over my cheek. "I know," I whispered. "I don't think I can do it anymore."

Will gathered me in his arms and let me rest my head on his shoulder. The warmth and the comfort of his arms around me broke the last shards of my fragile state. "You don't mean that," he whispered into my hair.

That was the problem. I did.

"I'm tired, Will. I just can't do it."

He gently pushed me back, holding me at arm's length so he could look me in the eye. Gently he brushed away my tears. "Aye, you can."

I waited for him to continue, to go into a great speech about how I could achieve anything I set my mind to. He didn't. He just looked at me with solid conviction.

"I know you can."

I sniffed, and he pulled me close again so I could cry into the security of his dark waistcoat. "I still love you," I murmured against his shoulder.

"I'd better not tell Fiona. She's the jealous sort," he said.

I let out an inelegant snort. He stroked my hair. "You won't give in. It's not in your nature. Which is why I love you."

I gazed up into his eyes. My skin began to tingle as a heady rush of pleasure wrapped around me like a soft blanket. "You still love me?" I had to hear it again.

"You know I do," he whispered as his lips met mine.

Will had kissed me many times, but I had never needed it so much as I had at that moment. His lips felt so comforting and thrilling all at once. I thought I knew his kiss, but the time that had parted us had changed us both, and I could feel all of it in the intensity of his lips upon mine.

It fed my soul with hope and determination. I never wanted to lose Will's faith in me.

He broke away with a heavy breath and touched his forehead to mine.

At that moment someone cleared his throat.

I pushed back from Will, my heart hammering with mortification that someone had witnessed the kiss. As I turned, my shock became horror.

David stood only a few feet from us with his arms crossed and a fox-like expression on his face.

I was ruined.

CHAPTER SIXTEEN

"WELL, WELL, WHAT HAVE WE HERE?" DAVID TOOK TWO careful steps forward into the shadowy alcove. I didn't like the look on his face. There was something dark there, almost like jealousy.

"Strompton," Will said in greeting, stepping in front of me and giving David a half tilt of his head instead of a full bow.

"William." David stopped directly in front of Will, and Will pulled himself to his full stature, lifting his chin. While they may have stood eye to eye, Will was clearly the more imposing of the two. That didn't mean David couldn't be dangerous.

"You know one another?" I said, trying to step around Will. The two of them looked like a pair of dogs with their hackles raised, just waiting to grab the other by the throat. No matter what I thought of David, I didn't want them to come to blows.

David gave me a tight smile. "Of course. He was His Grace's *servant* for months." He lingered on the word "servant" like it was a dirty thing in his mouth. "During the course of his menial tasks for the duke, he delivered quite a few letters personally to my sister."

I glared at David in challenge. He had to be a fool to think I didn't know his game. *His Grace*, my arse. He was talking about Oliver, who detested using that title unless he had to. After what Oliver, Will, and I had been through together, even the thought of calling him by his title seemed ridiculous.

"I have a new life now," Will said. "According to Amusementist tradition, you are to address me by clan." Will crossed his arms and widened his stance. David took a step away.

"Very well, MacDonald. It changes little." David sauntered back toward the lighted corridor.

"You're right," Will said, and pulled me closer. David looked back over his shoulder at us. His lofty confidence had been stripped away, leaving something raw yet powerful in its wake. He certainly retained his commanding presence.

"What do you want, David?" I asked. If he insisted on playing a game with names, I could play as well. He turned to me.

"The headmaster has called us all back to the main hall. He has something important to announce and instructed me to find you. I hardly have to remind you that your position here is tenuous at best, Miss Whitlock." He lingered on my name. "It would hardly do to behave in a manner unbecoming of your stature."

My stature. I let out an indignant huff. My stature. He may have believed that I held some great esteem in the Order, but I had not forgotten that I was the daughter of a clockmaker, an orphan, and a former penniless housemaid. If he intended to place me on some sort of romantic pedestal, that inclination wasn't about improving my *stature*. "My stature is no business of yours."

His eyes swept down my body, then drifted back up to my face. I felt his gaze, like the touch of a cool breeze that whispered through my clothing. "If you insist."

Will tensed behind me, and I held out a hand in front of him. For as much as it galled me to admit it, David did have a point. I didn't need to borrow more trouble, and the rumor that I had been sneaking off into shadowy corners to ruin myself with a Foundry boy would hardly make my life easier.

Besides, I couldn't keep the headmaster waiting. "Fine."

I took Will's hand and gave it a squeeze. I didn't want to say goodbye. He placed a tender kiss on the back of my hand, then let me go without a word as if he couldn't say it either.

David turned to Will.

"You should get back to the ship. They need someone to shovel coal." He offered me his arm with a short bow, but I grabbed my skirts and stomped forward into the lighted corridor without taking it.

Arrogant son of a bastard. If he was jealous of Will, then he was right to be. I had no interest in David. None. And I never would. Ever.

I kept my head high as we walked a few steps along the corridor. David stalked just behind me. I let him pass. Then at the last moment I turned to look back.

Will stood watching from the half shadows, waiting for me. I didn't know when I would see him again. I paused, watching him standing there, proud and strong like a true Highlander. He lifted a hand.

I touched the air as well, feeling a connection to him in

spite of the distance between us, and hoping he understood what he meant to me. He nodded, then disappeared into the darkness.

David suddenly realized I had stopped, and closed the distance to me. I dropped my hand even as I felt my heart fall with it.

"You could do better, you know." He took my arm at the elbow and drew me away.

I pulled from his touch. "No, I couldn't."

We walked the rest of the way in stiff silence until we climbed the ramp into the courtyard.

Samuel was standing there to greet us.

"You found her," he scoffed. "Which Scot was climbing up her skirt?"

I clenched my fist, and heaven knows how I found the strength to keep it at my side because I longed to swing it at his face. He was the saboteur. I knew it in my bones. I turned to David, knowing I only had moments before I'd have to endure Samuel's cruel taunts about the kiss I had shared with Will.

"She was alone," David said, his voice cool and casual. I was so surprised by his words, I nearly lost my balance. Why would he lie? I thought he of all people would crow any failing of mine from the rooftop, given the opportunity. He arched an eyebrow at me, then swept his arm toward the stair leading into the Academy. "After you, Miss Whitlock."

"She was lost then. Idiot," Samuel muttered under his breath.

Samuel could think what he wanted. I didn't care about the brute. David was the one who concerned me. I wondered what he would do with the knowledge of what he had seen. Blackmail? Perhaps. That seemed in line with his temperament. Before long he'd no doubt threaten to reveal the kiss to try to force me to ruin a project just so he could outshine me. Then he wouldn't have to dirty his hands with sabotage.

I supposed I'd have to wait for David to play his hand. I didn't like that he had leverage over me.

We entered the assembly hall, and most of the other apprentices were already gathered in the center of the room in front of the speaker's podium. Two roughly man-size objects were hidden beneath red blankets near the podium. Headmaster Lawrence stood between them, and to the right stood MacTavish.

At once the Foundry master turned to stare at us as we entered, his heavy-lidded eyes fixed on our little party. I couldn't read his expression. With his thick beard, only his eyes could reveal him. I didn't know what I saw there, but it made me uncomfortable. The headmaster glanced at us, then gave a sour look to the Foundry master before turning to us again.

Yes, we were last to arrive.

You would have thought we were walking to the gallows, if the faces of the two men were any indication.

Headmaster Lawrence straightened. "Now that we are all present and accounted for, I have an announcement."

Everyone looked toward the headmaster, so I used the opportunity to sneak along the back of the crowd until I was as far from David and Samuel as I could possibly arrange myself.

"The time has come to begin work on the Academy's contribution to the upcoming Amusement," the headmaster announced in a large and impressive voice. Immediately I felt the excitement in the air as I tried to recall what the Amuse-mentists had decided to work on during the Gathering. I had been too distracted by the bomb in my lap to pay much attention.

Now the bomb was being studied by the Order, but I wondered how much of a priority Headmaster Lawrence and the others had placed on it. No one had mentioned it to me.

But the bomb was a matter for another day. As I watched, Lawrence and MacTavish had grasped the coverings and pulled them aside with a flourish.

On the dais stood two perfect golden automatons. The one to the left was male. His face was a blank contour, his body covered in interlocking plates. At his elbows and knees, carefully protected gears allowed for movement in his joints.

To the right stood the other automaton. It was smaller, with more distinctive curves through the waist and the chest. Though her face was as blank as the other's, this one was clearly meant to be a woman.

Oh no.

"Allow me to introduce Adam and Eve. Over the years the Order has nearly mastered the art of the automaton. While we would not expect an apprentice to design such a complicated mechanism, we have a challenging task to ask of you." The headmaster got a gleam in his eye as he stroked his short beard. I felt my innards tie themselves into a sailor's knot, unravel, and then attempt the knot again more tightly.

"The two head apprentices will lead this project. Each will take one of the automatons. As for the rest of you, you are free to aid them as little or as much as you desire. Bear in mind the nature of the Order. Those who aid in success reap the rewards of success. Those who aid in failure . . ." He let his voice trail off in an ominous way. My palms grew moist.

I didn't need this. Not now.

"David, will you please step forward."

Of course the male would belong to him.

I watched as he lifted his head, inflated with his own self-importance. He didn't seem concerned at all as he accepted cheers and slaps on the back from his admirers. He stood before the headmaster with his hands clasped behind his back. I edged around the boys in front of me to get a better look. David's fingers were clenched rather tightly, and he seemed pale in the dim light of the hall.

"As the apprentice with the highest marks, the male is yours," Headmaster Lawrence announced.

David stepped toward his prize.

"Very good." Lawrence nodded his approval. "The second automaton shall be assigned to you,"—I hung my head, dreading to hear his next words—"Miss Whitlock."

Dear God, what was he thinking? If this was meant as the perfect bait to draw out the saboteur, fine. That was all well and good, but in the meantime I was saddled with a project that was about to clearly put me at odds with David.

My feet remained fixed to the floor, unwilling to take on such a burden.

"Come forward, Miss Whitlock." There was a stern reprimand in his voice, so I obeyed, but I couldn't bring myself to look him in the eye.

"As second-highest apprentice, the second automaton is yours. Congratulations."

I looked out at the faces of the other apprentices and felt he was congratulating me on a death sentence. At that moment in time I felt I'd rather face a tall man bearing a hood and a bloody axe rather than the lifeless golden woman before me.

Swallowing a lump in my throat, I glanced over at David, only to find his gaze meeting mine. His mouth formed a determined line as he gave me the slightest nod. I had no doubt he would soon be surrounded by volunteers to help with whatever it was we were supposed to do with our new charges. I wouldn't be receiving such support, and any support that was offered willingly would have to be suspect.

Whatever we had to do, I'd have to find a way to do it on my own in spite of the saboteur. I furrowed my brow. What *were* we supposed to do with the blasted things?

"Excuse me, Headmaster," I said. He turned to me like some great benefactor. "What is our assignment, precisely?"

He smiled at me benevolently. I wished he had decided to give his benevolence to someone else. "Why, teach them to dance, of course. How else are they supposed to attend the Automaton Ball?"

CHAPTER SEVENTEEN

THE ROOM BROKE INTO RAUCOUS CHATTER AS I STOOD there, ramrod straight. My posture matched that of the automaton so precisely, I wouldn't have been surprised if someone had tried to wind me. A crowd had already formed around David's machine. Boys were moving the arms and inspecting the gears as if Father Christmas had just gifted them all with a brilliant new toy.

My arms and legs felt frozen in place as I realized the scope of what I had to do. This was too much for one person. No single apprentice could manage this on his own. I needed help, and yet I did not have a fawning crowd at my disposal.

But not everyone was taken in by David's glory. I took a

step toward the thin group of stragglers who were unable to stand too close to the fire of his charisma. They were often burned by whatever failing David's friends had deemed unworthy in them. None of them had reason to sabotage me, and they also hadn't had access to my plans for the aviary. They were as safe a choice as I could make. I certainly didn't find them lacking, and if they wanted to be included in a project, I had one to offer.

Noah was the one nearest to me. While I remembered quite clearly how he'd broken his association with me at the beginning of the summer, I knew he was one of several caught in the middle as far as talent went. But his ambition was as great as any in the room.

"Noah," I began, carefully settling on the most advantageous angle to the problem I could think of. "A victory will reap greater rewards if there are fewer hands demanding a portion of the prize," I began.

He turned slowly, drawing his gaze reluctantly from the throng of people surrounding David. He could not hide the longing on his face. "I beg your pardon?"

"I could use your assistance with my machine. I promise, Samuel won't be invited." I gave him a brief smile, trying to remember those moments in our childhood when we had played side by side. The only trouble was, he had ignored me then, too.

My words caught the attention of Michael, the Irish boy. He was the son of a shipbuilder, and had been struck with an awkward gait and manner of speech that lacked a certain refinement. He glanced from Noah to me, as if unsure what he should do.

"Michael," I implored. "You have a talent for finding minute faults and correcting them. I'm certain creating switch panels to control the movement of a waltz will be an exquisite challenge. I know you are capable of it." I knew he was frustrated that no one seemed to have faith in his abilities.

Then there was Manoj, the boy from India. While we had never spoken directly, I knew he was very intelligent and skilled at piecing together fine gear-work. "Manoj? Will you not assist someone who needs aid?" I didn't know much about his customs or religion, but I did know he had a deeply embedded code of honor.

He crossed his arms.

I couldn't believe this group of boys would not wish to band together for their own improvement within the class. There had to be a way to get through to them. "If we succeed at this, it will be a triumph."

"The way I see it," Michael began, "there's nothing in it from where we're standing. Should we fail, our grandsons will bear the shame of it, but if we succeed, our automaton still won't be seen as superior to the other one."

I felt as if he had just doused me with a bucket of icy water. "What do you mean?"

"Well, because . . . you know," he hedged.

"Because I'm a girl." My face felt hot.

He shrugged.

Noah lifted his chin in a lordly manner. "I'm sorry, Miss Whitlock. Your latest tasks have been prone to failure." He tugged on the lapels of his jacket and then caught the eye of each of the others. Like sheep in a damned flock, they turned to him. "You have to admit that outcome is likely."

That was not my fault!

"What about you, Manoj? Are you brave enough to stand against this?"

He tipped his head down in a lukewarm bow of sorts. "My apologies. The others are correct."

"I suppose you will all abandon your duty to this Academy. You will willingly turn away an opportunity to create something together, and in the process humiliate us all when our automatons fall on their faces. For what?" I scolded.

"Well, you can keep your foolish pride." I glared at the sparse group. There at the edge stood Peter.

He smiled at me hopefully. I stood dumb, not knowing what to say. He was the only person I counted as a friend in the whole of the Academy, and the one person I'd been practically ordered not to trust. The room began to slowly clear as apprentices left in small groups.

"I'll help you," he said, as if it were a foregone conclusion.

My throat tightened up, and as he stepped closer to the automaton, I held my hand out. He paused, my fingertips only inches from his chest.

"I'm . . ." For the life of me, I didn't know what to say.

His gaze lowered as I watched the hurt and disappointment throw shadows over his sweet face. "You don't want my help, do you?"

By God, he thought I had no faith in him. The crushed look in his eyes broke my heart. "Peter, it's not that I don't want the help. It's just that . . ." What was I supposed to say?

He scowled, his expression turning from hurt to anger. "Yes, well, I'll save you the embarrassment. Forget that I ever suggested it." And with that he turned away and followed the other apprentices up the steps and out of the hall, leaving me alone in the cavernous room.

I clenched my fists.

"Dammit," I muttered.

I marched directly to the automaton and looked her in the blank face, seeing my own fury reflected back at me. "Damn. It." I kicked the machine in the bloody shin.

And immediately crumpled in pain as fire shot through my boot straight up my leg. I could have sworn I felt it in my fingertips as I hopped to one of the gallery benches and collapsed there.

What was I going to do?

Nursing my foot, I tried to weigh my options through the pain of my injury and my defeat. This was too much. I couldn't do this entirely on my own. I wasn't *meant* to do this on my own. This was supposed to be a group effort, and I had no help. I was forced to reject the aid of the only person who seemed to be on my side.

I held back a choice curse, biting on it like a sour thing in my mouth. The other apprentices were never going to willingly help, and it simply wasn't fair to expect me to try to do this by myself.

I couldn't do it.

Lifting my foot, I tried to nurse it, but my skirts impeded

me. Resting my foot on the step, I stared at my empty hands lying in my lap.

I had to try.

Simon Pricket's notes could only take me so far. I needed a way to figure things out on my own and the mettle to do it.

It left me only one choice.

I had to speak with the headmaster and ask him for permission to study some of the drawings in the archives. We weren't allowed to handle them without permission, since many were very old and crumbling. Still, if I laid out a tick sack and lived with the dusty tomes, perhaps divine inspiration would strike and I would discover a means out of this catastrophe.

As I walked down the empty halls, the heels of my boots clicked on the hard stone like the steady *tock, tock, tock* of my time at the Academy running out. But as I approached the headmaster's office, another sound reached me.

Voices.

Angry voices.

I slowed, not wanting to listen. It wasn't my business, really.

I heard something smash, then clatter to the floor, and I stiffened. Unable to move, I found myself bound to the spot by warring indecision—between my desire to investigate and my overpowering urge to flee.

"She is only in the position she's in because you favor her!" I knew that voice. Unfortunately, I knew the sentiment as well. It was Samuel. I immediately turned on my heel.

"No, she's in the position she's in because she has outmatched you on every single exam and has proven her capability both with her designs and with her ingenuity," Headmaster Lawrence answered. "Perhaps if you stopped relying on David's work as a crutch for your own, you could produce something of worth."

"I wouldn't have to rely on David if I felt I could rely on you," Samuel snapped back. "It's not fair. Everyone else has a father invested in his success. The only thing you ever do is criticize."

"With good reason!" I took a step back. I'd never heard the headmaster shout. I knew I shouldn't keep standing there, but I couldn't seem to move my feet. It felt as if my legs were made of lead. "I can't begin to express my disappointment when I took Miss Whitlock's plans from you. For one moment I had thought you had drawn them and actually produced something of worth, but that's too much to hope for."

The words seemed to hang in the air of the empty corridor. The sunlight slanting through the ancient window dimmed as a cloud passed over, marking the lengthy silence. The look of disgust when the headmaster had looked at my plan had had nothing to do with me at all.

"I don't know what you want of me," Samuel said. I had never heard such a tone in his voice, and the pain that resounded there almost made me forgive a portion of his former nastiness. Almost.

"I want a son who actually deserves the legacy I'm passing on to him," the headmaster answered, and I felt the blow of the words in my own chest.

It was awful, and I was well past the point where I should have left.

As I turned on my heel to leave, the door flew open. As fast as I could, I tucked myself behind it. I held my breath as I prayed to become invisible. The door slowly swung away from me, and I stood frozen and exposed.

Thankfully, the headmaster had turned the opposite way and was already rounding the corner and disappearing from sight.

I let out a slow breath. That had been too close.

I was gathering my skirts when a sound coming from inside the office stopped me.

Sobs—heavy, heartbreaking sobs. I peeked into the headmaster's office through the crack where the door hinges met the frame. Samuel sat in his father's chair with his face in his hands, his soul bleeding out onto the enormous desk.

I fought my urge to go in and offer him comfort. I was the last person he'd wish to witness such a heartbreak.

To be honest, I wished I hadn't. I wanted to hate Samuel. I really did, but seeing him so broken, I couldn't bring myself to do it.

I took a quick breath and hurried down the corridor back toward the main hall, trying my hardest to refrain from breaking into a run.

The skin on the back of my neck and arms tingled with the sensation that someone was following me.

Now, I may be counted as a hasty sort, but nothing has ever driven me to move so quickly. I admit, I skipped the last few steps to the assembly hall and shut the door firmly behind me.

The *boom* echoed through the cavernous chamber of the hall, adding a low accompaniment to the frantic beating of my heart. I felt as unsteady as a newborn foal as I stumbled over to the top seats of the gallery and perched on the bench.

Whatever lurked between father and son went much

deeper than scores on exams, and it was no business of mine.

Needing a steadying breath, I tapped my foot anxiously to alleviate some of the wobbly feeling in my knees. I certainly didn't wish to speak with the headmaster when he was already in such a foul mood and clearly disappointed in his son.

I got to my feet, descended the steps, and stood before my automaton, thinking. There had to be a way.

A door closed and a set of footsteps descended the stairs, only to stop behind me. I turned around, unsure of whether to feel fear or hope.

It was Peter.

Holding my hands steady before me, I dropped my gaze to my boots.

Peter turned his hat over in his hands. "Tell me why." His grip crushed the brim. "When have I failed you?"

I took his hat to keep him from ruining it. "You haven't failed me. You've been my only friend." My doubt came to the fore. I wanted to trust him so badly, it hurt inside. "I want for you to help me, but I can't let you, and I can't say why."

"That doesn't make any sense." He seemed genuinely perplexed.

This was madness. Peter was not the saboteur. The thought

of it was preposterous. He had absolutely no reason to be. I trusted him, the headmaster's suspicions be damned.

A door shut at the top of the gallery. I ignored it. It wasn't more important than what I was about to say.

"I'm sorry, Peter. You're right. I have no reason not to trust you," I began.

I heard a cruel laugh behind me, and I felt a stab of fear. I turned and looked up at the walkway along the top of the seats. Samuel stood there.

"How precious." Samuel clasped his hands beneath his chin and pitched his voice high. "'Oh, Peter, I trust you so!' You don't even know his name."

"What?" I turned to Peter. "What is he talking about?"

Peter didn't answer.

"Why won't you tell her, Peter?" Samuel crossed his arms, and I found myself looking back and forth between them, searching their faces for answers. Peter looked stricken . . . and *guilty*. Samuel flashed a cruel smile as he continued. "Or should I call you Rathford?"

CHAPTER EIGHTEEN

PETER WAS RATHFORD'S HEIR. DEAR LORD, PETER WAS Rathford's heir. After the fire, Rathford had taken me in under the guise of hiring me as a maid. In truth, he'd been trying to force me to use my grandfather's key to help him gain access to the time machine he had invented and hidden in the ruins of an old castle in Yorkshire. All he had wanted was to go back and prevent a terrible tragedy, but he hadn't been considering the impact his time travel would have had on the world as we knew it. My grandfather and a handful of others locked away the time machine so only my grandfather's key could reveal it.

I had had to stop Rathford by any means possible.

It was my hand that had shattered the heart of the time machine. I'd played no small part in Lord Rathford's destruction.

I was responsible for the death of a member of Peter's family, and worse—I knew Rathford had been given the Black Mark even though it was Lord Strompton who had truly deserved it. I didn't understand. By rights, Peter shouldn't have been part of the Order.

This was what the headmaster had meant when he'd said that Peter had a motive for sabotage.

Revenge.

I was hardly aware of movement. I couldn't even look at Peter, too overcome by my shock and horror.

"Leave, Samuel," Peter demanded, his boots sounding heavy as he ascended the stairs along the gallery benches. I couldn't help watching the confrontation from my position at the center of the hall.

"Why should I?" Samuel pulled a timepiece out of his waistcoat and wound it with casual disinterest. "I have as much a right to be here as any." He tucked the watch back into his pocket and crossed his arms.

"Because if you don't leave now, I cannot guarantee you'll pass through that door with all your teeth," Peter responded.

Even from my vantage at the bottom of the stair, Peter seemed larger, more powerful than I'd ever seen him. Samuel still towered over him by half a head. He sized Peter up, then straightened his cuffs as if he hadn't a care in the world. "Enjoy your evening," he said as he bowed his head at me in a condescending way.

With that, he left, going along the walkway behind the top row of gallery seats and heading toward the corridor that led to the courtyard.

Peter looked pale as he descended once more to the floor of the gallery. "Meg," he began, but I didn't wish to hear it.

"You lied to me." I looked him dead in the eye. It was true. I couldn't trust him.

Peter recoiled. "I did no such thing."

"Why didn't you tell me you were Rathford's heir?" My voice sounded breathy. I tried to pull myself together.

"Our names aren't supposed to matter." He shifted.

I looked at him in disbelief. "We had an entire conversation that first day about who you were, and where you came from, and you didn't see fit to tell me you were Rathford's heir?" My voice echoed off the high ceiling, and I bit my tongue. After a hasty breath I continued. "How can you say it doesn't matter?"

A dreadful feeling clawed at me.

He has something to hide. . . .

Peter's eyes narrowed as his normally sweet face hardened. I recognized the look in his eyes. I'd seen it before, a dark and calculating desperation. "My name changes nothing." Peter flexed his hand, the one that had been injured.

"Doesn't it?" My dark thoughts led me down a twisted path full of shadow and doubt.

Peter had reached out to befriend me within minutes of my climbing the ramp that first day. He was the one who'd sought me out to comfort me and offer me his friendship when no one else had.

I'd thought he was as outcast and alone as I.

I was a fool.

He'd needed to get close to me.

Peter rubbed his brow, as if his thoughts pained him. "Meg, listen to me," he insisted. "It has never mattered to me."

"It matters to the Order." I took a step, this time closing the distance to my automaton. I couldn't let him touch it. "I exposed your family to scandal. Your family prospects hang upon a thread because of me. How can that not matter to you?"

"Because I am your friend." He looked up at the ceiling, then back down, holding his hands out to his sides. "This is precisely why I kept silent about all this. There are some secrets that aren't worth the bother of telling."

I fisted my hands at my sides. "You truly are Rathford's heir. He liked secrets as well."

"I barely knew my father's cousin!" Peter shouted, his face turning red. "He ruined us. We had an honorable name until he did what he did. Now we are nothing." He seemed to choke on his words as he dropped his head. He rounded on me again. "Our only hope for redemption lies in me and my reputation here at the Academy."

He looked at me as if expecting me to say something, but I had no words for him.

With a disgusted shake of his head, he turned away. "Fine. Be unreasonable. I only offered my help. I know when I'm not wanted." He straightened his coat with a stiff jerk. "Good luck to you. The assignment is impossible."

"I'll find a way." I clasped my hands together in front of me. I could feel the presence of the automaton staring over my shoulder. She was mine. I wouldn't let anyone ruin her. "Goodbye, Rathford."

Peter snatched up his hat, and with a furious anger

burning in his once kind eyes, he marched up the stairs and out of the hall, slamming the door behind him.

The sound echoed through the chamber like the crash of a great tree succumbing to a battering storm. Then stillness settled on the air once more, heavy and stifling.

In the chilling silence I turned to my automaton. Naked and faceless, she stared back at me as if waiting for the chance to come alive. I didn't know how I would help her to walk, let alone make her dance.

I didn't even know how I would move her from the room.

Holding my hands as if in prayer, I touched them to my lips and closed my eyes until the quaking in my body subsided and I could breathe again.

"I am in a fine mess," I whispered to myself as I took the automaton's hand and gently lifted it. When I let go, it swung back to her side with a ratcheting series of clicks.

I turned a slow circle, but I was entirely alone. The rising benches seemed to loom over me, while the empty podium whispered, *You have no place here.*

And through all of it, I still had trouble believing Peter could be the saboteur.

I just couldn't be certain who was friend and who was foe.

During the next week the automaton consumed my life. The headmaster had it moved to a spare room in the monastery where I could work on it in peace, but the empty room felt like a prison cell.

To aid us, our lessons turned to the finer points of automaton construction and direction, but I couldn't see how any of it would help me in my task. There were two main methods of control for the mechanical beings: Either they ran on tracks, like the ones I had encountered on the clockwork ship during the Rathford incident, or they had a complicated switch system. I needed to create a control system that made my automaton move with the ability to react to whatever David's automaton was doing.

In this I had the more difficult challenge. David could make his automaton lumber around the room like a plodding ox and it would be suitable, but if my automaton couldn't follow that movement, mine would be the one in the wrong.

What I needed to know was how a complicated automaton, like the Minotaur from the labyrinth at Tavingshall, functioned. That mechanical beast had had absolutely no difficulty tracking the motion of Will and me as we'd run for our lives while it had tried to gore us. I had survived one round with that monster. I was not keen on trying it again just to study how the bloody thing worked.

By the end of the week, I had achieved nothing. My automaton still stood, motionless and silent, in our dim little room.

Frustrated, I left her and sought out one of the instructors so I could search the archives. Perhaps some early drawings of the Minotaur from the Tavingshall labyrinth could be found there. That was a much safer prospect than visiting the beast again. I started with the headmaster's quarters, but he wasn't there, so I checked our main classroom.

Oliver was inside setting up a miniature rail system across the front table. My heart jumped. I hadn't spoken to him since the accident, but he was one of the few people I could trust completely.

He looked up at me, the patch still over the one eye, though his skin now appeared quite normal. "Hello, Meg. I was just setting out our next lesson." He gave me a friendly smile. His words felt like a warm blanket wrapped around me on a very bitter day. It was good to know he wasn't angry with me for the aviary disaster.

"I see you intend to put us through our paces. How is your eye healing?" I asked, feeling terrible that he was still injured.

He frowned just slightly. "It could be faring better, to be honest. Lucinda claims the patch has made me a better shot." I tried not to smile as he carefully fixed a miniature figure onto the track. Oliver had no talent for firearms.

"I'm so sorry you were injured."

"I've seen worse." He gave me a grin that made me think back on our adventures together. He had come out of them badly gouged and nearly drowned, and he had broken his arm. In context I supposed this wasn't so bad.

"Could I beg a question?" It felt good to speak to Oliver.

"Of course." He gave me his full attention.

"I can't help wondering why it is that so many of the Order seem prone to madness." As I looked at Oliver I couldn't help remembering how mad he had seemed when I had met him. "Rathford, Strompton—and others." I knew I shouldn't mention Haddock or the saboteur.

Oliver seemed thoughtful. "I suppose it's part of the nature of who we are and what we do. Give a man the power of God in heaven and it becomes too easy to believe he has the right to use that power how he will." Oliver looked as if he'd swallowed something distasteful. "It's good for us to have some humility."

I nodded. "Is that why you nominated me? To humiliate them?"

"Now, Meg, that's unfair. I'd hoped you'd give us all some perspective." He grinned and shook his head as if he couldn't believe how well his scheme had played out. "And you have." He clapped his hands together. "Now, how are you faring with your project?" he asked.

"Not so well as I would have hoped." I didn't know if he knew about the saboteur. I decided not to mention it, just in case the headmaster didn't wish me to. "I was hoping for permission to access the archives."

I bent down to inspect the track he'd laid out. It was complicated. I didn't see how we could create something that elaborate in the ballroom. No one would be able to move without being forced to step over the rails and wheels every few feet. While it might work, it certainly wouldn't be either functional or particularly elegant.

"Permission granted," Oliver stated without looking up. He squinted his good eye as he turned a crank on one of the control wheels, and the figure jerked along the track. "This needs some work. That will be a good task to set the class on tomorrow."

"Oliver?" My heart fluttered a bit with my nervousness. I had one advantage over my classmates. While I didn't have my family to aid me, I did have good friends. "Would you help me with my automaton?"

Oliver stood to his full height, then let out a heavy sigh as he placed his palms on the table. "I'm sorry, Meg. I wish I could, truly, but I cannot. As a full instructor here, I'm unable to aid you. It would be seen as favoritism, and I would lose standing in the Order. I'm afraid I'm already suspect due to our close association."

I swallowed a bitter knot in my throat. "I understand." Letting my gaze fall to my feet, I turned to leave the room. "Thank you, Oliver."

He didn't say anything as I slowly shut the door and returned to my cell. I retreated to the corner and inspected the drawings of control systems that had been provided to me by Headmaster Lawrence. I let my elbows rest on the smooth wood of the table as I stared at the incomprehensible maze of lines and annotations scrawled across the paper.

As I drew in a shaky breath, a heavy tear splattered on the parchment and soaked in, blurring the ink lines as it spread slowly outward.

A soft rap sounded on the open door. I quickly swiped a hand across my eyes as I drew myself up and wrested my composure back into order. I didn't know who would be bothering me so late. It was well past the time for the others to return home. I had arranged for Bob to come to collect me well after nightfall so I would have extra time for work.

"I don't wish to . . . ," I began as I turned, but my voice caught.

In the doorway stood David.

CHAPTER NINETEEN

I STARED AT HIM FOR A FULL SECOND. MY HEART BEAT. Two seconds, three. He watched from the doorway, leaning on the heavy wood frame and closing me into the room. Fear crawled under my skin, and I shifted closer to the table. "What are you doing here?"

David cocked his head and moved into the room. He stepped to the side so he no longer blocked the door, and held up an imperial hand as if silencing an imaginary crowd. I took a step closer to the door. His pale eyes caught the light of my lamp and glittered, cool and icy, like the surface of a frozen lake. "I mean no offense. I thought it might be nice to see how my competition was faring."

He gave me what I assumed was his most winning smile. The fact that it only turned up half his mouth irritated me, as if I were only worth half the effort.

"You know full well what I'm capable of," I said, even as I slowly clasped my heaviest wrench.

"Indeed," he said, taking another step toward my automaton. He lifted his chin, peering at the automaton with great interest. "But this is a very daunting task."

"Which is why you should return promptly to your own project and cease gaping at mine." I cradled the head of the wrench in my palm, the heavy weight of it cool against my skin.

David's lopsided smile ticked up as if he were amused. It was the kind of grin a cat gives a mouse when he has it by the tail. "I've heard rumors that you've had some trouble finding volunteers to assist you."

I gripped the handle of the wrench tighter even as it felt like someone had jerked the stays of my corset too tight. "Are you here to gloat?" I asked, lifting my chin and taking a step toward him. "If you are, you can leave."

He lifted his hand again. I wanted to smack it back down. I was not his servant he could silence with the wave of his hand. He may have been an earl outside of these walls, but within them we were both apprentices to the same Order. I would not stand for it. "Excuse me, David, do you see a fly?"

"No." His brow furrowed as he looked at me, perplexed.

"A bee perhaps?" I tilted my head to match the arrogant angle of his.

"No, not at all."

"Then there's no call to flap your arm about." I laid the wrench on the table with a heavy thump. "Now, unless there is a point to this visit, kindly get out."

He had the temerity to laugh. "There's no need to be prickly about it. I only wished to offer aid."

I let out a huff. "You, aid me?" I crossed my arms, and David's eyes flicked down, only to lazily drift up again. "Somehow I doubt the sincerity of your offer."

He shook his head, a very subtle motion that I almost didn't notice. Then the corners of his lips ticked downward before he resumed his painted-on half smile.

He stepped to the table and glanced at the drawings for the automaton. "I have more help than I need, and I'm sure I can convince some of those willing to work with me to assist you instead, so long as I make it clear that this is all a single effort. After all, the two automatons have to work as a combined unit, and so really it is only one project if you think about it logically, not two. We're all in this together, after all. The greater glory of the Academy is the only thing that matters, isn't it?"

I let out a short breath, then a second when I found it difficult to breathe in. It took almost all my effort to trample on the fire of my anger, but I managed. That fire must have shone in my eyes, because a shadow of doubt flickered over his expression.

"For the glory of the Academy?" I began, my words feeling sharp on my tongue. "Or the glory of you?"

His grin faded to a tense line as the crease in his brow deepened. For the first time his façade cracked. He leaned forward slightly, clearly confused, as if he were an actor on the stage who'd suddenly forgotten his next line. "I beg your pardon?"

"You heard me." I dropped my arms and pushed past him to gather up my plans and pull them to my side of the table.

He planted a palm on one of my sketches, and we both froze, facing one another. "But I'm not sure of your meaning."

I let out a bitter laugh. "Oh, no, my lord. I'm sure you wouldn't understand my meaning." I snatched the paper out from under his palm, rolled it up with the rest, shoved them under my arm, and proceeded out the door. With any luck my driver would be early and I could leave at once. David followed closely on my heels as I marched down the corridor.

"Now see here. Stop all these hysterics and let's have this out plainly."

It was as if I'd suddenly stepped into some sort of snare. My feet rooted on the spot, and I turned to him. "I'll cease all my *hysterics* when you cease your insufferable arrogance."

"Arrogance!" It was his turn to bark out a laugh. "I'll have you know I'm quite modest," he said as he straightened his fine silk waistcoat. "It's not my fault that I have many admirers. I didn't ask for them. It's wrong of you to judge my character so harshly when I've been nothing but fair to you."

I clenched my teeth so hard, my jaw ached with it. I tried to hold back the flood of words that came rushing to my mind, but it was no use. The tide was too great. "Fair to me? Have you really?" I turned and resumed my pace down the corridor. He caught me by the elbow. I wrenched my arm from his grasp, accidentally dropping the drawings to the floor.

I clenched my fists at my sides but did not stoop to retrieve the drawings. I wouldn't give him the pleasure. My eyes stung from the strain of my anger. "Everything is so bloody easy for you." The curse fell softly from my lips, but David flinched.

There was no trace of a smile on his face now. He

reminded me of his father. "I have done the same work and faced the same challenges as you have," he said. "Nothing has been easy for me here, and blasphemy does not become you."

I shifted my weight to stand more firmly. "Oh, I'm certain nothing has been easy, with your lordly title, your wealth, your education, your connections"—I waved a hand toward his face—"your *bloody* good looks."

He raised an eyebrow at that, and I had the same feeling one gets when one finds herself inadvertently standing in a heaping pile of horse excrement. He looked as if he were about to say something, but I continued before he could. "All of the other apprentices would sell their souls to be in your good graces, and frankly, I find it pathetic. You think you are being so magnanimous coming here and offering to take all this off my poor little hands. Well, you're not. I don't appreciate the offer, and I don't trust you. Frankly, you can go to hell."

I stooped and began snatching my drawings off the ground. I couldn't speak. My words caught in my tightened throat. I tried to look at anything but the perfect shine on David's pristine boots.

He knelt, then picked up the last fallen paper and handed it to me. I jerked it from his hand and bunched it with the others. "Goodbye, David. Good luck with your automaton. May the best Amusementist win."

I turned on my heel and left without looking back. My heart was pounding so hard, I could feel the press of it against the constraint of my dress with each beat. I descended the stair into the courtyard and then the ramp down into the carriage bay, and I let out a heavy breath of relief to see Bob Brindle's sweet old gray standing there waiting patiently for me.

"You a'right, miss?" Bob asked as he helped me up into the cart. "You look flustered a bit."

"I'm fine, thank you." The lie came so easily, even as my body sank into the unforgiving seat. "Just take me home."

The next day I returned to our lectures expecting to find David in his usual place beside me, grinning and winning the favor of the instructors, as always. Instead his chair was empty.

Disconcerted, I tried to keep it from my mind as I focused on my studies, but I found myself glancing over at the door every few minutes, expecting to see him walk in. My innards fluttered with nervousness each time I did. I didn't wish to speak with him, not after what had happened the night before.

At the same time I couldn't help wondering what his

reaction would be. Would he go about his business as if the whole untidy row had never happened? Or would he be contrite?

It wasn't likely.

My unease carried with me through to the end of lectures and seemed to fill the room as I settled in to work on my automaton. Time faded into the silence as I studied the old drawings I had pulled from the archives. I didn't realize it had turned late, until I found myself squinting over my papers, having forgotten to light my lamp. I only had an hour or two before Bob returned to take me home.

With a sigh I struck a match and held it to the wick of the old oil burner. I didn't like being in the Academy in the dark. I felt I could always hear footsteps.

"Good evening, Meg." David's voice came from behind me.

I screeched and nearly knocked the lamp over onto the priceless old drawings from the archives. David lunged forward with lightning reflexes that had probably been honed by his fencing lessons. They paid off as he righted the lamp with one hand.

"What are you doing here?" I didn't bother to hide my exasperation. I was too weary.

"I came to make amends." He flashed an uneasy smile

that for the first time used both sides of his face. Then he brought forth a box with a gorgeous silk bow.

I eyed it suspiciously. Of all the nerve. After I had soundly admonished him for taking advantage of his position and money, he was attempting to buy me off.

When I didn't squeal like a suckling pig and snatch the thing from his hands, he seemed uncertain what to do with himself. Finally he set it on the table.

"I realize," he began, tucking his hands behind him and standing taller, "my proposition last night may have been taken in the wrong context."

"Is that so?" I doubted it. He wanted me out of the way so the entire project could be his. "I think I know what you meant by it."

"Do you?" He rubbed a bare forearm, and I noticed he had rolled his shirtsleeves. "None of this is simple. The truth of the matter is, I need you."

I couldn't have heard him correctly. "I beg your pardon?"

David held out his hands. "I meant, I realized before I came here yesterday that I cannot succeed at this project without you. That's why I asked if you needed my aid. I didn't mean offense."

I turned to lean against the edge of the table. "I refuse to yield my automaton to you."

"Nor should you, but surely you've come to the conclusion by now that if we don't work together, *both* automatons will fail spectacularly."

He was right. I had figured I would be forced to adjust to his automaton before he'd ever stepped through the door. I was simply surprised he had enough humility to see that as a problem as well. Knowing it was foolish, and potentially dangerous, I decided to hear him out. David was the last person in whom I wished to place my trust, but I couldn't continue on under this heavy cloud of suspicion. At least for the first time he seemed genuine. "What do you propose?"

He looked at his hands before meeting my eyes. Determination shone in his eyes, and in that moment he almost reminded me of his sister. "A truce, and a pact. We give it our best effort and between the two of us decide who has the better means of controlling the automatons. If we both use the same system, then both machines will work together, and we will avoid one of us designing a system with rails and the other a system with switches." He lifted his chest, clearly bolstered by the fact that I was willing to listen.

"That is fair enough," I said, though I still didn't trust

him. It would be so easy to shut me out and demand that I follow his system, but I supposed that was a bridge to cross when the time came.

David glanced at the plans on my desk. "After that we can each work on our own, but before we hand the automatons over to the instructors, I propose we work together for that final week to make sure the two machines function as one, for better or worse. I will not touch your machine, and you will not touch mine. That way we can assure fair play."

I nodded slowly. With those two rules in place, the task almost seemed manageable. I wouldn't have to worry about developing a system that allowed my automaton to react. It would only have to follow instructions. The latter was much less demanding than the former. In spite of the many ways in which things could still go wrong, this plan was better than nothing, and if we had a chance to test the automatons together before the ball, then I would have some measure to assure that he wouldn't change his at the last moment to spite me. "So long as we agree to a mutual inspection of the machines just before the ball to insure against tampering, your proposal seems fair."

David smiled again, a grin that managed to warm his eyes. "Thank you, Meg."

He carefully lifted the box and offered it to me. "This is for you. Please accept it."

I felt like a statue, unsure what to do or how I should move. He held the box in his hand before me, and like Pandora I reached out to take it. As much as I hated it, I knew that if David showed me favor, the others would too. I didn't want to need that, but I did. I was tired of feeling so alone.

With hesitant fingers I pulled the ribbon. It slid away like silver water, and I opened the lid.

A music box rested inside. Gently I placed the outer box on the table and lifted the music box out. Atop the gorgeous pedestal a pair of dancing figures that looked as if they had just stepped out of the court of Louis XIV remained still and silent, waiting.

"Turn the key," David said as he stepped closer to my shoulder. His voice was hushed, and intent.

I swallowed and turned the delicate golden key, knowing full well that what it revealed could be dangerous. A lilting waltz filled the room, the delicate notes trapped within the stone walls.

David took a step back, then gave me a courtly bow. He straightened slowly and held out his hand. "May I have this dance."

Flustered, I turned and straightened the papers on the table. "Don't be ridiculous. I have too much work to do."

The music continued to float through the air, drifting and falling like a leaf caught in the wind. David reached out and took my hand.

I looked up, shocked, but I couldn't pull my hand away. My feet turned clumsy as I tried to keep my balance.

David's clear blue eyes met mine as though he were a golden prince from a long-forgotten bedtime tale. "Miss Whitlock, would you do me the honor of having this dance?"

"I really couldn't. It's getting late."

David took a step closer, wrapping his arm around my waist as he lifted our hands out to the side. "Come, Meg. Dance with me."

Heat—wicked, wanton, sinful heat—flushed through my blood. I couldn't think through the haze of it as I felt the strength of his legs through the thick layers of my skirts and his hips so close to mine. "I can't," I whispered in a tight voice. "I don't dance well."

His hand pressed into the small of my back as he drew me closer. I felt his breath tickle over my neck and ear. "Then I will teach you how."

CHAPTER TWENTY

"I DON'T THINK THIS IS A GOOD IDEA," I SAID, BREATHLESS. He was too close, too commanding. No one had ever held me like this other than Will. I couldn't do this.

"Nonsense," David said, as if confidence were his birthright. "How can you expect to teach an automaton to dance if you've never done so yourself?"

I tensed, and worried that my palm had turned clammy.

David smiled as if he knew a secret and didn't wish to tell. "Relax, Meg. It's only a dance."

And with the sudden pressure on the small of my back, I turned without thinking to follow his lead. I could hardly remember what my feet should be doing, but somehow they managed. My body was completely within David's control. With his slightest touch we turned in dizzying circles, spinning around and around the lonely automaton standing naked in the center of the room.

It was terrifying and thrilling at once. For a brief moment I wondered what my life would have been like if my parents had survived. Like all young women of my status, I would have attended parties and danced with many young men, just like this. They would have been my suitors. I wasn't sure what about that thought troubled me so.

The music box began to slow, and our dance slowed with it. David leaned closer, looking over my shoulder as we moved across the room like one being. "You're a remarkable woman, Miss Whitlock," he said.

I leaned back to look at him. His eyes were bright and focused only on me as he said, "You're worth more than you are giving yourself."

The last slow notes trickled out of the music box, and I took a step back, but he kept hold of my hand and drew me close again. "That's enough, David."

"Is it?" He closed my hand in both of his and lifted it to the center of his chest. I could feel his heart beating rapidly beneath my palm. "I wonder if you have really chosen, or if you have given your affections because it is the only choice you thought you had."

I wanted to pull my hand away, but he held me fast, and his words felt like ice in my heart, freezing me to the spot. "My affections are mine to give to whom I will," I said.

David eased closer, closing the distance between us. My heart leapt like a frightened doe crashing through the tangled brush with baying hounds at her heels.

"Has he told you you're beautiful?" David whispered so close to my ear. His cheek brushed mine as he tilted his head, bringing his lips so near. "You could have the world if you wanted. I would give it to you."

I couldn't breathe, let alone speak. I felt aflame, and terrified at the same time. I shouldn't have felt anything. I should have been able to push him away. But I didn't want to. I wanted him to let me feel his lips against mine. I was drunk with it.

I was weak.

I was selfish.

But I couldn't.

I dropped my chin, and took a slow step backward.

David let out a heavy breath, then brought my hand to his

lips. They caressed the bare skin on the back of my hand with sinful intent before he let me go.

"Until next we meet, Miss Whitlock." He gave me a courtly bow, then turned and strode from the room. At the doorway he paused and glanced back over his shoulder, his taunting half smile flashing at me. Then as suddenly as he'd appeared, he was gone.

I stood in the silence, trying to comprehend what had just transpired.

David. Of all people, David.

What had I done?

With my hands shaking I flapped them in front of me as I furiously paced the room.

What had I *almost* done?

I couldn't think through the buzzing in my ears. My heart continued to gallop through my chest as my stomach leapt from my shoes to my throat over and over. As I paced toward the table, my gaze caught on the music box.

What had I *wanted* to do?

Oh dear Lord, I had paved a path to my own ruin, and I had done it gladly. It would be impossible to face him again. All at once I tried to reconcile everything I thought I knew about him with what had just happened, and no matter how I tried, I could not.

My only consolation was that no one would ever know.

But I would know.

I stopped in front of the table and forced myself to regain my composure.

Fretting about things wouldn't make them go away. I ran a hand over the drawings from the archives. Now that David and I had a pact to work together, I no longer needed to study how to make my automaton react to stimulus. I could return two-thirds of the drawings I had taken out of the archives. Technically I wasn't supposed to be in the archives without supervision, but I was only going to replace what had been given to me. Surely the drawings would be more secure in the archives than sitting out on my table, and the walk down to the cellars would do much to steady my nerves.

It was late, and the Academy was empty. The last light of the deep red sunset lingered in the dim panes of the old mullioned windows. Holding the delicate drawings with care, I turned down a narrow hall and descended the stone stair at the far end.

Alone in the oppressive dark, I wandered down the wide

corridor to the large archives deep in the old cellars. Torches remained lit through the wine and ale cellar, the lights flickering over the large wooden casks. It would have been like any dusty old wine cellar, except for the large iron armatures and gears affixed to the racks that allowed the Amusementists to sort and retrieve any cask they wished with a simple pull of a lever.

Something snapped, like the crack of a whip against the stone floor. I leapt forward and nearly dropped my lamp as I turned quickly around. The shadows stretched, reaching out from under the casks of wine and ale. I thought I heard a crackling, like a fire, but I saw nothing.

Fear was playing tricks on my mind, and I had no time for them. Steadying myself, I marched straight to the archives and slipped through the large wooden door at the far end of the wine cellar.

The archives were dark, but with the small circle of light from my lamp, I managed to place everything I was holding on one of the long tables. I lit four of the large lamps bolted into the wide stone columns in the center of the massive room. Shelves stretched between the columns filled with old books and journals and large slots for rolled drawings.

I had to hurry to return each of the drawings to its rightful place. Bob would arrive soon to take me home, and I didn't have time to waste. I saved the oldest roll for last, as I had to climb a tall ladder secured to rails on the shelves to reach the slot where it belonged, and I didn't much care for ladders.

Gathering my skirts, I managed to hold the drawing and carefully climb the rungs even though my toes caught the hem of my dress twice. I didn't wish to fall, and from my perch atop the ladder I could imagine my own body crumpled on the floor, with my head split on the hard stone. I didn't want to think of how long it would take before someone found me, or what the rats would do to my dead body.

I shuddered as I placed the drawing in its slot. Then I began scrambling down the ladder. My toe caught the inside of my hem again, and I slipped. I gasped, and I clung to the ladder with both hands as my feet fell free. The ladder slid along the rails, swinging me four feet to the right as I clambered to regain my footing.

With my heart in my throat, I managed to find my perch and pulled myself right onto the ladder once again. I stood there, panting, with my eyes closed tight and my fingers gripping so fast to the rung, I didn't think I would ever pry them free again.

When I opened my eyes, I found myself staring at a thin

book with a leather binding as black as pitch tucked at the end of the records and bound minutes from Gatherings. There were no words written on the spine. That alone was odd, and enough to draw my curiosity. I pulled the book from the shelf, and with my whole body shaking from my near fall, I descended the ladder.

I took the book with me to the table and fell into the chair, grateful my shaking legs had remained steady enough to allow me to reach it. I didn't yet have the strength in my knees, or the composure, to climb the stair back out of the cellars, so I opened the book to distract myself until I felt I could walk again.

I flipped through the beginning of the book, which looked like more minutes from meetings. The pages had been transcribed, but most of it was written in Italian. That would do me little good. I was proud of my French and German, but my Italian was abysmal.

I fanned the pages, but only half the book had been recorded in. The rest was blank. As I let it rest on its spine, the pages fell open to the last entry that had been recorded. It must have been creased there recently.

What I read there sent a chill down the back of my arms. The latter entries had been written in English.

Decision for the issuance of the Black Mark against Ulysses Rathford stands, for the crimes of murder and rogue invention.

I skimmed over the next two pages of evidence against Rathford, which included a sketch of the same machine I had helped destroy, and testimony from Oliver regarding what had been found in the dungeon of the castle in Yorkshire.

When I came to the end of the entry, I had to read the last paragraph three times before I fully comprehended the scope of the judgment.

According to the testimony of Oliver Stanley, Duke of Chadwick, Rathford's actions were entirely of his own making and unknown to the rest of the Rathford line. Because of this estrangement from his current heir, an exception shall be made for the Rathford name so long as the current son proves worthy in the Academy. Should he fail, the name will be struck from the history of the Order for all time.

Poor Peter. If this was known to him, he must have been suffering under terrible pressure, and I had only added to it.

I wished there were a way I could know for certain he was not the saboteur. I wanted things between us to go back to the way they'd been at the start. I wanted my friend back.

I couldn't linger on that thought for long before I realized what I held in my hand. This was the record of evidence of every Black Mark. It could reveal the truth about what had happened between my grandfather and Richard Haddock.

I quickly flipped back through the pages, scouring the looping script for any sign of the name . . .

Haddock.

There it was, as clear and bold as the hand of the Devil himself. I hastily read the entry.

Decision for the issuance of the Black Mark against Richard Haddock for conspiracy to profit from an invention of war.

Inventing weapons was strictly forbidden by the Order. There was no way for the Order to survive if they could not remain neutral in war. The membership was international, and the last century alone would have set half the Order against itself. It was one of the reasons for the strict rules of secrecy. No one wanted to be labeled a traitor for associating with an enemy of the Crown due to the Order, and no Amusementist was willing to dissolve the Order for the politics of war.

I wondered what Haddock had *intended* to invent, and how my grandfather had played a role. I read through the testimony against him, but whatever Haddock had tried to invent was so dangerous that even in this record it was only ever referred to as "the machine."

In Haddock's defense he had claimed that the machine had not been intended for war but instead had been meant to be used to clear land for the installation of future Amusements.

The committee hadn't believed him. It was unclear in the entry if he had succeeded in creating this "machine." I wondered about the bomb and if it was part of the weapon.

My eyes skimmed over the next section to see what fate had befallen Haddock. When I reached the final paragraph, I nearly dropped the book.

In an attempt to escape imprisonment during trial, Richard Haddock was brought to justice by the hand of Gerhard Reichlin. The Reichlin clan has ascended in honor for the capture and defeat of so heinous a criminal. Richard Haddock's name shall be struck from our history for all time.

The Haddock line is dead.

At the bottom of the page was a spiral symbol like a ram's horn with a red skull stamped over the black ink.

I closed the book and took a deep breath. Haddock had just cause to seek revenge on both sides of my family. The thought chilled me. It was a very good thing he was well in the grave.

Unless he wasn't truly dead.

If the committee had been mistaken, and Haddock somehow had survived, no one had more reason to seek out the death of my family than he did. He had been an Amusementist, and clearly a remarkable inventor if my grandfather had sought him out as a mentor.

If he had survived, it was possible he had found a means of extending his own life. Maybe that was the purpose of the clockwork mask. While such an invention seemed impossible, I had seen a machine bend time itself. Extending life seemed simple by comparison.

I had much to think about as I replaced the book and extinguished the lamps. Bob would be furious with me for keeping him so long. I had to return to the carriage bay. Finding proof of Haddock's death would have to wait for morning.

Shutting the door with care, I stepped into the wine cellar. The lamps were still lit.

"Hello?" I called. "Is anyone still here?" I didn't like leaving lamps burning. They could cause a fire. I turned a slow circle, listening for a response.

Snap!

I heard the loud crack again, like a gunshot, followed by a pained shout and the crackling. It wasn't in my mind. Someone was in trouble.

Gripping my lamp tightly, I ran toward the noise, only to find myself facing a wall of large casks lined floor to ceiling against the stone. It was a dead end—or was it?

Dimming my lamp, I walked through the shadows, moving a hand along the faces of the enormous casks. In the darkness the third one on the bottom row had a strange glow, as if a light were shining through a crack in the wall just behind it.

I felt along the face but couldn't find a trigger or a latch for a hidden door. Reaching between the casks, my hand found the thick bung plugging the cask. Beneath the plug, I found the seal. So I used my key to open it, and the face of the cask swung outward.

Through the open face of the barrel came an eerie green light. I placed my lamp at my feet and ducked as I stepped into the enormous cask.

There was no back end to the barrel. Instead it opened up to a narrow hall. I followed it until I reached a half-open door. The green light flared like whips of lightning as the crackling and snapping grew more intense.

I peered into the room beyond, and immediately I drew my hands to my mouth in horror.

Headmaster Lawrence sat on a chair bolted to a platform raised four or five feet from the ground. He was shirtless, his pale skin reflecting the green glow of a large glass orb above him. A metal crown connected to the chair with long coils of wire circled his head. His eyes were closed, and his face was drawn taut with agony. I could barely hear over the sound of energy whipping over and through the orb as whirring gears turned along the outer arms of the ghastly machine.

Another *crack* cut through the air, and I leapt back. I could see what looked like a projection of an image within the glass orb. I squinted against the light, unsure what the image was.

Slowly it came into focus. The scene was of a glowing river of fire flowing, as dark iron buckets suspended from heavy chains dipped into the inferno and heaved the thick molten metal up into the air. A bird appeared, large with a gray head and a finely barred breast. His dark wings flapped above the ironworks around him. It looked like a falcon.

No, not a falcon, a cuckoo with a bright yellow bill.

I wasn't sure what to make of the bird, or the machine. Was it intended to expose a man's dreams? Headmaster Lawrence gave a shout, though his eyes remained tightly closed. The machine itself was a nightmare. I had to help him.

I took a step forward, but then suddenly the molten metal from the buckets tipped and poured over the flying bird. It burst into flame, turning black and skeletal before falling into the fire.

The headmaster laughed.

I backed away.

Feeling unsettled, I ran as fast as I could through the cask and shut the door. I didn't wish to know what Headmaster Lawrence was doing.

His dreadful machine was one Amusement I wanted no part of.

CHAPTER TWENTY-ONE

THE NEXT MORNING I WOKE UP IN MY SOFT BED WITH warm sunlight slanting over my bedcovers and a fresh pitcher of flowers from my modest garden sitting on my dressing table. A bird sang merrily as it greeted the dawn.

It was a beautiful morning, a morning that should have made me feel pleasant and eager to live life.

Instead I couldn't tear the lingering images of my disturbing dreams from my head. I shivered, cold to the bone. I wished to be back at the Academy, and already I was plotting excuses to spend more time in the archives searching for any information I could find about Richard Haddock.

Something was very wrong with me.

The blasted bird kept singing, taunting me with what life would feel like if I could just leave the Order. But I knew I never would. I had given up too much already. I had refused a marriage and had chosen a path that only seemed to grow darker the further I traveled on it.

As I listened to the bird sing, I questioned whatever corruption of my spirit drew me toward danger like a moth to the flame.

And I had the sudden urge to take in a stray cat.

Dressing quickly, I wove my hair in a heavy braid and tied it in a simple knot at my neck. There were no lessons at the Academy for the day. My obsessions would have to wait.

As the morning drifted on, I effortlessly balanced the records in the shop and took inventory of the various colorful toys adorning my shelves. It all seemed so quaint.

Four different customers had come into the shop, filling it with the giggles, laughter, and the occasional begging of children without a care in the world beyond the desire for the toys in their arms. I wished I could be like them, to only see the beautiful things before me, and have no knowledge of what mysteries remained hidden just beyond the shelves.

When I scolded a small boy for filling his pockets full of colorful glass marbles he had no intention of paying for, they spilled out of a hole in his pocket and clattered over the polished floor, much to his dramatic chagrin. As I stooped to gather them up, the silver key that always hung around my neck felt heavy as it swung away from my heart.

Just then the bell on the front door rang. A flock of colorful skirts paraded into the shop amid a cackle of familiar laughter.

I took a steadying breath. I should have known I wouldn't be able to escape. The young boy scampered out, and I wished to follow him, the shop be damned.

"Miss Whitlock, whatever are you doing crawling about on your hands and knees?" The voice of the vapid Thornby daughter drifted through the room. Condescending. Just like it had been at Strompton's memorial.

Lord have mercy.

I rose, keeping the slick glass marbles held tight in my fists. The girl wasn't alone. She had three of her friends with her. I hadn't met them. I didn't care to either. They looked at me as if I were some sooty blemish on their hems. I tried to recall the Thornby girl's name. It was something plain, like Alice—no, it was Mary.

"May I help you?" I asked in my politest voice even as I kept a furious grip on the marbles.

Mary drifted over to the marionettes and idly tugged on one of the strings. "We're only looking," she said in an overly sweet voice. "Just trying to determine if there is anything here of *worth*."

The others giggled, and I felt the marbles grow hot in my hand. I gave her my most imperial look and stepped behind the counting desk. I released the marbles into a small box. "Everything you see is of fine quality, provided you can afford it."

Mary turned, her nose crinkling in an unattractive way. "I can have whatever I wish," she said as she ran her finger along the lace trim of one of the dolls. She picked it up and toyed with the coils of hair beneath the tiny bonnet. "I do love acquiring fine things." She let her cool gaze drift over my modest dress. "But I suppose you have little time for refinement, what with all your work."

"I manage," I said, quickly calculating my ledgers. Perhaps if I ignored her, she'd spontaneously burst into flame.

"Hmph. If you insist." She placed the doll back on the shelf and turned to me. "Just the other day the Earl of Strompton spent all morning purchasing a fine thing indeed. According to Prudence he spent a small fortune on a very ornate music box before proceeding on to the monastery."

That took me aback, and I couldn't hide it. Lucinda had warned me of the propensity for spying within the ranks of the Society, but this was ridiculous.

Mary clearly felt she'd scored a touch, and decided to lunge again. "Seeing as how a music box trussed up in a silver bow is hardly an average purchase for a young earl, I had to wonder who the gift was intended for."

I arched an eyebrow. "His mother?"

"Oh, you think you are so clever. You should be careful, dear. Men don't enjoy the company of plain women with keen minds." Now her entire face had taken on a crumpled look, and her forced smile reminded me of a small growling dog.

Plain. Honestly. She'd have to do better than that. As if she were some great beauty. "If that is true, and men do in fact prefer the company of frivolous women with dull minds, you should have no shortage of suitors." I shrugged and went back to my figures.

Mary planted her palms on the counting desk and leaned across it, pure rage alight in her yellow-green eyes.

"Don't be coy with me. I know what you are. You may think you are so superior with your nomination to the Academy, but you are nothing but a greedy whore. I know about your gypsy lover, and now you have your sights set on Lord Strompton. I will ruin you if you even think you are worthy of Lord Strompton's attention. The headmaster may have taken you under his wing, but it's the headmaster's wife you truly take after." Her voice hardly came above a whisper, but I felt the slap of it.

I began to quake, feeling suddenly ill as if I had taken a physical blow. Tears burned my eyes, but I absolutely could not release them. How dare she call me a whore. She was the one parading about town with her expensive dresses, tittering friends, and nasty rumors. I was not the one hunting down a rich husband like a mad dog. And here I was on the verge of crying in front of this horrid wretch. I absolutely would not. I would not give her the satisfaction, even though I felt as if she'd just stabbed me with a knife.

She wasn't worth it. I had to swallow the bitter taste in my mouth. I had a few choice words I could call her. My unspoken insults felt like poison on my tongue, but I refused to sink so low. I'd use the truth instead.

I stepped around the counting desk, keeping one hand on it so as not to tempt myself to strike at her. "Lord Strompton will seek the affection of anyone he desires. If you feel the need to come here to badger me about what he chooses to do with his money and gifts, that says very little about me and volumes about his feelings, or lack thereof, for you."

Mary huffed, then tried her best to fix a stiff smile on her face, but it did no good. I could see the hate in her, and her frustration showed in the way she crushed her reticule. "Come, ladies. I see nothing of value here." And as one they marched back out the door, the bell jangling merrily.

I exhaled, letting my hands shake. I had won the battle, but it was clear the war was far from over.

The question was, how far was she willing to take this? She seemed the sort to attempt to ruin me through gossip. A single rumor might be easily dismissed, but there was nothing anyone could do to combat a battalion of lies coming from multiple people. I had no doubt her friends would gleefully set their tongues wagging.

For as terrible and scandalous as those rumors could be, especially the one concerning the headmaster, it was my own words that concerned me. I had practically admitted that David was courting me, and it wouldn't be long before Mary's friends spread that rumor all through the Society with or without her prompting.

Our wedding would be planned in a fortnight.

Will would not appreciate hearing the news that I was

intended for an earl. Even if it could never be true.

Save for one dance, David and I had hardly exchanged a kind word. No one had any reason whatsoever to believe I held affection for him.

My neck and arms tingled. I crossed them. David was a troublesome problem as well. As soon as he heard about what I had said to Mary, there would be no stop to his pursuit. He'd made his intentions clear.

I would be caught with the only man I wanted hating me, and the one I did not want courting me. It was practically Shakespearean, though not nearly as humorous. I just hoped things wouldn't end tragically.

I didn't need this. I didn't need any of this. I didn't need the dark stain of my own self-doubt slowly spreading through me like ink soaking through paper. I didn't need scandal and deceit. I didn't need the countless small tools, springs, and bolts I constantly had to fish out of my pocket every evening. I'd had enough.

No person in their right mind would continue this torture for absolutely no gain. I had no friends at the Academy, only scorn. I had no accolades, only sabotage, and the admiration given in the form of David's claim on me, I certainly hadn't asked for. It wasn't making my life any easier.

Enough.

I grasped a piece of parchment out of my counting desk and wrote a simple and concise letter to the head of the Order. My script looked unsteady and scrawled, but it was legible enough. I wasn't foolish, and I wasn't going to torture myself for nothing, when a perfectly wonderful future awaited me in Scotland.

That was the heart of the matter. At one point I thought that becoming an apprentice to the Order would be a magnificent thing and make me feel whole somehow. So far the Academy had given me nothing but strife.

I was done with it.

Mrs. Brindle walked in just as I finished sealing the envelope. She took one look at me, and concern immediately fell upon her face. "Is everything all right, dear?"

I stood tall, my head high. "Of course." I handed her the letter with a crisp flick of my hand, though it quavered in the air. "Please post this letter for me immediately, and then send word to Lucinda that she'll need to find a new shopkeeper. I'm leaving for Scotland in the morning."

<hr/>

Early the next morning I had the modest things I owned packed into one small case. I set it by the door and waited for Bob to hitch the cart. I had a train to catch to Inverness.

Not a single book had been placed in my luggage. I'd left Simon Pricket's journals where they belonged, in his workshop. I would have no need of them anymore.

Just as I was finishing out the last of my accounts, the door opened, the bell clanging at my nerves.

"We're closed," I snapped.

"Not to me, you're not."

I looked up to see Lucinda standing in the door. She had the stern look of a governess who was very disappointed in her pupil. One part of me wanted to rush to her and confess all my woes. The other part hated her for standing there, because I knew her intentions.

"You can't stop me." I shut the book on the accounts.

Lucinda didn't even blink. "I suppose it's fortunate I was in London, then. I can see you off."

"Thank you." Suspicious, I felt her watching my back as I left the shop to gather my bonnet and gloves near the fireplace in the parlor. Lucinda followed me there and remained in the doorway, blocking my path.

"It's not like you to run away." She removed her bonnet

and held it lightly by the ribbons. How nice of her to settle in. She could put her bonnet right back atop her head, because I wasn't going to stay.

"It's over. I've had my fill. I was foolish to think I was ever capable of doing this." I hastily jammed my bonnet on, not caring a whit for how my hair looked beneath it.

Lucinda seemed bemused, but I didn't bother to straighten it. "From what I understand, you are one of the finest students in the class." Lucinda removed one glove, then the other. "According to Oliver you show remarkable promise, and have even bested some of his early apprentice designs."

My shock forced me back a step. But it didn't take me long to recover from it. "It isn't the studies. Set a problem before me, and I will find a solution. That is nothing more than stubbornness and a willingness to read."

"And yet you're unwilling to solve this problem."

My face grew hot. "Don't lecture me. I've had enough of it. I'm not here to live out your ambition to be part of the Order. You don't know what I've had to endure."

Lucinda reached out and took my hand. "Then tell me." She led me to a seat, and sat down next to me, keeping my hand folded in hers.

Until that moment I hadn't known how alone I'd truly

been. Everything came pouring out of me in a rush. I told her about the scorn from the other apprentices, the accidents, my guilt at having hurt Oliver, then the sabotage. I knew the headmaster wouldn't want me to say anything about that, but I had to tell *someone*, and I trusted that Lucinda wouldn't tell a soul, not even Oliver. I told her my fears that the man in the mask was hiding in every shadow, waiting to strike, and confessed how the mystery of what had transpired between Haddock and my two grandfathers made me realize I knew nothing of my family's history.

With tears in my eyes I told her how alone I felt, and that I couldn't trust the only friend I thought I had in Peter.

And finally I recounted the argument I'd had with Mary Thornby in the shop the day before. Lucinda seemed surprised at the mention of her brother's recent behavior toward me, but thankfully she said nothing, only listened. At the end of all of it, I felt hollow and empty, aching for something I could not even define.

When no more words came, Lucinda bowed her head. "I apologize, Meg. I've not been a very good friend to you."

"It doesn't matter." I wiped a hasty hand beneath my eyes and turned from her.

"No, it does." She handed me her handkerchief. "I have been too caught up in my own affairs."

Speaking all my frustrations aloud may have alleviated some of the pressure in my head, but words were of no real use anymore. "You can't change anything. The fact is, I'm one person, and I'm tired of facing an army of those determined to see me fail."

"I don't wish to see you fail." Lucinda gave me a determined smile. "And I know you won't. You concentrate on your studies. Leave Mary to me."

"I wish I could. I thoroughly insulted her, and she won't soon forget it. She said I take after the headmaster's wife. I don't even know the woman, but it sounded like an insult," I said.

"What did she say exactly?" Lucinda asked as she knit her brow.

Unfortunately, the exact words had haunted me all night. "She accused me of being Will's lover, then had an outrageous notion that I somehow had designs on your brother as well. Then she said that Headmaster Lawrence may have taken me under his wing, but it's his wife I take after."

Lucinda laughed.

"It's not amusing."

"Do you have designs on my brother?" she asked as she tilted her head slightly, with a wickedly curious gleam in her eye.

"Heavens no!" A shiver trickled down my back. I ignored it.

"Well, then, there's nothing to worry about." Lucinda patted my knee. "Lawrence's wife, Emma, has always been a kind soul. It would be a far greater insult to take after Mary Thornby. We should feel sorry for her, really. She has harbored feelings for David since she was three."

"Which makes her dangerous," I said, taking off my lopsided bonnet and placing it on the table. "What happened to the headmaster's wife?"

Lucinda took a long draw of breath, then let it out in a resigned sigh. "Mary was dredging up long-dead gossip. The rumors about Emma died down at least fifteen years ago, perhaps more. I don't even know why Mary brought it up, other than that she wanted to evoke a sense of scandal." Lucinda waved a dismissive hand in the air. "If she had any sense at all, she would have realized you've never heard of it. So much for verbal warfare. She can't even load the cannons properly."

I chuckled at that. However, it did prove Mary was all too willing to use gossip as a weapon. "What was the rumor?" I asked.

Lucinda's expression turned serious. "If I told you, I'd be no better than the rest. There was never any proof of anything salacious, only conjecture based on the thinnest of suspicions, and I couldn't believe it of Emma. All you need know is that you should never feel ashamed for how you feel about Will."

I wasn't ashamed of Will. I never would be, but it was difficult to remind myself what I should be feeling when so many other things seemed to get in the way of it. David's words still lingered, that I only loved Will because I had no other option. I didn't believe it was true. "According to Lady Chadwick, David and I should have been betrothed."

I don't know why I said it. I supposed I needed to know what Lucinda would say on the matter and if she, too, would push me toward her brother.

Lucinda looked at me as if she knew exactly what I was really asking her. "Thankfully, your mother had enough sense to deny my father's wishes, twice, both with her own betrothal and then again with yours. It's why she kept you from the Order." Lucinda's gaze drifted as her expression became heavy with the weight of her thoughts. "My father is dead. He no longer has a bearing on either of our lives. I should have realized that before the spectacle I made of myself at his memorial. I was so caught up in my revenge against him and my mother, I very nearly ruined my own brother and sister. That wasn't my intent."

She sighed. "Marry whom you will, Meg. I have never once regretted my first marriage, and I know your mother never regretted her decision either."

I bowed my head and stared at the callus beginning to form on the side of my first finger. "I miss Will."

Lucinda nodded. "I know you do. He's a good man." She smiled. "Not that my brother isn't."

She stood and held out her hands to help me to my feet. "You have already done more than most ever could have. Even if I had had the chance to become an apprentice, I doubt I could have done so well as you. I know it is difficult, but these challenges will not last. The saboteur will be caught, and things put right once more. One day this difficulty will fade and your achievement will shine through."

I didn't know what to say to that, and doubted I could even speak.

Lucinda picked up her bonnet. "Now, are we bound for the train?"

She was right. I had come too far to give up now. If I gave

in, then all the struggle I had suffered would have been for naught. I shook my head.

"Good, then I should return this." She produced a letter from her reticule and handed it to me.

It was my letter of resignation from the Academy. Mrs. Brindle had never posted it.

CHAPTER TWENTY-TWO

I ENTERED THE ACADEMY WITH A NEW SENSE OF PURPOSE. As I passed before the statue of Athena holding her sword aloft, the shifting light from the moving colored glass made it seem as if she were watching me closely. I held my head high and nodded to her, one woman to another. They may have enshrined her on a beautiful pedestal, but I intended my mark on the Academy to be every bit as deep as hers.

The apprentices met in the assembly hall, but it was clear we weren't to remain there. Instructor Barnabus bunched us into a large cluster and told us not to take our seats.

I lingered around the edges of the group. The boys all talked quietly, leaning toward one another so they could speak in hushed tones. Every time I drew near, they fell silent and stared at me until I was forced to move on. I caught sight of Peter, but he turned his shoulder to speak with Noah. Samuel broke ranks and sat down, kicking his feet out and crossing his arms.

David was about to say something to him, when he glanced at me. He wore his fine silk waistcoat, and shirt-sleeves that he'd rolled up to expose the lower half of his arms. Smudges of grease marred his otherwise perfect hands. With his hair tousled he looked a bit rakish, like the proverbial nobleman who longed for adventure and so became a pirate. His eyes warmed as they met mine. He may very well have been handsome, but I wasn't impressed, truly.

He took a step toward me, and I turned and walked with purpose toward Manoj and Michael.

Thankfully, Headmaster Lawrence appeared at the far door and everyone turned to give him their full attention. I wasn't sure if anyone else found the dark circles under his eyes, or the sallow appearance of his skin, as troublesome as I did.

No one else knew what endeavors he was engaging in in the cellar. I worried for him. He drew himself up with a large breath, then said, "Follow me," without any further explanation.

We did as we were told, forming two neat lines as we walked out of the lower hall and then turned down the long corridor that led toward the cellars.

To make things worse, I was walking next to Peter. He refused to speak a word as we stepped side by side down the long spiral stair into the cellars.

Instead of turning toward the archives, we passed the casks, and Barnabus opened the large arched wooden doors on the far side. I tried not to stare at the cask that hid the entrance to the secret chamber where I'd seen Headmaster Lawrence working on his machine. I had to tell myself it was just a wine barrel like all the others.

Once we were all within the cavernous chamber, Barnabus shut the heavy doors with a resounding *boom*. The chamber we were in was vast, easily as large as the archives or the wine cellar, with heavy stone pillars supporting the floors of the Academy above us. There were no windows, and for the most part the room was empty.

An automaton stood at the center of the room, his head bowed as if he were quietly sleeping on his feet. He was easily the largest automaton I'd seen, fifteen feet tall with limbs like tree trunks and hands that could crush a man's skull like an egg.

I wasn't the only one to gape at the enormous machine. The rest of the apprentices had surrounded it, admiring it from just outside the automaton's reach.

"Allow me to introduce you to Alfred." The headmaster's voice echoed against the walls. "He was one of the earliest functional automatons the Order ever created." Headmaster Lawrence circled the giant with his hands clasped behind his back.

I knew about Alfred. Simon had written extensively about him. It was one thing to study a drawing of him. Seeing him in person was quite another experience.

The headmaster continued as I stared. "While our capabilities with automatons have improved over the years, we still find Alfred useful in teaching new apprentices the mechanics of automaton locomotion and control. Michael, if you would assist me please."

Michael, being the tallest of us, followed the headmaster around to the back of the automaton, and between the two of them they turned a large wheel affixed to his back. The clacking of whatever coil powered the giant rattled off the bare walls. None of us dared to even whisper as we watched, transfixed.

It took several minutes to wind the machine. When the

wheel began to strain and clack against the pressure, the headmaster and Michael finally stopped. Michael staggered back, his arms hanging loose at his sides as if he no longer had the strength to lift them.

"Now then." The headmaster smacked his hands together and straightened his waistcoat. "If you look closely at the automaton's chest, you'll see a series of small levers. Each serves a basic movement, and depending on the combination . . ." His voice droned on. I recognized the lesson immediately. I'd already read it eight times, both in Simon's journals and also from some records in the archives while I'd been trying to determine the best method to control my own automaton. My mind still heard the words as I recalled what I had read, but I no longer really listened to what the headmaster was saying. It was already imprinted deeply in my well of knowledge.

I found myself staring at the automaton's face. Unlike so many of the automatons the Amusementists had created, Alfred did not have a smooth, blank mask. Instead gracefully rounded lids covered its eyes, waiting to roll up and wake the sleeping giant. Its squared jaw hung slack, giving it an oafish expression when combined with the sharply pointed brass wedge that served as a nose.

The giant looked alive in a way that the other automatons simply did not, as if it had thoughts and was waiting for the moment of freedom from slumber to express them.

It was so large, greater even than the Minotaur. I tried to shake off my memories of that mechanical monster, but I could not. It had moved so fluidly, as if it were alive and thinking. It would have been beautiful if it hadn't been so intent on crushing me.

This automaton could easily crush half the monastery.

". . . And so, as you see, with this configuration of motion, the automaton will take three steps forward, then stop." I turned my attention to the headmaster just as his hand wrapped around the handle of a lever in the center of the automaton's chest.

He pulled it, then took several quick steps toward the door.

The class parted like the Red Sea, giving the giant a clear path. Alfred trembled as if shaking off the bitter cold of sleep. Slowly its tarnished lids rolled up, revealing large, shining black spheres.

The automaton's shaking increased as it lifted one leg and let it fall to the floor with a heavy *boom*. The boys around me gasped and moved farther from the lumbering automaton.

We jumbled together, and the press of the crowd moved us away from the door.

Boom.

Another step. The automaton now stood between us and the only means of escape. My heart began to race as I pushed with all my might to get free of the crowd. I ended up next to David. He glanced at me and gave a short nod, as if all of this were critical to our automaton project, but at the moment all I could think about was how ominous each footfall sounded. They echoed like thunder when it breaks directly overhead.

Boom.

The chamber broke out in cheers. David clapped regally.

My fear was irrational. I should have been studying the automaton as well. Books could only do so much, and I did understand things better once I could see how they fit together.

The giant continued to tremble, though its feet remained fixed to the floor. I let out a relieved breath.

The footsteps had stopped. Thank the Lord, they had stopped.

"Now for the next movement," the headmaster began, but he wasn't able to finish.

Slowly, like a great bear sniffing for his prey, the giant's head turned and its body twisted. Its enormous hands clenched into fists the size of anvils as the metal eyelids lowered and those cold black eyes fixed on me. A light appeared inside them, like twin candles were trapped within the glass orbs. Then they glowed red.

"Erm, Headmaster, is it supposed to do that?" Noah asked.

Suddenly the giant threw its tarnished head back and let out an unholy roar that filled the room until I could feel it shaking my bones.

"Run!" I screamed, gathering my skirts and throwing my shoulder into the boy next to me to force him to move.

The giant lifted its fists and starting swinging its arms as he charged straight toward us like a mad ape. The boys scattered like ants. The door was closed, and a press of bodies pushed up against it, preventing anyone from pulling the door open. The headmaster shouted for them to move back. In the confusion Noah fell.

"Noah," I called, fighting my way back to him, even as Manoj grabbed my arm and tried to pull me away. The giant took a step to the side, then turned and stomped toward Noah. I wrenched my arm from Manoj, and ran. I reached Noah before the giant, and yanked him to his feet, throwing him toward Manoj. Then I dived forward as the giant's foot landed where Noah's head had been. The impact cracked the stone.

I tumbled off to the side, rolling over the ground before quickly scampering to my feet in spite of my skirts. The giant turned and faced me. He ground his heavy metal jaw.

It was behaving just like the Minotaur.

Because someone tampered with the automaton and gave it the same commands.

I needed fire. It was the only thing that had confused the Minotaur and rendered it blind.

"Meg, run!" David shouted as he loped to the side. I gripped my skirts and dashed as fast as I could to the back wall, where the large brass braziers were burning.

The giant charged after me like a locomotive, its momentum too great to stop. Panting for breath, I reached the wall and made a sharp turn to the left. The giant crashed into the brazier, spraying burning oil up and over itself.

I screamed, and David caught me, pulling me toward the eastern wall.

We fell together against the stone as the headmaster pulled the door open just enough for the others to escape.

I looked back at the giant, and to my horror the burning oil remained lit as the automaton rose and looked in confusion at the fire burning on its hands and curling over its shoulders.

"Perfect," David said as he hauled us back toward the door. "The blasted thing is on fire."

We ran for the door as the last of the boys slipped through.

"Hurry!" David shoved me through the door. The giant roared again. Then I heard the heavy fall of his feet as he thundered straight for the door. With David right behind me, we ran past the huge casks of wine and ale.

The large arm of the mechanism that lifted the barrels loomed over us. It was attached to the ceiling, but if it swung just right across the center aisle—

I skidded to a halt. "I have an idea." I took in the connections of levers and gears. If my timing was right, it could work. We just needed to put tension on the wheel used to position the arm, then release the stabilizing levers suddenly.

David stumbled. "Are you mad?"

"If we don't stop the automaton, it will burn the archives and bring the entire monastery down on top of it," I shouted. As if to prove my point, the giant crashed through the heavy wooden door, splintering it as if it were nothing more than kindling twigs. "Take that over there!" I pointed to the control lever to our left.

The giant swung its fist into one of the large casks. The wood shattered, and a flood of deep red wine broke in a wave over the automaton. I covered my head with my arm as sharp pieces of the barrel rained down on me.

"Look out!" I shouted. The giant fixed its burning gaze on David, then swung its fist again as David ducked just beneath it. A shower of ale exploded from the broken cask, and David slipped as he reached the control lever for the claw that grabbed the casks.

He used it to haul himself up to standing.

I frantically turned the large wheel to my right, putting tension in the arm. "When I give the command, pull your lever!"

The giant ripped its hand from the remains of the broken ale cask and turned back toward us.

"Now!"

I pulled as hard as I could against my control lever, but it was stuck.

"Meg!" David wrenched his lever until the lock on the arm came free.

I threw all my weight against my lever, battering my hip. The lever shifted and the lock on the arm released.

The heavy lifting arm swung across the aisle, crashing directly into the giant's face.

The automaton lost its balance and fell with a splash into the shallow lake that looked like foaming blood.

I didn't have time to lose.

Lifting my skirts, I ran through the slogging mess and climbed onto the chest of the giant.

The automaton reached a hand up and brought it toward my head, the fingers outstretched to grab and crush.

I grasped the lever on his chest and switched it.

The giant's fingertips brushed my ear as the spring wound down with a high-pitched *whirr*.

And the giant closed its eyes.

CHAPTER TWENTY-THREE

I COLLAPSED FORWARD ONTO THE CHEST OF THE GIANT, just trying to catch my breath. My clothing felt heavy, soaked and pungent with the smell of malty ale and red wine. I closed my eyes and gave my thanks to heaven that I hadn't been crushed.

Now that the danger was over, I didn't think I could lift my body again. All the strength had drained out of it.

"Meg." David climbed up beside me. "Meg, are you injured?"

He rolled me over by the shoulders and helped slide me down to the floor. The cold wine seeped farther into my heavy petticoats. David reached out and brushed my sticky hair off my face. "Speak to me."

"I'm unharmed," I answered. His fingertips felt too gentle as they skimmed over my ear. I pulled away, struggling to my feet in spite of my ruined skirts. Blast it all, I wished I could be rid of them. They were nothing but a nuisance. David lent me an arm even as a crush of people poured out of the mouth of the stairwell and into the flooded room.

I watched my classmates look around with expressions of shock, horror, and the occasional elation that comes when boys discover a really large mess. As I watched them I was certain of one thing. Not a single one of us was capable of creating this disaster. The saboteur was no student. He was a master.

Peter approached looking relieved. "That was bloody brilliant."

"Watch your language," David warned. "That's no way to speak in front of a lady."

"It was a *bloody* nightmare is what it was," I grumbled. David could keep his strict language mores to himself. Michael stopped in his tracks and guffawed; Manoj smiled.

Peter offered me his handkerchief, but David pushed his

own in front of it. Unfortunately, David's was dripping wine. I took Peter's and gratefully dried my face.

"What caused this?" Manoj asked as he inspected the fallen Goliath. The machine appeared to be dead. The wine helped the effect.

"Someone instructed it to take more than three steps." I inspected a rip in the sleeve of my dress. Any reasonable person would call the dress a loss, but I didn't have the funds for another. I'd have to mend it somehow. Lovely.

That's when I noticed Noah looking ashen and still amid the excitement of the rest of the apprentices.

He cleared his throat. "Thank you," he said, then pivoted on his heel and pushed through the crowd and back up the steps.

I sighed in resignation. I'd saved his life, but that would be all the gratitude I would receive. Even after nearly killing myself to save the Academy, I was still an embarrassment to him.

It didn't matter anymore. There were some battles that I just couldn't win. I had greater problems to solve.

"Miss Whitlock, David," the headmaster called as he pushed his way through the crowd of boys. He took one look at the fallen automaton, then took in the carnage of what remained of the large casks of wine, some still spilling their contents out through cracks in the sides of the wide barrels. "Thank the Lord you are unharmed."

"For the most part," David said.

"It was very brave of you to rescue Miss Whitlock. However did you manage to shut it down?" Headmaster Lawrence asked David. I couldn't believe what I was hearing. No, I could believe what I was hearing. That was what angered me the most. David straightened, sticking out his chest, though his once immaculate shirt had been stained a lovely shade of purple.

Of course he would take the credit. Why wouldn't he?

"Actually, it was Meg who stopped the automaton. She thought to use the cask arm to knock it over. Then she was the one to leap upon it and disable it." David lifted his chin as the rest of the boys turned to me all at once.

I felt as shocked as they looked, and hoped my mouth was not hanging as slack-jawed as theirs were.

The headmaster's gaze swung to me. "Is that so." He looked me up and down, his expression pensive. "Well, that was very foolish of you. You could have been gravely injured. Whoever did this had intended irreparable harm. I'm surprised you weren't killed."

I tucked my head in an appropriately subdued way so he wouldn't see me roll my eyes. "Yes, Headmaster."

"Now go home and make yourself decent." He clapped his hands loudly, drawing the attention of the boys. "The rest of you will stay and help set this right."

The room collectively groaned.

I didn't bother fighting. It wasn't worth it, not now with my ruined clothing and the throbbing pain in my hip. I limped a bit as I climbed the stair. Occasionally an instructor or a fellow student would rush past me down the stair or along the corridor. I paid them no heed as I wandered back toward the courtyard. Now that the fight was over, I ached in every part of my body.

As I passed by the room that held my automaton, I caught a glimpse of the light from the corridor reflecting off the pristine shine of her metal face. I paused only for a second. I'd had my fill of automatons.

Shaking my head, I stepped passed the slightly opened door. The Academy needed to invest in some locks, especially with a saboteur around.

A leather-covered hand grabbed me by the face, covering my mouth as a strong arm wrenched me backward.

I felt a jolt like lightning snap through me as I grabbed

the hand at my mouth with both hands and pried the smallest finger away.

Wrenched to the side, I struggled. I took the finger and pulled it straight back until I heard a loud snap. The man cried out and pulled his hand away. I screamed as loudly as I could, then held the hand and pulled it to my mouth so I could bite through the leather glove.

With all my force I kicked and stomped, landing a heel on the arch of his boot and throwing my head back into his face. A sharp pain sliced through my head. I felt as if I had just smashed it into something metal. After a second pained shout from the man, the arm around my waist let go, and I charged forward like a hare flushed from the briar.

I bounded through the corridors and down the stairs into the open courtyard. Spinning around, I gasped for breath. There was no one behind me. I was alone.

Carriages rattled in the bay. Without further hesitation I ran down the ramp into the large tunnel. Several Amuse-mentists were arriving. Headmaster Lawrence must have sent for them to help. I recognized the Chadwick crest at once.

"Oliver!" I ran to him and threw myself forward. He caught me and held me steady as I shook in his arms.

"Meg, what happened? I heard there was an accident."
He took in the sight of my disheveled clothing.

"An attack," I coughed out, so overwrought I could
hardly speak. I just wanted to feel safe. I feared I couldn't feel
safe again. "There's a saboteur. The man . . ." I started coughing again. I couldn't breathe.

"Here." He helped me into his fancy coach, uncaring that
my skirts were still dripping with wine. He spoke briefly with
the driver, then came back to the door. "The coach will take
you home."

"Wait," I tried to call out, but he was already running up
the ramp. I wanted to tell him about the man in the mask, but
I couldn't speak. My throat felt closed shut.

The carriage began to roll down the long tunnel. I
wrapped my arms around myself and just tried to stop
shaking.

By the time I reached home and managed to fill a bath
with scalding-hot water, my panic had abated some, but not
my fear.

Whoever had grabbed me had been waiting in the room
where I had been spending several hours a day by myself.
He'd been watching me and knew my patterns. He had to
be the saboteur. He had changed the automaton so it would

cause chaos, then had taken that opportunity to attack. I felt hunted, not even safe in my own skin.

Even though I had no proof, I was certain of one thing.

The saboteur had to be the man with the clockwork mask.

The next morning before sunrise a note arrived calling me to an emergency Gathering of the Order. When I arrived at the monastery, rumbling voices from the main hall permeated the corridors as I joined the river of men flowing steadily toward the Gathering.

I flinched any time someone brushed up against me. The lingering fear from the attack had not abated. The man with the clockwork mask had managed to sneak inside the monastery. I felt I had to be aware of every detail around me, which was exhausting. I had not had a restful sleep. Nightmares of my attacker lurking in every shadow haunted me.

"Meg!"

I let out a gasp as I leapt and spun around. It was Peter. I placed a hand over my heart. "You startled me."

Peter pushed past Instructor Ivan, then matched my stride.

"Do you have any idea what could have caused the automaton to attack?" he asked. "Some of the other apprentices were speculating about it while we were mopping things up yesterday, but each theory is as implausible as the next."

"You mean they don't intend to blame me again?" I couldn't resist the barb. It was early, and I hadn't yet had my tea.

Peter just gave me an impatient look. Well, since it was all about to be revealed anyway . . . "There's a saboteur at the Academy. The accident with your hand, the aviary, and now this, they're all connected."

"A saboteur?" Peter's eyes grew so large, I could see the whites.

"I'm sorry, Peter. I thought it was you." I hurried forward as his steps faltered, putting a gap between us, but it wasn't enough. He quickly caught up.

"That's why you didn't wish for me to work on your automaton. Oh God, honestly! How could you think that of me?" He grabbed my arm and halted us both. The stream of people continued on around us.

"I couldn't believe it, not really, but you were the one who built the first faulty machine, and the headmaster caught you studying my plans for the aviary, and, well . . ."

"I'm a Rathford." Peter let out a heavy breath.

"I'm so sorry, Peter. The headmaster ordered me to keep my distance and not tell any of this to you. Will you forgive me?" We began to walk again. I settled a little, with him by my side. It felt good to have him with me again.

"Already done. What do you think they're going to do? Do you think they'll close the Academy?" he asked.

"I don't know."

We turned the corner and passed through the doors into the assembly hall. The benches were beginning to fill, and while there weren't as many people as the first time the Order had gathered, I was still astounded at how many were there with less than a day's notice.

Peter and I walked down the steps and took a seat with the other apprentices at the far end.

A loud rapping came from the podium, and we turned our attention to Leader Octavian. The room quickly fell silent.

He adjusted his spectacles on his thin nose. "As you all know by now, a very serious incident happened during the training of our apprentices yesterday. I would like to take a moment to thank Headmaster Lawrence and Barnabus for ensuring that no one was injured, though the damage was extensive," Octavian began as his voice wheezed through the machine that amplified it throughout the room. I gave Peter a sidelong glance. The headmaster and Instructor Barnabus had practically been the first ones out of the room.

"It is my understanding that the automaton had been tampered with. His original control system is missing, and the control system for the clockwork Minotaur was put in its place."

The murmurs began again. Leader Octavian held up his hand. "Headmaster Lawrence, if you would, please."

The headmaster stood behind the podium looking imperial and grave. "There have been no less than three acts of sabotage at the Academy thus far. The first two were directed at Miss Whitlock."

The voices of the Amusementists grew louder. The headmaster rapped on the podium with the gavel, but one of the men near the front stood. "Which is precisely why she should not be allowed to continue at the Academy!"

I felt as if a mule had just kicked me soundly in the chest. A chorus of "Hear, hear!" followed his words as they winged around the chamber. This was what the saboteur wanted.

"Except that she's the most brilliant mind to come through the Academy in the last hundred years," Headmaster Lawrence snapped back. Whatever ghostly mule had kicked me managed to land a second blow. The other apprentices shifted nervously around me, trying to glance across the row at me, or over their shoulders. Even David turned to look. Samuel cuffed him on the arm, and he turned back. I straightened my spine and drew in my breath through my nose. I would not crack. Not now. Peter took my hand and gave it a squeeze.

The headmaster continued. "Her attention to detail is impeccable, she has an innate understanding of how things work, and her creativity is unmatched. To remove her from the Academy would be a sin against everything this Order claims to honor."

"But she is a danger." A thin man with large spectacles rose from the crowd. "Two people have already been injured, and yesterday one of our sons could have been killed."

The angry shouts grew louder at that, burying my hope. I had intended to address the Gathering and tell them about the attack to my person yesterday, but if I did, it would only be greater cause to remove me from the Academy. I didn't wish to prove my detractors correct. However, they were right, someone could have been killed. I didn't know what to do.

"Miss Whitlock is not the problem here," Headmaster Lawrence protested. "If needs be, I will assign her an escort at every waking moment. The fact remains, this latest attack was against the Academy as a whole. My fear is that if we remove Miss Whitlock, this person will slip quietly into obscurity before we can discover his identity. And we don't know for certain if Miss Whitlock is even the cause for these attacks, so much as a convenient scapegoat."

"I find that difficult to believe, considering she brought a bomb into our midst," a man in the back shouted.

"A bomb someone from this Order created." Headmaster Lawrence came out from behind the podium and walked casually to the center of the room, turning in a slow circle to take everyone in. "Look around. We have a madman in our midst once again. He is in this room at this very moment. He could be sitting next to you, and yet we intend to blame Miss Whitlock."

The eyes in the room suddenly turned shifty as the Amusementists risked furtive glances at their neighbors. Several fixed on the man who had initially suggested my removal. He shrank down like a chastised dog. The headmaster wasn't through castigating them. "The attacks are escalating. We must find this person and drive him from our midst before it is too late. We turned a blind eye to madness before, and it led to murder. Can we afford to do so again?"

The murmurs seemed humble now. I was glad for it.

As soon as I was able, I'd tell the headmaster about the man who'd attacked me. He'd know what to do.

Oliver stood, the patch over his eye marring his face. "I agree with the headmaster. Whoever decides to attack one of us attacks all of us. The last time something like this happened, we all turned and ran to protect ourselves. By doing so we allowed more to be murdered. We cannot afford to make the same mistake twice. This saboteur must be found and brought to justice." There was a smattering of applause. Oliver gave a half shrug. "At the very least we should force him to pay for the wine."

The applause grew as the Amusementists laughed. Finally someone spoke over the crowd. "What do you propose?"

Headmaster Lawrence returned to the podium. "I'm so glad you asked." He pulled a lever and immediately the hall dimmed and a roll of heavy linen unfurled against the stone wall behind him. A contraption rose from the floor, flashed with sudden light, and projected an image upon the linen.

I gasped, then brought my hand to my mouth.

"Meg, what is it?" Peter whispered.

I recognized at once the machine being depicted. The sketch was rudimentary, but there was no mistaking the design. I had seen it in real life in the secret room in the cellars.

"I propose a simple test!" Headmaster Lawrence announced, beaming with pride. "I have been struck by a bolt of inspiration. All we need is a machine capable of seeing the thoughts of a man. With it we will be able to discern truth from lie and purge our house of the sickness that dwells within it."

I leaned forward, confused, as I listened to the uneasy whispers of those around me. Why was the headmaster lying? He claimed this idea had only just come to him, but I knew the truth. A working model of it was right beneath our feet. And if the headmaster had been thinking of birds and fire when I had spied upon him, the machine was fully functional.

Perhaps it wasn't *fully* functional. The headmaster's thoughts hadn't made any sense.

Suddenly a horrible realization came to me. If no one else knew about the mind machine, then the headmaster had been working on it in secret. That had been expressly forbidden at the last Gathering. He was working on a rogue project.

The eleven men in black waistcoats sitting in the very first row of benches huddled together to speak. I strained to see them more clearly, as if that would help me hear their words.

Finally a withered little man stood.

"As members of the approval committee, we feel it is too soon to jump to such drastic measures. A man's thoughts are his own, and that sanctity of the privacy of one's own thoughts should not be violated for the ease of discovering the perpetrator of this crime." He coughed and leaned on his cane. "Instead we shall continue to investigate the origin of the bomb and launch an investigation of the incident with the automaton. It is best to rely on tried methods for revealing the identity of the perpetrator of this heinous act."

Headmaster Lawrence clenched his fists. "What happens when there is another attack? What happens when it is something we cannot ignore?"

The old man looked to his fellows along the bench. "We will take things as they come. In the meantime I call upon all of us to remain wary."

"Indeed," Headmaster Lawrence said, his expression thoughtful. "Indeed."

CHAPTER TWENTY-FOUR

ON MY FIRST DAY BACK AT THE ACADEMY, I STOOD BEFORE Headmaster Lawrence, watching him pen a letter. I had been there for fifteen minutes at least, and he hadn't acknowledged me.

Things seemed to have returned to normal now that the disaster in the cellars had been set right, but I knew better. The spilled wine may have been gone, but the threat was not. I cleared my throat.

The headmaster ignored it.

The man had some nerve. I was likely the only one in the entire Order who knew he was working on a rogue project.

I almost wanted to confess what I knew, just to get a rise out of him.

A clock ticked from somewhere behind him, a constant reminder of the wasting time.

"I wish to speak with you, Headmaster," I finally said.

He lingered over a final word on his letter, then looked up at me through a pair of thin spectacles. "Miss Whitlock, ah, yes." He removed the spectacles and placed them on the table, but did not bother to stand. "What can I do for you?"

"You told me to come to you if I witnessed anything suspicious." I took a step forward and placed my fingertips on the edge of his desk.

"And did you?" He leaned back in his chair as far as it would allow.

"I was attacked by a man in the corridor outside my workshop only minutes after the incident with the automaton. I believe it was the man in the clockwork mask, the same man who planted the bomb in my toy shop earlier this year and was responsible for the death of my parents. He is the saboteur. I'm certain of it."

The headmaster stood even as his expression softened into a doughy look, the one people seem to give whenever they don't believe a word you say but don't wish to call you addled. I stood straight, holding my head high and my gaze steady even though I still felt myself shaking inside whenever I thought about the attack.

"My dear girl." He smiled, his neatly clipped beard emphasizing his placating grin. "What happened the other day was quite traumatic, and everyone was in a rush. As a sheltered young lady you're clearly not used to such commotion. You must have been bumped or jostled, and in the aftermath of the accident misunderstood the situation."

Dear Lord, the man was being obtuse. Not to mention patronizing, blind, and reckless. "I didn't misunderstand anything. I was grabbed from behind." There was hardly any room to misinterpret my attacker's intentions.

"Did you see his face?" he asked.

"No. He was behind me."

"There. You see?" The headmaster leaned over his desk toward me. "As I said, you were *distraught* when you left here, and perhaps you took too heavy a blow to the head." His voice took on a subtle but threatening edge, as if ordering me to accept his words as truth. That edge didn't leave his tone as he continued. "This monastery is well protected. It is nearly impossible to infiltrate these walls. Only trusted servants who have been in the service of Amusementist families for generations know the password to enter the carriage bay. The dock for the ship, as well as the tunnels, are all secure. We made sure of it when the sewage system was constructed not that long ago. There is simply no possible way for a man with something as conspicuous as a clockwork mask to enter this building."

Secure? There weren't even locks on the doors. I didn't know how the man in the clockwork mask had entered the Academy, but I knew for certain that he had. I had been attacked. That inconvenient reality was not about to disappear because the headmaster didn't *want* to believe it. "What if he knew the password?"

"Impossible. He'd have to be an Amusementist. While we may have a flair for the dramatic, we keep careful lists of all those trusted with the password, and none of us jaunts about in a clockwork mask." He brushed his sleeves, then tugged on his lapels. "To further prove my point, someone outside the Order would never have been able to modify the automaton to such disastrous effect. The saboteur is a member of the Order, of that I have no doubt."

"What if he was an Amusementist but is not one anymore?" I asked as Headmaster Lawrence circled around the desk to stand directly in front of me.

"I'm not sure what you mean." His pale eyes narrowed.

"What if he bears the Black Mark?" I asked. "Surely you've noticed the insignia etched on the corner of the bomb."

Headmaster Lawrence's gaze darted to the side in a suspicious manner before settling back on me.

"All those who bear the mark are dead." The headmaster reached out and opened the door. "And if there were an intruder, I would have seen him by now." He waved over at the spying glass like the one I had seen in Rathford's old study. "When we discover the saboteur, I assure you he will not be a ghost but a man of flesh and blood."

"But, Headmaster—" He placed a hand on my back to lead me out the door.

"I've heard enough. The Academy cannot invite any more scrutiny from the Order. You are not to speak of any of this. I won't have the Academy ruined over the silly fears of a young girl. Good day, Miss Whitlock."

And with that I found myself alone in the corridor with the door shut behind me. At least he had admitted the true reason for dismissing what I had to say. He didn't wish to lose respect within the Order. I turned and slammed the heels of my palms against the immovable stone beside the door.

I didn't know what to do next, or whom I should confide

in. Oliver was away for a time on business, and no one else would understand the threat the man in the clockwork mask posed to me and the Academy as a whole.

Now, with the headmaster's revelations, I was even more convinced that Haddock had somehow survived. This time he'd caused an uproar by making an automaton attack. What if, the next time, he reverted to his first trick and simply planted a bomb?

One thing was certain—he had walked these halls.

I was no longer safe here.

With every slow step down the corridors, I felt the presence of someone stalking me. If I looked forward, I felt the urge to turn suddenly and look back, or step more quickly to somehow outrun the shadow I felt lingering behind me.

As I approached my workshop, my fear outweighed my sense. My attacker knew I worked here. He knew I often worked alone. He knew I worked late.

As much as I wanted to prove to the headmaster that I was right, I didn't wish to do it by getting killed.

The door was open and the room dim as sunlight tried to pierce the overcast sky and break through the old glass. Dammit, I would invent a lock for the door. This was ridiculous.

I pushed close to the wall in the hallway, the fabric of my sleeves catching on the stone. Silently I crept toward the door, determined to spy into the room unnoticed to see if my attacker was there.

I peered around the door, gripping the edge of the wood tightly.

A man leaned over the table, peering at my drawings. He had his back to me. My breath caught as my heart hammered. All I could think to do was run, but my feet wouldn't move. My hand gripped the wood too tight.

That's when I saw the wrench lying on the floor next to my automaton.

With a shout I rushed forward, snatched it up off the ground, and swung it over my head like a railway worker driving stakes with a mallet.

The man cried out in terror and collapsed in a jumbled heap of awkward limbs. He fell to the side only moments before the heavy head of the wrench would have smashed through his skull. The wrench crashed into the table, and I nearly dropped it as the pain from the blow lanced through my arms.

"Dear Lord, Meg! Are you trying to kill me?" Peter stared up at me, his round face blanched with terror.

"Peter! Oh, I'm so sorry." I dropped the wrench, which

nearly landed on his foot. He scrambled backward, but I offered him a hand. "I thought you were an intruder."

Once he picked himself up, he dusted off his coat and sent me an incredulous look. "A bit paranoid, aren't you?"

"Not nearly enough, I'm afraid." I could feel my relief pounding like a drum in my ears. Thank God, I hadn't landed that blow. And now I was no longer alone. For that I would be eternally indebted to Peter. I didn't have to feel afraid so long as he was there. I straightened the things that I had knocked over by hitting the table, including David's music box. Thankfully, it hadn't broken. "What are you doing here?"

"Before narrowly avoiding a sudden and painful death, I was looking at your notes and plans." He picked one of them off the floor. He must have dragged it with him when he'd fallen.

I gathered another. "Why?"

"Because I wish to help you, you ninny. Remember?" He smiled then, a broad smile that I hadn't seen in ages. My heart swelled, and I took his hands in mine. "That is, unless you still suspect me of sabotage," he added.

"Of course I don't, and I'm so glad." Peter might not have been the best student in the class, but he had always valued my ideas and helped me stay on task.

"My housekeeper asked me to send her best wishes, and my cook wrapped this for you." He reached over to the corner of the desk and produced a hastily wrapped package. I unfolded the paper and broke into the biggest grin I'd ever had. In my hands rested Agnes's infamous treacle tart. During the height of Lord Rathford's madness, when Agnes and I had both slaved in the kitchen, she had been forced to make it every week, and I had been charged with throwing it away, untouched, the next day. It seemed I was finally allowed a piece.

I didn't know what to say. I felt tears form in my eyes even as I began to laugh. "Would you like some?"

Peter chuckled as well, and he shook his head. "It's too sticky and sweet for me."

"Hey, what's this? You didn't tell me there'd be dessert." Michael stepped in through the doorway, followed closely by Noah and Manoj. "Is it tea already? We haven't begun to work yet."

I stared, shocked. I hadn't really expected Peter to come, but at least we had been friends. I wasn't sure what the others meant by this visit, and I was cautious.

"Noah," I greeted, though in truth it sounded like a question.

Thankfully, he answered. "After what happened with the

automaton in the cellars, we felt it only right to offer our help in your project."

I couldn't believe what I was hearing.

"Impressed, were you?" Peter said for me as he cuffed Manoj on the arm.

"Actually, yes," Manoj answered.

"Well, that, and Samuel would have none of us, so it's really this or nothing," Michael confessed. "Are you going to eat that?" He pointed at the tart. I laughed and handed it to him. My insides hopped about like my stomach had been filled with an abundance of overly joyous frogs, and I felt a bit unsteady after nearly hitting Peter with the wrench.

"Thank you," I said, looking Noah in the eye, then turning to Manoj. Michael looked like a squirrel with his cheek puffed full of tart. "All of you."

For the first time I felt like I was a part of something.

And it was wonderful.

"So, what have you been working on thus far?" Manoj asked.

I pushed back my sleeves. "Come over here. I'll show you."

We worked on the automaton every afternoon for the next three days. For the first time since I'd been nominated, I looked forward to arriving each day. While we didn't seem to be making much progress, the work was no longer a chore. I was enjoying myself.

Even Noah managed to smile on occasion.

The others had noticed the music box sitting on the table, and taunted me to no end about it. I attempted to defend myself. After all, eventually we'd need music for the automaton to dance to. They only laughed at me. The truth was, I didn't know what to do with it, and so it sat, waiting.

That afternoon after looking over my notes, I turned my attention to Manoj. He was in the process of trying to plan out a specific series of motions for the automaton to follow, and have it result in a dance. So far, we'd only managed to have the automaton trip over her own feet.

"Perhaps you are not the right one for this task," Michael suggested to Manoj.

Manoj glared at him. "What exactly are you implying?"

"You don't dance." Michael shrugged. "Well, not like us anyway."

"And you don't think," Manoj muttered in response.

"I heard that." Michael turned to us, while Manoj tried to act innocent.

"Don't listen to him, Michael. It's nonsense," I said, studying some figures Noah had written down. "You have an astounding capacity for thought." I smiled at him and wondered if this was what it was like to have brothers.

"Thank you, Meg—" Michael began, but I cut him off.

"About food," I added.

Manoj laughed deep from his belly, and Michael threw a rag at me.

Peter shook his head at us as he leaned back in a chair with his boot braced up against the edge of the table. He watched Noah pace by the window. Peter's eyes narrowed as he touched a finger to his chin. He rocked himself on the back legs of the chair. "We need an interactive system, so that when the automaton hears a certain strain of music, she turns right. When she hears another, she turns left." He paused. "You know, the Minotaur system is the most reactionary—"

"No!" all the rest of us shouted at once.

"Honestly, Peter, the last thing we need is another automaton that thinks," I said. "The last two I've met haven't exactly proven themselves trustworthy."

"Unless you trust they're going to kill you," Michael added.

There was too much truth to that. "What we really need is a system with a rigid set of commands," I said. "We need something that can tell the automaton precisely how to move, and when. Then we only need to concern ourselves with starting her at the right moment, so she dances to the music." My gaze fell on the music box.

I felt something, a stirring in me, both in my mind and in my body, as if something great were about to happen. I rushed to the music box and lifted it into my hands. "It's so simple. Why didn't I think of it before?" I turned the dancing couple at the top of the box, and they slowly twisted back as a tiny comb within the box played notes that had been precisely recorded on a tumbler.

A tumbler.

"What do you know of the Chadwick coach?" My voice sounded breathy as I pulled a chair next to Peter and faced the others.

"Is that the one that records how it gets from place to place, so it can drive itself?" Peter asked.

"Ah, yes. Instructor Oliver explained how it functioned just the other day," Michael said, drawing nearer and sitting down on the stool next to me. "It works off a tumbler, I think."

"It does. I've seen it myself." I grabbed for a spare bit of paper to start sketching what I could remember from the controls of the coach. "The motion of the coach records itself on a tumbler. If you place the correct tumbler in the coach and start it from the correct location, the coach knows how to go from place to place. It follows the turns recorded on the tumbler."

Noah stopped pacing. "We can avoid an automaton control system entirely. It could work."

"It's brilliant," Peter said. "And much less likely to run rampant through a ballroom filled with our instructors."

"If we must record this tumbler," Manoj said as he walked slowly around the automaton, stroking the beginnings of his beard, "that puts us in a difficult position if we can't make the automaton move to begin with."

That was the tricky part. I joined him, facing the automaton. With the coach you could drive it, and so record the directions as you drove. We couldn't do the same for the automaton.

As I stared, my face reflected back at me from the smooth golden visage.

That was it.

I turned to the others. "I have an idea."

CHAPTER TWENTY-FIVE

I COULDN'T BELIEVE I WAS ABOUT TO RELY ON WHAT David had taught me. "I can dance."

"That's lovely, Meg," Michael said. "I can play the fiddle. That doesn't exactly help us, now, does it?"

"Don't be an ass." Peter threw a bolt at him.

I ignored them, turning instead to the automaton and lifting her arm out to her side. "All we need is some kind of machine to record my motions onto a tumbler. Then we can transfer the tumbler into the automaton and she will repeat my motions exactly."

"That could work," Noah said, stepping closer to inspect the automaton. "How well do you dance?"

My gaze drifted over to the music box on the table. I could hear the song playing sweetly through my memory as I recalled the feel of David's palm pressing into my back, and my hand firmly enveloped in his.

I touched my lip, remembering how close I'd come to disaster. "I can dance well enough for David."

"I won't ask how you know that. It's irrelevant in any case. Even if you were a prima ballerina, it wouldn't solve the problem of David's automaton moving completely independently of ours." Peter leaned his elbows on his knees and let his hands fall between them.

"David and I already have a pact. Whichever one of us designs the best control system, the other will use it as well. This will work." I felt my ears go hot, and everyone's gaze landed very suddenly on me.

"You made a pact with David?" Peter asked, though it didn't sound much like a question.

"I didn't think it worth mentioning until now." Perhaps once or twice I had felt I should say something. After all, they were putting a lot of effort into the automaton, and if David's design functioned better than ours, all that work would have been for waste. But I was confident in us, and so I'd held my tongue.

"I thought we weren't allowed to consort with the enemy," Manoj said.

"He's not our enemy. He's our classmate," I said, but Michael arched his eyebrow in a skeptical way.

"What did you have to do to convince him of this arrangement?" Noah looked suspicious, then slid his gaze to the music box.

Now, that had gone quite far enough. I didn't like what he was implying. "Yes, David and I have a pact. We both realized, just as you did, that it would be impossible to succeed unless we agreed to work together. Nothing more. Since you lot decided to wait so long to grace me with your presence, I had little choice but to accept." I crossed my arms. "Now with this plan we can go to him and force him to admit we have the superior idea."

"Samuel will love that," Michael said.

Peter tried to hide a smile. "Knowing David and how he thinks, he will likely overcomplicate things."

David, complicated? I never would have imagined. I had to stop thinking of him. "So, how do we keep things simple?"

Manoj took a step back, then spread out his arms and legs. He moved them slowly, pondering his own limbs as he swept them elegantly around him. "We need to create something that can move with you, joint for joint. The body bends in many ways."

"Yes, but thankfully, in a waltz none of the upper body has to move at all," Noah said, joining Manoj and observing Manoj's feet as he turned.

I turned to stare at the window. A spider crawled along the edge of the panes. His eight spindly legs rose and fell, moving gracefully through the air as he climbed. "Could we create another set of arms and legs? They would have to be something I could wear outside my clothing on my back, connected to my hands and feet." Spindles and gears began to link themselves together in my mind.

"Like another skeleton, only on the outside." Peter pushed his chair forward and grabbed a piece of paper from the table. He sketched furiously, and when he was done, he had drawn me standing with an armature reaching out and tying to each joint in my arms and legs. "Something like this."

"It needs refinement." Manoj took the drawing from him and considered it. "But it could work."

Michael peeked over Manoj's shoulder. "My grandfather worked with many different control systems. I can ask him to help. I believe he was good friends with the late Lord Chadwick."

"Good," Noah said. "I can ask my father as well."

I took the drawing from Manoj, though I didn't look at it. My father and my grandfather would have known exactly how to make such a machine. I didn't have the benefit of their help. I feared I never would again and all links to my past had been brutally severed by someone who wanted to destroy me, too.

I felt a hollowness inside, one I knew I would have to live with forever.

"Meg?" Peter placed a hand on my arm, and I looked down at the drawing. "What do you think?" he asked.

I took a breath. There was nothing I could do but move forward. "I think it is an excellent plan." I looked at the faces of the boys around me. I knew them now, much better than I had before. For such a long time they'd been only names. Now they felt like family, a new family. "Let's get to work."

It took us quite a while to develop a full drawing for the armature. Michael's grandfather was an immense help, since he had been one of the Amusementists who had developed the original tumblers for the Chadwick coach. With his aid we were able to create a working model for our motion-recording device, and Noah's father helped us craft the model.

After seven spectacular failures with our model that required finessing the motion of the joints and calibrating the recording mechanism, we found success.

Confident in our final drawing for the armature and tumbler system, we sent it on to the Foundry, then turned our attention to converting the internal mechanisms of the automaton to suit our new control system. It was not an easy task.

After working on it for weeks, I was intently fighting with a particularly stubborn spring when I heard people walking very quickly down the hall. They were talking excitedly, but I couldn't hear what they were saying. I was curious, but I was really close to having all the pins adjusted perfectly, and I was the only one who could manage it, with my small hands.

"What is happening out there, Peter?" I didn't bother to look up as I twisted my fingers in knots trying to adjust the last pin with a sharp but sturdy awl. I was wearing a set of magnifying goggles that illuminated the interior of the automaton, but I couldn't see anything in the room at large. I waited. No one answered.

I lifted my head, only able to see large dark forms around me. "Peter?" Something loomed in the light of the doorway. A cold stab of fear lanced through my heart.

I lifted the goggles.

My eyes cleared and my heart flew to life with new purpose.

"David, what are you doing here?" I said, pulling the goggles completely off and stashing them with the awl in my pocket. I wiped my hands on one of the old rags lying at the automaton's feet. I tried to settle the fluttering feeling in my chest. It was only the lingering effects of my shock, nothing more.

David stood in the doorway, his posture both at ease and regal. He looked as if he had just stopped by on his way to Camelot. "I came to offer my congratulations," he said, stepping into the room with his casual grace.

I tucked the rag into my pocket with the awl and goggles. They joined what felt like a bolt, a marble, a spoon, and I didn't even want to know what else. I yanked my hand out and smoothed the front of my dress. "Yes, well, we don't know if it works yet."

His intent gaze met mine as he took a step forward. "It will."

I swallowed. I wasn't sure how to respond to that. "Thank you?" I muttered, while immediately chastising myself for sounding like a complete fool. Thank you. Honestly, I couldn't think of anything wittier?

David smiled, then turned to the table where all our drawings were. "Your plan for the control system for the automaton is genius, and I intend to use it as well. I have had no luck with my own attempts. My plans were far too . . ." He circled one finger in the air.

"Complicated?" I leaned against the table.

He smiled. "Yes, exactly that."

I let out a sigh. Creating something David wished to be a part of was an accomplishment in its own right. We were more than competitors. We were fairly matched.

"I brought you a gift to thank you for your hard work and to celebrate your brilliance." He held out a small velvet-covered box.

"David, really I mustn't." I held my hands out and stepped back, gathering my tools and arranging them in their box. "I shouldn't be accepting gifts from you. People have already begun to talk."

"About what?" He looked as if he had as much concern about rumors as he did for the sun falling suddenly to Earth that very moment and burning us all in a great ball of fire. "You have achieved something great, and I had this made for you so you will always remember this achievement. You should be proud of what you've done."

I didn't like the feeling that there were words left unsaid at the end of his sentence. With trembling fingers I took the tiny box and opened it. Inside was a miniature tumbler. I lifted it out of the velvet and held it up to him.

He reached out and collected the music box he had given me, then rummaged on the table for a tool before removing the small screws on the bottom of the box. When he had it open, he held his hand out for the tumbler. I placed it gingerly in his palm, and he expertly fitted it into the pedestal of the music box.

Once he had it reassembled, he turned the figures at the top of the box, and slowly they began to spin.

This time the melody that came from the box was the tune that had been selected for our automatons at the ball. I watched the figures turn, and imagined our dancers doing the same in front of all the Amusementists. Profound pride swelled within me until it inhibited my ability to speak.

"It's very thoughtful. Thank you." I smiled, if only because I knew he understood.

"Dance with me, Meg." He gave me a courtly bow, then held out his arms. "Just once more."

I knew I oughtn't. I knew I was practically skipping down a very treacherous path, but his gift had been so thoughtful, and his praise so sincere. I couldn't deny him.

Stepping into his waiting arms, I placed my hand in his. We started a turn.

"What is this?" A dark voice with a heavy Scottish brogue spoke from the doorway.

Confused and terrified, I leapt away from David as if I'd just been burned.

There in the doorway with his arms crossed and a wary expression on his handsome face stood a certain Foundry worker.

"Will!" I ran to him and threw myself into his arms, my heart hammering with joy and fear all at once. I wanted to kiss him until I had no breath, but his arms felt tense around me. "I didn't know the ship was here," I confessed.

"Clearly." He kept his eye on David, who casually polished the edge of the music box with his thumb even as the lilting song continued to play.

"MacDonald, how good to see you." David gave Will his slanting half smile. "How is Scotland this time of year?"

"Strompton." Will didn't return the smile.

"David, please." I turned to my fellow apprentice. "I'd like a moment."

"Very well." He gave us a nod. "We can continue another time." He left the room without another word just as the music began to fade.

"What are you doing here?" I asked Will, hoping to brush past what had just happened with David.

"We were sent down to deliver orders for the ball. I helped with the pieces for your drawing. I took extra care with them." He glanced at the naked automaton. Her chest was open, exposing the inner workings. We only needed to place the tumbler where her heart should be once we had it recorded. "I was looking forward to seeing her dance."

"You'll be at the ball?" I couldn't believe it. I was thrilled Will would be there to see the culmination of all the things I had been struggling so much for, and yet his reserved demeanor was giving me pause.

"MacTavish has chosen me to be part of the builders' crew. That means I'm invited to attend."

I wondered what it would be like to dance with Will at a gilded ball, but then realized he probably wouldn't know how. It wasn't as if he'd ever had the chance. "That would be wonderful."

He glanced down the hall. "I don't have much time. I wanted to see you again. I've missed you." He entered the room, inspecting the automaton and smoothing his hand over a panel on the arm, as if testing the curve of the metal.

He waited, as if expecting me to say something, but nothing would come out. Of course I had missed him. I wanted to say it. But for the first time I didn't feel empty or hollow inside. I hadn't even realized he was in London. I loved him, but I had been busy, and to be honest I hadn't thought about it much.

It was awful of me.

His brow crinkled as his gaze swept to the table. He stiffened.

I followed his gaze to the music box sitting so elegantly near my drawings. He looked at it with a deep longing as he walked over and touched the flying skirt of the fine lady. "This looks very expensive."

"It's only a music box," I said. "It merely plays the tune the automatons should dance to. It's inspiration more than anything."

"*He* gave it to you, didn't he?" Will's voice cracked on the last bit, and my heart broke at the sound. He was hurt, even if he'd rather die than show it.

He clenched his jaw and dropped his gaze to the floor. After a moment he looked up at me. The look in his eye reminded me of a fierce wild thing caught in a trap. "Your silence says too much."

"It's nothing, Will. Nothing." Even as I said it, I thought

of the dance and how I had longed to kiss David. I thought about how I had been eager to step into the circle of David's arms just a moment before. It wasn't nothing, but it wasn't something, either.

Whatever I felt for David, it wasn't as real, as deep, or as lasting as what I felt for Will, and so I couldn't trust it. But I didn't know how I could explain what I did feel to Will without making things worse. I didn't wish to feel anything, but I couldn't help myself. If I truly loved Will, shouldn't I be blind to everyone else? I feared what I felt meant I didn't know how to love at all. What if all the love I had known was nothing more than infatuation?

"Whatever is going on between you and Strompton shouldn't be nothing, that's the problem." He turned toward the door. I grabbed him by the arm and held him.

"What do you mean by that?"

"You could be a countess, Meg. You could have wealth and luxury, and anything you wanted. He could give that to you. You are suited to him." Will's shoulders dropped as if weary of the weight of his own thoughts. "I can't give you any of it. Not fortune, not prestige, not family, nothing."

I reached up and touched his face, turning his cheek so he'd look at me again. "I want none of it."

Will stood for a moment, thinking, as my hand lingered on the edge of his tight jaw. He closed his eyes. "Tell me you feel nothing for him, and I'll believe you. Tell me you haven't considered him at all. That you haven't thought of what it would be like as his wife."

I opened my mouth to speak, but my throat closed tight and the words just wouldn't come. I had thought of it. I had thought of the fine manor, and the money, and the dresses. I would have all the time in the world to work on my projects. David and I together would be like a perfectly arranged marriage of royalty. How could I not consider it?

"That's what I thought." Will let out a long breath, then strode for the door.

"Will, stop!" Lord, men could be so foolish. I didn't love David. David was a temptation, nothing more.

He paused and turned back to me. "I've battled dragons for you," he said, and I felt tears rushing to my eyes. "I've lifted your wings and helped you fly. But it will never be enough. You have always been destined for something greater."

And with those words he turned and walked away.

"It's enough!" I shouted down the corridor as I watched him turn the corner without looking back. "I love you." I let out a heavy breath. "Only you."

As I said it, I knew it was true. I felt it, not like explosions or lightning, or fire in my blood. I felt it like air, all around and within me, quiet and unassuming and yet as powerful as a storm.

Standing alone in the middle of the hall, the cold of the stone walls closed in on me.

What had I done?

CHAPTER TWENTY-SIX

I COULDN'T LET THINGS END THIS WAY. I COULDN'T LET Will leave for Scotland thinking I wanted to be with David instead of him. It wasn't true. It simply wasn't true.

And he had to know.

I broke into a run, bolting down the corridor, then rounding the corner, only to crash into Samuel. The force of it knocked us both down.

Scrambling to my feet, I held a hand out to Samuel to help him back up. "My apologies."

He grabbed my wrist and squeezed painfully tight. "Your apologies aren't good enough."

He pulled me closer, looming over me with his broad frame.

"Let her go," Manoj said directly behind me.

Samuel looked up and sneered. "And what if I don't? Miss Whitlock knocked me over and she owes me, Punjab."

Manoj pulled a curved blade from his belt. "My name is Manoj, and I said let her go."

Michael came up next to him, followed by Noah. "If you want an apology, I've got one for you," Michael said, casually rubbing his fist. "I'd be glad to knock you down first."

"You're outnumbered. Drop her," Peter said from close behind us. As Samuel turned around, he loosened his grip enough for me to twist my arm up and break his hold.

I stumbled back toward the boys, and Noah caught me and drew me behind Manoj and Michael. Samuel turned around slowly and leered at Peter as he straightened his coat. Peter crossed his arms and glared back, his head held high.

Even though my heart was nearly beating through my chest, I felt such pride in my friends.

Samuel stomped off, muttering under his breath.

"Thank you," I said to the others, my voice breathy. "Thank you for everything."

Peter gave me a knowing grin. "Go find him."

I ran.

My feet flew, and I thanked the Lord I had shortened my hems for practicality and to remove the worst of the wine stains, and had been making do with a very thin petticoat the last few weeks because of the heat. I didn't have to worry about tripping as the heels of my boots struck the stone over and over, echoing off the tight corridors.

As I entered the catacombs, I saw that the main corridor had been blocked by a group of Amusementists trying to maneuver a cart with a large engine up the ramps. When I tried to push past them, I overheard one say, "I'm glad this is the last of it."

My hope plummeted. The ship would be leaving any moment.

About halfway to the underground dock, I had to catch my breath. I may have loosened my corset for comfort, but it still never allowed me to take too deep a breath. I leaned against the cold and slightly damp stone. The shouts of the men on the boat drifted through the thick air along with a blast from the whistle. The ship hadn't left yet. I was almost there.

"Wait," I gasped. "Wait."

Finding my strength, I ran the down the final corridor. One more turn, and I'd be at the docks. Slowing down, I stayed focused on that last turn and the torch burning there as if encouraging me to chase toward its light. The open archways to the storage rooms on either side of me passed in dark shadow.

I was going to make it.

Something slammed into me from behind. An arm wrapped tight around my torso, and before I could scream, a sickly-sweet-smelling cloth pressed over my nose and mouth. It burned my lips and cheeks as I thrashed against my attacker. I couldn't shake free. I couldn't breathe.

"I have you now, my dear," the man whispered into my ear. I fought and fought but the glowing torch at the end of the corridor began to loop around in large circles and turned fuzzy. The bell of the steamship clanged, the sound slow and watery as it pushed through the spinning haze. I could hear a soft ticking behind me from the gears embedded in the man's face. "Let's go on a little holiday, shall we?"

His words sounded stretched, like they had been shouted through a long, dark tunnel. I closed my eyes as all my strength left me, and I remembered no more.

When I woke up, at first all I knew was that my body ached all over. I tried to open my eyes. Nothing. Darkness surrounded me. I tried to open them again. Panicked, I attempted to sit up, but I found myself on my back, my knees curled toward my chest, and my neck propped forward. I smacked my hands out, and they hit walls. I was closed in.

Terrified, I couldn't scream. I imagined myself in my own coffin, trapped and helpless as men in long black coats lowered me into my grave. In my mind I could hear the thumps of shovelfuls of dirt hitting my casket, burying me, with no escape from death. Everyone already believed I was gone.

A high wail broke out, and only then did I realize I was the one screaming, and the thumps were the sounds of my arms hitting the wood surrounding me. This was no dream. I was caught, and if I couldn't control my panic, I would die.

I tried to kick at the lid, but it wouldn't give, and I didn't have enough leverage. I only had enough room to move my arms.

My breath came in quick gasps. The air around me was choking. I was feeling ill and too hot. I had to escape. My eyes focused on a keyhole just to my right. I curled more tightly into a ball to try to peer out of it, but it was no use.

Pressing my hands into the sides of the rough wood

surrounding me, I took as slow a breath as I could. I had to get out, and I had to think. I wasn't in a coffin. Coffins didn't have keyholes. It had to be a trunk, a large one.

I was being smuggled.

I wasn't dead yet, and so long as I wasn't, I had to fight. I needed to pick the lock. Wriggling my hand into my pocket, I prayed something in there would actually be of use. I pulled out a marble, then fumbled with a tin soldier tangled in a bit of twine with the damn spoon. Then I felt the goggles.

Thank you.

I pulled them out and did my best to strap them onto my head, but my neck was burning with pain, and I still couldn't breathe. As I turned the switches, the goggles began to glow, illuminating the interior of the chest.

The planks surrounding me hadn't been shaped or planed well, so there were small cracks and gaps between some of the boards. Swirling knots plagued the wood, and the chest smelled like salt water and mildew. The casing around the keyhole seemed sturdy enough, even though rust had taken hold along the edges. Hopefully, the rust had weakened it. I tried to fit my finger into the keyhole but couldn't. I needed something to prod around inside it. Digging deeper into my pocket, I felt a smooth wooden handle.

The awl.

It had poked a hole in the bottom of the pocket and nearly fallen through. I struggled to pull it out, but it was caught up in the folds of fabric, and I couldn't push my elbow down far enough to remove it. Finally I managed to free it. I tried to fit the point into the keyhole, but with the angle, the point of the awl kept hitting the inside of the rusted casing. I tried again, twisting my wrist to angle the point down. The awl scratched against the inside of the lock casing but couldn't reach the locking mechanism. It was no use. The awl was too strong and couldn't bend to manipulate the pins inside the lock.

Panicked, I drew my breath short. I didn't wish to imagine what would become of me if I couldn't escape. I would surely end up dead, but that fear seemed the least of the sufferings I'd have to endure before I was murdered.

I gritted my teeth.

It's not over yet.

There had to be another way to escape. I pulled my knees in as tight as I could to my chest and kicked out. My boots thudded against the planks of the trunk. I thrashed my shoulders, trying to sit up just a bit more, to somehow press the walls of my prison outward with the force of my will.

My foot curled and tightened painfully, drawing into

itself until I wanted to scream with the agony of it. I had no way to stretch it out. I kicked again and felt a tear slide over my cheek. There had to be another way to get the lid off. I glanced to my left, and with the magnification of the goggles, I noticed a small triangle of burrs in the wood. They were nothing more than tiny breaks in the grain. A few splinters cracked away from the plank. I reached over and smoothed my finger along the wood. The skin on my finger caught on a sharp protrusion.

Nails.

Of course, they were the points of the nails that held the hinges. I fought with my skirt until I could stuff my hand back into the constricted pocket and feel around. After a moment I was tempted to rip the front of the pocket off and use that, but finally I touched the rough weave of the rag I had been using with the automaton. My elbow hit the wall three times before I could pull out the rag. I ignored the ache as I wrapped the rag over the end of the awl. After fitting the tip of the awl against the point on the nail, I slammed the heel of my hand into the fat wooden handle.

My hand felt as if it had shattered, but I swallowed the pain and hit it again with all the force I could manage in my awkward position. I heard the distinct *tink* of the short nail hitting the ground.

Thank you, dear Lord. I tried to take a deep breath. My arm ached, and I wasn't sure if I had the strength to continue to strike. I didn't have good leverage, and the nails near my knee would be even worse.

I couldn't give up.

Just five more.

The second one came easier, but I feared I had broken a bone at the base of my thumb. My entire hand thrummed with pain and I had managed to gouge my palm. For the third I tried twisting the awl against the nail, and eventually it came out, but the effort left my shoulder aching.

My strength was running out. Somehow I manage to curl my body tighter to reach the other nails. Biting my lip to steal the pain from my hand, I pounded the heel of my palm against the blood-slicked awl. I had no other choice. Each time I curled to reach the nails, my corset constricted and I couldn't breathe.

Finally with a gasp I slammed my fist into the awl a final time, thankful for the terrible wood and weak hinges of the trunk. Holding my breath, I pulled my body as tight as I could and kicked with all my force. The lid burst into the air, then clattered back down onto the trunk. I shielded my face with my arms, and a corner of it hit my shoulder. I shoved it away with my boot.

I lurched up and took several deep breaths. The stench of river water nearly overpowered me, but I breathed it in gratefully. With a sore and bleeding hand, I perched the goggles on top of my head.

I was free.

Feeling dizzy, I attempted to stand, but my head swam and my cramped muscles protested as a thousand needles seemed to jab into my skin at once. I fell back down, bracing my arms on the sides of the trunk. I kept my hands out, as if their presence outside of the trunk could somehow prevent me from being forced back into it. I felt helpless and weak, and my captor could return at any moment. I had to find my damn feet.

I scrambled out of the chest, tipping it over and rolling out onto the floor.

After coughing until my lungs burned, I lifted my head and cautiously pushed myself up. I was still in the catacombs, in what looked like an empty storage room. The smooth stone walls were the same as the rest of the underground tunnels, but I had to be very near the river. Seeping water had stained dark streaks down the walls near the door.

I stumbled to the door and fell against the damp wood.

I shook the latch until the entire door rattled on the hinges, but it was no use. It was locked from the outside. At least my prison was now less cramped, though just as terrifying.

The light from a flickering lamp inside the room created shifting shadows in the darker parts of the chamber. A blanket lay crumpled in the corner next to a small crate. A rat was perched on a plate beside a half-eaten loaf of dark bread and the rotting skeleton of a fish. Shaking, I took a step back and almost knocked into an old whisky barrel. Atop it rested several delicate tools, a mirror, and a small brown glass bottle. I hastily wrapped my injured hand in the rag as I took a closer look at the items.

I picked up the bottle and inspected the label. Just as I'd suspected, it was chloroform. I pushed hard on the stopper, then tucked it into my pocket.

Whoever the man in the clockwork mask was, it seemed pretty clear he had been living in this wretched place for some time. Hunting me.

I had to escape before he returned.

My hand went to my neck, where I kept my grandfather's key.

The familiar weight was gone.

I staggered, still dizzy from the chloroform. The key was

gone. My father had died with that key in his hand, trying to keep it from the man in the clockwork mask.

I had to get it back.

I ransacked the dingy, foul-smelling alcove, throwing the blankets against the wall. Grabbing the crate with both hands, I swung it with all my might against the wall. It smashed open as the plate clattered against the stone. The rat squealed, then scampered to the door, where it wriggled its fat black body through a tiny gap in the wood. I'd never been so envious of a rat.

I kicked the broken remains of the crate, but it was empty.

The clockwork key was gone.

What was I going to do?

My palm stung. I inspected the wound and concentrated on pulling out a large splinter. Once free of the wood, I stanched the blood and inspected the lock on the door.

I heard a scratching on the other side.

He had returned.

Shaking, I leapt across the room and tried to conceal myself behind the whisky barrel. I heard the unmistakable click of a bolt sliding back, and the door creaked open.

I tried to peek around the barrel.

The man in the clockwork mask stepped through the

door with my key hanging like a trophy around his neck. The brim of his hat and his high collar obscured his face.

Just then he looked up.

The human side of his face was as familiar to me as my own. From his salt-and-pepper hair to the thick eyebrow, the curve of his shoulders, and his long arms—everything was familiar to me. Especially the single dark gray eye locked on me. All the wind left my lungs in a sudden burst as I stood up, dumbfounded. "Father?"

I shook all over, hardly able to stand upright as I stared at his face.

The man's resemblance was uncanny, but his face was slightly wider, with more of a hook to the nose, and large sideburns over a pockmarked cheek. On the other side of his face, the gears turned slowly in the intricate mask as the lifeless metal eye watched me.

He laughed—a cold, cruel sound. "Your father? Hardly. I've never had the pleasure of being called a Whitlock."

His voice was not the voice I knew. His voice was higher-pitched than my father's and gravelly, with an accent I couldn't place. He may have borne a resemblance to my father, but this man was a stranger. Any resemblance was just an illusion.

"Where is my grandfather?" I shouted at the doppel-gänger even as I drove my hand into my pocket to retrieve the bottle of chloroform.

"Don't worry." There was a harsh and mocking quality in his voice. "I'll take you to him." He lunged for me, and I saw the gleam of a knife in his hand.

With all my strength I threw the bottle of chloroform. It shattered against his metal mask.

Quickly I tucked an arm over my face and breathed into my sleeve. The knife clattered to the ground.

The man in the clockwork mask clutched at his face. He staggered, smashing into the barrel, and reached for me.

I screamed as he charged forward and nearly pinned me to the wall. Even through my sleeve I could smell the cloying sweetness of the chloroform. Ducking to the side, he crashed, his shoulder and head hitting the stone wall hard. Then he collapsed.

Keeping my breath shallow, I reached out with shaking fingers and tugged on the chain to my grandfather's key. As soon as I'd pulled it free of him, I grabbed the knife and scrambled for the door.

I charged through and ran down a long tunnel, fearing I'd run straight into a wall with every step. It was pitch-black.

Having lost my bearings, I hadn't a notion which way to run. I had to get back to the monastery as quickly as possible before the man in the clockwork mask woke. I needed Headmaster Lawrence. Any water that came through the catacombs drained to the river, so I turned my feet in the direction that felt uphill. I pulled the goggles off my head and turned them on, though I didn't wear them. Using the eerie green light emanating from them, I could only see the path directly before my feet.

Holding them aloft like a strange candle, I tried to find my way out of the maze.

I had just about given up hope, when I saw a dark figure holding a torch at the far end of one of the tunnels. No, he couldn't have woken already. I tucked myself back into a dark corner and hid the light from the goggles in my skirt.

I was out of tricks, and I knew I couldn't overpower a full-grown man. I grasped the knife in my hand.

"Meg?" a familiar voice called into the darkness.

David.

CHAPTER TWENTY-SEVEN

I RAN TO HIM, AND DAVID CAUGHT ME, HOLDING ON TO my wrist to direct the knife away from his side. It felt so good to have his hand on my arm and to know I wasn't alone. Tears streamed down my face, and I tasted blood on my lip.

David reached for my cheek, but his hand lingered a hairsbreadth away, as if fearful. Whatever mask of confidence and swagger he'd had had been stripped and replaced by an expression of utter horror. "Meg, what happened to you? You've been gone for hours. Your driver is beside himself."

"I was drugged and locked in a trunk." I hastily wiped

away my tears. It was not the time to allow myself to be overcome by what had just happened. Tucking the knife into my pocket, I took his torch. The heat of the flame kissed the cheek that still burned from the chloroform, and irritated the sting.

"How? Who would do such a thing?" What little color had been left in David's face drained away.

"It was the man who murdered my parents. He's here," I said. "He's the saboteur. He's been trying to flush me out into the open since the beginning of summer when he planted the bomb in your sister's shop. He's been living here in the catacombs, trying to create enough commotion that he could take me without anyone noticing."

I had been too predictable. He'd known I would seek out the steamship after my little display with Will the last time the ship had arrived. He had probably seen us kiss, lurking in the shadows like the rat he was. He knew I would come. I'd run like an unsuspecting rabbit into a well-placed snare.

"Were you harmed?" David inspected me all over, looking for injury.

I shook my head. "Just my hand. It's not bad."

"Where is he now?" David asked, peering at my palm.

"I gave him some of his own medicine. He's unconscious

on the floor of one of the storage rooms. It's down that way." I pointed with the torch.

"Come," David said, pulling me forward. "We must find the headmaster and alert him."

We ran through the catacombs until finally we reached the ramp that led up to the carriage bay. I nearly stumbled in my haste to escape the darkness of the tunnels below.

"Miss Whitlock!" Bob Brindle ran forward, his round face pale with worry. He swept me up into a protective embrace that nearly caught his shoulder on fire from the torch, and I worried for the knife in my pocket, but the thick folds of my skirt seemed to hold it harmless, for now. "Were you lost?"

"Taken. It was the man with the bomb." I didn't need to give any more explanation than that.

Bob extracted a pistol from his coat pocket and took the torch from my hand. "Where is he?"

Even as I was about to explain, David's man came up beside us with his own pistol in hand. "Follow me," he said to Bob, and the two descended the ramp.

David returned to me looking grim. "Don't worry. They will find him."

It didn't take long to reach the headmaster's office. Most of the monastery was abandoned even though the sun had not yet set. Only a few torches lit the halls. Their flickering shadows unsettled me, and I wanted to bathe myself in light.

David pounded on the door to the headmaster's office. It opened, but to our dismay Instructor Barnabus was inside. He slowly took in my disheveled appearance, then slid his gaze over to David. There was no hiding the suspicion in his eyes. "What is this about? Shouldn't you both be home by now?"

He straightened a large pile of drawings and orders from the Foundry and tapped the bottom edge of them against the desk. He placed them neatly down and closed the counting book.

"Miss Whitlock has been attacked by the saboteur," David said.

Instructor Barnabus's demeanor changed immediately. He took me by the injured hand, led me to the largest chair, and deposited me in it like a fragile doll. "Dear heavens, child. Who is it?"

"The same man who planted the explosive in my shop. The man in the clockwork mask," I said, relieved that someone would finally take the threat seriously.

Instructor Barnabus turned the shade of a ripe beet. "This is the last I wish to hear of your delusions, young lady. There is no man with a clockwork mask. You have used this ploy to gain attention and wrongfully secure your place at the Academy. Now, I don't know what your intentions are, but you, David, should beware lest she use her wild deceptions to corner you into marriage."

"I believe her," David said without flinching.

Barnabus made a series of puffing, blowing noises through his long mustache. "Well, I for one don't have the time to waste on wild fantasies. I am due for supper with my aunt."

"They are not wild fantasies. There is a murderer out there!" I said. He had to listen. The fate of the Academy was at stake. Instead he shuffled us out the door and locked it.

"If that were the case, I'm sure the proper authorities would have found him by now. I am already late and have no more time for this. Good night." He walked down the hall, his head bobbing along as if he hadn't a care in the world.

I released the breath I hadn't known I'd been holding. Barnabus was a braying ass. He'd been against me from the start, and now that unfounded judgment was going to get someone killed. "What do we do?"

David looked at me, then the door. "Give me the knife."

I handed it to him, and he wedged it into the jam and knocked the hilt with the heel of his palm. The latch released and the door swung open. Honestly, there wasn't an effective lock in the building. David ushered me inside as he handed the knife back to me. "Stay here. I'll try to find the headmaster. If he returns, tell him what you told me. I'll be back soon."

I wanted to say "Thank you," but he was out the door, charging into the fray like a gallant knight. I closed and locked the door behind him, though after David's demonstration of how easily the lock could be defeated, it hardly seemed necessary.

In the aftermath of everything that had happened, I now felt exhausted and just wanted to sleep for seventy years, but I couldn't. We were still in danger.

I sank into the headmaster's chair, as it was the biggest and seemed the most comfortable, then drew my feet up beneath me. Time seemed to stretch on forever as I listened to the clock tick behind me. I glanced at the spy glass and thought about using it to try to find the headmaster, but decided against it. The controls were much more complicated than the one in Rathford's workshop.

I found an old leather glove with holes in two of the fingers, and a bit of wire, so I used them to make a sheath for the knife and then tucked it back into my pocket.

As I tied off the wire, I accidentally pushed over some

of the drawings and orders that Barnabus had stacked so neatly on the desk. I picked them up to right them, but then curiosity got the better of me. I leafed through them, interested to see what my fellow classmates had created, and also what the full members of the Order had requested from the Foundry.

It was remarkable how much I had learned in so short a time. I could now glance at a drawing and for the most part picture the final construction clearly in my mind. I turned over another page, and froze.

Tucked in with various orders for parts for automaton control systems and even whole body parts for automatons themselves was an intricate little drawing. I could picture the final mechanism quite clearly, because I had seen it before.

A knock sounded at the door, and I startled.

"Meg, it's me," David said from the other side. I snatched the drawing off the table and rushed to the door. I threw open the lock, and he stepped inside. "I'm sorry, Meg. I couldn't—"

"David, look at this." I thrust the drawing in front of him.

"What is it?" he asked, moving closer to the single burning lamp and tilting the page at a better angle.

I swallowed the lump in my throat as he inspected it.

"It looks a bit like a spider, doesn't it?" He tilted his head, considering the drawing. "Oh, no, look. It's a striker. There's a note for a bit of flint here. How clever. With every rotation of the main shaft, it moves down this thread."

My heart sank. It was the piece of the bomb that Will and I had destroyed. Only now it had been fortified by a solid casing around the outside. "That's what I feared."

"What is this thing?" David asked, looking concerned.

"It's a triggering mechanism for a bomb. I destroyed it. It seems someone had it rebuilt. Is there a completed order for it?"

David searched through the papers. "Here it is. It was delivered today. It doesn't say who requested it."

Dear God. This was the work of the saboteur. It had to be. He'd used the Foundry orders from the Academy to cover his intention to repair the bomb. We had to find it. The headmaster had been tasked with studying the bomb. He'd know where it was.

"The workshop," I whispered. I looked up at David. "I know where the headmaster might be." I grabbed his hand and the lamp and led him out the door and down into the cellars.

I went straight to the false cask and unlocked the bung.

The front of the cask swung open, and David looked at me in shock. "How did you discover this?"

"Trust me, you don't wish to know." I crept through the narrow hall, but everything within the workshop was dark and still. "Headmaster?" I called. Nothing. I lifted the lantern and looked around.

David was drawn toward the mind-reading device. "This is the device from the plans the headmaster showed us after the incident in the cellars. Why would he complete a rogue invention?"

For the first time I could see the workshop in its entirety. At the table there were several pictures of Samuel at different ages, Headmaster Lawrence, and a woman I assumed was Headmaster Lawrence's wife.

"David, look at this. These pictures are strange." I picked up one to show him. Lines had been drawn all over the faces, with notes on shapes and proportions in reference to the other pictures. I glanced down and noticed the wood of the table I had exposed when I had picked up the picture. It had been gouged with a knife.

Handing the picture to David, I swept the others away, and gasped.

Lies, lies, lies, lies . . .

The word had been carved deep into the wood in angry gouges hundreds of times.

Suddenly all the pieces fell into place. I could hear the echoes of conversation.

Mary's tinny voice, *You take after the headmaster's wife. . . .*

A woman in love. Mary was taunting me for being in love. The headmaster's wife must have been as well.

Lucinda's calm explanation, *Mary was dredging up long-dead gossip. The rumors about Emma died down at least fifteen years ago, perhaps more. I don't even know why Mary brought it up, other than that she wanted to evoke a sense of scandal. . . .*

She was involved in a scandal. Something terrible had happened.

All you need know is that you should never feel ashamed for how you feel about Will. . . .

Will, a man from the Foundry.

She loved a man from the Foundry. The headmaster's wife loved a man from the Foundry.

I remembered the way MacTavish had stared when I had entered the assembly hall for the unveiling of the automatons. He'd looked so sad. Samuel had been standing directly behind me.

MacTavish.

"Dear Lord," I whispered, recalling the vision I had seen in the mind-reading device.

"Meg, what is it?" David asked. For the briefest moment I had forgotten he was there.

"Headmaster Lawrence is the saboteur. And now he intends to destroy the Foundry."

CHAPTER TWENTY-EIGHT

"I THOUGHT THE MAN WHO ABDUCTED YOU IS THE saboteur." David placed the picture back down on the table. "This doesn't make any sense. What does the man in the clockwork mask have to do with the headmaster?"

"Nothing." I shook my head in disbelief. "Other than providing the headmaster with a bomb. That's why the headmaster was so quick to dismiss my warnings about the man in the mask. He knew he was the one who was guilty."

"This doesn't make sense." David turned to take a step away, then turned back just as quickly. "The headmaster would never do such a thing. Someone could have died in that last attack."

"And notice, *he* was practically the first person out of the room. It all fits now, all of it." Goodness, why hadn't I seen it before? I had been so blinded by my quest to discover the identity of the man in the mask and so certain he was the one behind the attacks. "The man who attacked me never sabotaged anything. He's been lingering in the shadows hoping to take me when no one would come looking for me. He's only acted when he's had a clear opportunity. It was Headmaster Lawrence who gave him the chance to strike. It was Headmaster Lawrence who had his own agenda all along."

"I fail to see why a man would seek to destroy something he's clearly passionate about and loves." David turned around, as if looking for something in the room that might make the headmaster less guilty.

"The Academy is not the only thing he has loved. Several years ago there were rumors surrounding his wife. Namely, that she had been having an illicit affair with a man from the Foundry." I picked up a picture of the headmaster's wife. The eyes had been roughly scratched out, as if the hand that had done it had been driven by malice. "This all happened at a time that would have made Samuel's parentage suspect."

"Are you calling my friend a bastard?" David's voice rose, but I held my ground. "We grew up together. I know him better than anyone. He used to be a fun chap when we were young. He was kind—"

"Then why is he so angry now?" I asked. David's demeanor changed, as if he were holding back a secret. I pressed on, "There's not much love lost between him and his *father*, is there?"

David's expression turned tight and grim, his eyes as hard and cold as ice. "You have no idea what it is like to never live up to the expectations of a father who is determined to demean and belittle you at every given opportunity." He turned away from me, giving his head a shake, as if trying to free his mind from his own thoughts. "You don't know how it breaks you."

"Do you?" I asked, holding very still.

He turned back to me, and seemed twenty years older in that moment. "This isn't about me."

I took a deep breath. This discussion would get us nowhere. I needed to lessen the charge of it. I started sifting through the photos. "Let's look at what we know for certain. Clearly, the headmaster is obsessed with discovering the truth about something regarding his family, as evidenced by the pictures. He has created this machine without approval from the Order to extract secrets forcibly. He has been using the Academy as the perfect mask for ordering whatever he needed for the device from the Foundry. After the disaster with Lord Rathford, if he were caught with this machine, he would be given the Black Mark. The only way to continue to pursue his course of action was to come up with some excuse to propose a truth-detecting machine to the Order, an excuse that would force them to see the need for it."

One of the pictures caught my eye. I picked it up and studied it. "That's when I came along and everything fell into place."

David crossed his arms and huffed. "You mean that's when everything suddenly exploded. I was there when you were nominated. I've never seen such an uproar."

"That anger was the perfect front for sabotage," I said. "Those fat old blowhards made it clear that they would do anything to stop me from defiling their precious halls. My nomination was a convenient excuse to make everyone who opposed my nomination suspect."

"Which made everyone suspect," David concluded. "No wonder he seconded your nomination. And to think, I admired him for breaking convention even though it would cause him grief."

"Exactly."

David shook his head. "The Foundry is too important. No

grudge is worth that. And how do we know which Foundry worker he suspects?"

I turned around the picture I had gathered. It was MacTavish. I remembered Oliver's warning about madness in the Order. "The headmaster's not in his right mind." I pointed at the globe above the chair. "I accidentally witnessed the headmaster using this machine on himself, and in that globe I saw a cuckoo flying through the Foundry. Cuckoos lay their eggs in the nest of another bird and force that bird to raise the young as their own. As I was watching, the bird caught fire, and Headmaster Lawrence laughed."

"By God." David looked appalled.

I hadn't made the connection at the time, but now it made perfect sense. "Remember what the headmaster said when he proposed his machine in front of the assembly? He warned them that next time the saboteur would choose a target they could not ignore. Leader Octavian ordered the headmaster to study the bomb. The headmaster has access to it. He has the means to repair it, and he has a personal vendetta against the master of the Foundry."

"Without the Foundry there are no Amusements." David took my hand and grabbed the lantern. "Come. We have to find him."

I wanted desperately to capture the man in the mask, but suddenly this was so much more important. Headmaster Lawrence's plan could destroy everything. Hundreds of lives could be lost, including Will's. I had to stop him.

We left the secret workshop, and the barrel door swung shut behind us. A light was shining through a crack in the door to the archives. David and I ran toward it. Instructor Nigel was on top of one of the high ladders.

"Instructor," David called out. The man turned on the ladder and peered down his nose at us through his monocle.

"What on earth are you both still doing here?" he asked as he descended the ladder.

"Have you seen the headmaster?" I called up to him. "We desperately need to speak with him."

Instructor Nigel paused on the ladder and tipped the spine of a thin book out to consider it a moment. "He's no longer here and won't return until our next set of courses. He has business to attend to."

"Where?" David asked even as I felt the cold weight of dread settle within me.

"Scotland, of course." Instructor Nigel made a face at the title he had selected and returned it to the shelf. "He boarded the steamship this afternoon."

I looked to David, and he seemed to share my thoughts. Our worst suspicions had just been confirmed.

"Instructor Nigel," I said, "is there any way to quickly get a message to the Foundry? We've discovered the identity of the saboteur, and he must be stopped before unspeakable disaster occurs."

"By God, who is it?" Instructor Nigel asked.

"The headmaster," both David and I answered in chorus.

Instructor Nigel's monocle fell out as he gave us a disbelieving stare. "Of all the ridiculous things. That's impossible. It's absolutely preposterous."

"Listen to us," I demanded. "There's a secret workshop here in this cellar. He's been inventing a rogue machine and using the sabotage to cover his actions. The men at the Foundry are in very real danger."

"Nonsense. You have been reading too many childish stories." He replaced his monocle.

"I can show it to you!" I shouted.

"See here, that is quite enough. Nothing is more important to Lawrence than this Academy. Now, if you are quite finished with your ridiculous theories, I must ask you to return to your homes immediately. I won't say a word about the both of you being here together at this hour, but it stretches the bounds of propriety." He came the rest of the way down the ladder and made a shooing motion with his arms. "Off you go. You wouldn't want the Society tongues to start wagging."

I shook my head even as David urged me to move. My reputation was the least of my concerns. Headmaster Lawrence was well on his way to the Foundry, and if his plot succeeded, Will would be dead.

As David and I left the archives and started up the stairway, I felt desperate and hopeless at once. I didn't know what to do, but we would find no help at the Academy. We were on our own.

I followed David out to the courtyard, where Bob and David's coachman came charging up the ramp.

"What news?" David called out. I clung to his hand out of fear.

Bob shook his bald head. "The bastard's gone. We saw him staggering through the tunnels and gave chase, but the rat managed to escape through an old passage that had been closed off years ago. We followed him up to the streets, then the docks. He boarded a ship just as it cut ties."

"Where was it heading?" I asked.

"The Continent," the coachman answered. "I'm sorry. There was nothing we could do to stop him."

The Continent.

If he was returning to the place where my grandfather was being held, my papa could be anywhere in the whole of Europe. How would I ever find him? All this time I had hoped he was safe and simply didn't know he could return. Now I knew he was in the hands of a killer and a madman. I didn't know how much time my grandfather had before the man in the mask decided to kill him, if he hadn't already.

Oh, God!

What could I do?

"Damn it," I cursed, and pulled away. I stalked in a large circle around the courtyard. David stepped into my path.

"Let him go. We have more pressing concerns at the moment." He reached out to take my hand. I held it back.

"He killed my parents! My grandfather may be dead or being tortured by his hand. The man is insane. I can't let my grandfather die. He's all I have left."

"Hundreds more could die if we don't stop Headmaster Lawrence, including MacDonald." David's words felt like a slap across my face. "If your grandfather were here, what would he tell you to do?"

I hung my head. He'd gladly sacrifice his life for the Foundry. I choked back a sob, then pressed my lips together as I made a vow. As soon as this was over, I'd dedicate all my efforts to finding Papa. I would stop at nothing until I did.

Tonight I had another score to settle.

"How are we going to stop the headmaster? The ship is gone, and even if we could find another to take us to Scotland, the Foundry steamship is the fastest thing on the water," I said, turning in a small circle. "We can't take the train. It doesn't leave until morning, and then we'd have to stop at every village between here and Edinburgh. It's impossible, unless you have some magical way to whisk us through the air more than five hundred miles in one night."

David's expression changed suddenly as he glanced at the key around my neck. "I just might." He turned to his coachman. "Are the horses well rested?" David asked as he pulled me toward the carriage bay. It brought me back into the moment and the danger at hand.

"Yes, my lord." The coachman followed close on our heels, flanked by Bob.

"Good." He waved off Bob and escorted me to his coach. "I think we need to pay a visit to Uncle Albrecht."

CHAPTER TWENTY-NINE

"WHO IS UNCLE ALBRECHT?" I ASKED AS I FELL INTO THE seat of the coach, and David leapt in and sat across from me.

"He's my great-uncle on my mother's side," David said as he offered me a hand and helped me upright. He continued, "He's a little difficult to describe. You'll know what I mean when you meet him."

I didn't like the sound of that. "Is he at least part of the Order?"

David gave a slight shrug. "He used to be."

"How can he *used to be*?" I asked, letting my skepticism get the better of me. "Does he have the Black Mark?"

"If he did, we wouldn't be talking about him. No. He's

just eccentric. At the moment he's been restricted by the Order for causing a bit of a commotion that nearly exposed us." David said it like it was a good thing. "He's had to give up the key to his Amusements until further notice."

The horses climbed up the ramp that led out onto the streets of London. The sun hung low in the sky, reminding me that I'd spent most of the day locked in a trunk. In the coach I felt safe, and for that I was eternally grateful.

I wasn't quite certain we should be calling on a feeble old man who was probably a touch more than daft, but we really didn't have any other choice. I watched the London streets fly by as the coach hurried through town, heading south and then east into Surrey.

I concentrated on making myself presentable as best I could as the crowded streets of London broke apart and gave way to country lanes following over rolling hills, pastures, and woods, bathed in the light of the setting sun.

It didn't take long before we reached an old Tudor home, nestled near a quiet brook. David and I stepped down from the coach and peered at the faded old house. The entire eastern side had been overcome by ivy. It was the perfect picture of the idyllic English countryside.

Until a *boom* loud enough to rattle my teeth broke the

silence. A flock of blackbirds took to wing from a cluster of trees.

David laughed. "I guess he's home. This way."

I was only mildly surprised David didn't show more concern. "Are you certain he's all right?" I asked as I followed David down a garden path around the house to a very large stable nestled in a slight dell. It was easily as large as the Chadwick stables, but the size of the house didn't seem to warrant it, unless David's uncle had once been a horse breeder.

Billows of steam were rising up from stacks on the nearest side of the long building. David rushed to the door. It opened, and a wiry old man stumbled out. A shock of pure white hair sprouted from the center of his forehead, but the rest of his hair seemed to have abandoned the lonely patch and had taken up residence in a circle about his ears. He coughed dramatically as he came to sit on a large rock near the doors. Then he took out a flask from the pocket of the leather apron he was wearing and took a swig.

His bushy eyebrows hopped up and down as he wiped off a pair of spectacles and replaced them on his nose. He leaned forward and peered at us.

"Guten Abend, Onkel," David greeted with a very distinct

Prussian lilt. David's uncle brightened at once and sprang to his feet like a prancing fawn, not an old man. I guessed we didn't have to worry about him being feeble.

"David, my God! It is too long a time since you have come to visit," the old man responded in an even heavier Prussian dialect. "So, my favorite nephew is well?"

"Yes, of course," David said, switching back to English. "You're trying to find a way around your restrictions again, aren't you?"

David's uncle didn't seem to notice the censure or the change in language. At least he didn't heed it as he continued on as if David hadn't responded at all, walking back toward the house. "And who is this you bring here? What a pretty girl. I hope you have come to tell me of a marriage. If that is not so, you should ask her to wed."

I felt my cheeks go hot. David blushed as well, as he led his uncle toward me. "Allow me to introduce Miss Margaret Whitlock, *Onkel*." David leaned his head closer to the old man. "She speaks German," he whispered, "though her Swiss dialect is horrendous."

"Ach, I am caught," Uncle Albrecht said in English. He smiled, and his silvery eyes twinkled. "So this is the young lady apprentice. I must admit, I was expecting something different. Your forgiveness, please. I so rarely have a chance to play the matchmaker."

"Of course . . ." I hesitated, not knowing what to call him exactly.

"Uncle Albie, *bitte*. Our families have always worked well together. At least on the Reichlin side." He took my arm and led me through the back garden toward the house.

"I beg your pardon, but what was the loud noise we heard earlier?"

The old Prussian laughed. "My smithing skills are not what they used to be. I had a pressure vessel, how should we say, not meet my standard. Do not fear. I had it quite contained, though none of this would happen if I still had access to the Foundry." He opened the door to his kitchens and attempted to usher me inside. "So you will stay for tea? I will make my best attempt with my regular teapot. I'm having only a very little bit of trouble with my clockwork one."

I started to answer, but David spoke over me. "I'm sorry, *Onkel*, but this is not a social call. We have discovered a plot against the Foundry, but at present no one will believe us. We have to get to Scotland tonight, or the disaster that will unfold could destroy the Order altogether."

Uncle Albrecht let the door swing closed as his affable

disposition turned suddenly serious. "Who would wish to harm the Foundry?"

"Headmaster Lawrence is seeking revenge upon MacTavish for a suspected affair with his wife. He has a bomb," I explained. "He intends to use it."

Albrecht's bushy eyebrows furrowed so close together, they became one. "If what you say is truth, this is very serious. I would help, but after the incident over Kent, I'm afraid I cannot." He looked toward the barn with longing. "I can no longer direct the steam from the boilers into the envelope. Without a working key I'm afraid our feet must remain firmly planted."

I brought my hand to the key around my neck. "If you have a means to get us to Scotland by morning, I have the means to unlock it." I lifted the key, and the old man's wrinkled face lit up.

"Henry's master key. He taught you to use it?"

I nodded.

"Excellent." He clapped his hands together. "I am far too long without causing trouble for the Order. Come, this way. David, go inside and gather food, water, and warm blankets— oh, and don't forget my tonic. If we are going to Scotland, we will need them."

I followed Uncle Albrecht back to the stables. I didn't know what we might find there. I thought perhaps he had invented a train that did not need a track. Or perhaps there were mechanical horses in the stable that never tired. When we had traveled north in the Chadwick coach, we had made good time, but it had still taken us days to reach Yorkshire. We had to get to the Highlands. I didn't see how it was possible.

Albrecht opened the doors, and we stepped inside. I immediately choked on the thick air, heavy with smoke and steam. It clung to my skin and made my hair stick to my scalp. We had entered a good-size room. On either side of the room stood enormous boilers, six in all. Scorching-hot fires burned within them as the hiss and whistle of escaping steam permeated the air.

"I've been trying to find a way around the lock but have had little success, as evidenced by the noise you heard. With the lock in place I cannot vent what steam I have, except through the stacks," Albrecht shouted over the noise. "The lock is here." He reached a box connected to the juncture of several of the pipes. They radiated out from it like the rays of the sun.

"Why did you light the fires in the first place?" I asked,

swiping my hand over my cheek to pull away the wet strands of hair clinging to it.

"I am an Amusementist," he said while checking the pressure valves on the enormous boilers. "I was working on improvements to the water intake system. What else am I to do with my time? Here, here." He ushered me closer to the box.

I pushed away the medallion with the Amusementist seal. It was hot from the steam. Opening my key, I watched the internal mechanism rise from the casing and spin until it had opened completely, like the flower that graced the seal.

I fitted it into the box, and the song began to play. A set of pianoforte keys rose up from beneath a long, narrow grate at my feet. Several large pipes also rose, forming a wall behind the pipes sprouting from the boilers.

Albrecht moved close to my side and without thinking much about it played his personal code phrase of music on the keys. Answering notes bellowed out of the pipes like those from a monstrous pipe organ.

Suddenly gears began to turn, and the whistling hiss became a rush of moving steam. Something rumbled, and the building began to shake. I ducked, fearing the old ceiling would come down. I ran out the door and onto the grass beyond.

Albrecht galloped out of the doors, looking both enormously pleased and satisfied. I didn't see what he had to be so happy about. The rumbling was about to tear his stable apart. As I looked up, I realized it *was* tearing his stable apart. The roof of the building had split and was rising slowly, opening up like the hinged lid of a basket.

A great undulating form seemed to be rolling or boiling within. David came up beside us with a crate of supplies. He leaned back a bit to get a better view. "The last time you flew it, it seemed much larger."

Whatever the pulsing thing was, it could not possibly get any larger. It was enormous, filling the entire barn.

"Oh, my dear Lord," I murmured as the mass began to take shape and rise.

An immense oblong balloon rose out of the barn and into the falling dusk. Mist swept off the fabric in waves as the cool evening air met with the heated balloon. A gondola, shaped suspiciously like a pirate ship, hung from great cords of rope attached to the keel framework of the balloon above. The fabric swelled and ebbed as it strained against the confining ropes, and I couldn't help thinking of the body of a great dragon breathing and belching smoke as steam vented from the ship. Slowly a pair of guide wings unfurled as the airship reached the limit of its tether.

I didn't have words. It was glorious.

"*Na ja!* We will sail the skies. It has been too long a time. Come! Come!" Albrecht entered the stables, waving his arms for us to follow.

As we passed through the door, I whispered to David, "Are you sure about this?"

He looked at me as if I were the one who had gone daft. "Of course. No one can take us to Scotland faster."

We climbed an unsteady wooden stair into what should have been the loft of the barn. The airship bobbed lazily before us. "I'm not worried about arriving quickly so much as arriving in one piece."

"Worry not, Miss Whitlock. This ship is perfectly safe." Clearly, the old man's hearing was as sharp as he was spry. "One day the sky will be full with airships. You will see. Once people learn to float among the clouds as one with them, there will be no other way to travel. There is no disaster that could possibly taint the glory of an airship." Albrecht led us over a swinging rope bridge and onto the deck of the ship. He opened up a large chest and pulled out some long, heavy leather coats, along with caps, gloves, and goggles.

I glanced at the boilers and imagined the ship plummeting

to earth in a ball of fire. No disaster indeed. A pair of gloves smacked me in the chest, and I instinctively caught them. Albrecht removed his leather apron and donned one of the long coats. "David, use the starter to get the fire going in the propeller engines." He tossed David a cap. "I must adjust the condensation feed from the envelope. Miss Whitlock, if you would, please wind the navigation system at the bow of the ship."

I pulled on my own coat. It felt reassuringly heavy on my shoulders and warm as it wrapped over my entire body and nearly reached the hem of my skirts. I buttoned the front and pulled on one of the thick leather caps. Stray wisps of my hair refused to be contained and tickled my cheeks.

Near the bow of the ship, I found a large map on a table surrounded by an extremely intricate machine. The joints and arms created a lace-like impression as I tried to follow the connections to several different instruments and gauges. To the right was a large wheel. I turned it slowly even as the fading light of dusk finally died.

Albrecht joined me and lit a lamp hanging from the machine. In the light I could make out a very detailed map of Great Britain. Albrecht inspected the machine, making a few adjustments, then placed the ball of a pointer attached to an arm suspended from the machine on a point on the map. "We are here." His thin finger touched the map. "As we fly, this machine will track our progress. If all goes well, we will reach the Foundry by morning." He tapped a second location on the map. Loch Ness. It seemed so far, and so much could go wrong.

It didn't take long before we had the ship in full working order.

I heard a churning, chugging sound, not unlike a locomotive, and the great blades of the propellers at the back of the ship slowly turned.

Albrecht perched his goggles merrily on his thin nose, then reached for a large lever at the center of the deck. He pulled it, and I let out a gasp as the deck lurched. Ropes from along the rail all released at once, falling away to the ground like dying serpents. Albrecht jumped into a seat next to the map and deftly turned each of the four different wheels surrounding him. I ran to the rail, mostly to hold on to something as the deck tilted sharply to the sky and we rose, the dark countryside falling away beneath us.

My heart hammered and my throat went dry as I clung to the rail, watching the dark shadows and glimmering lights from windows in the houses below sink farther beneath me. We drifted along past as if we were sailing on a very clear lake. The trees were nothing more than the rocks at the depths, and the lights, reflections of golden stars in the water.

I had never witnessed anything so utterly beautiful and terrifying at once.

CHAPTER THIRTY

ONCE WE REACHED A DIZZYING HEIGHT, THE DECK OF
the ship leveled out and we floated along amid the clouds. I
refused to let go of the rail and gripped it tight enough that
my knuckles blanched as I watched the lights and shadows
move along beneath us.

"We're at thirty-five knots, *Onkel*," David called from the
engines in the back. "All system pressures are normal."

"Good, good." Albrecht hummed a tune to himself as he
checked the map again, then adjusted one of the two smaller
wheels.

The great fans were spinning behind us, catching the cooling mist trailing off the envelope. The loose tendrils of my hair brushed against my face as the mist rained down on us. With the breeze it was quite cold in spite of the large, heavy coat I was wearing. I shivered.

David appeared next to me and wrapped a quilt over my shoulders. I could see the glow of London like a blanket of fire on the dark countryside.

"It's beautiful, isn't it?" he said, leaning his forearms on the rail as if he were sailing on a ship and not suspended thousands of feet in the air by hot gas.

As I took in the sight of London, burning like some glorious beacon in the night, I had to admit he was right. The last time I'd flown, I had nothing but a pair of wings on my back with thin straps of leather holding them on, and a fervent prayer I wouldn't drop from the sky.

That had been a wholly different experience. With the solid rail beneath my hand and the deck steady under my feet, it was the world around me that seemed to defy what was possible. The clouds drifted over us, close enough to touch, and I wondered if they felt soft, or if, like ghosts, they'd elude such earthly connections.

"It is beautiful," I admitted, pulling the quilt closer around my neck. "Perfect, really." I watched my breath turn into fog before my face. I felt no danger here, no thrill for my life. All was still and so very cold.

As I thought back to the time I had flown with the wings, I remembered the touch of the light of the dying sun on my skin, and the feel of Will's hands on my face as he kissed me, hot, desperate, and so alive.

I had soared.

Now I drifted.

We sailed on for a time in companionable silence before David spoke again.

"What is it about him?" he asked. He didn't bother to say more as he turned to me. The moon glowed behind him, lighting his hair with a silvery hue and turning his blue eyes to elusive mercury.

I didn't wish to answer. I wasn't sure if I knew. Will had nothing, and yet was willing to give. He was cautious, and yet was willing to stand in the face of danger. He was scarred, and yet he knew joy. In my heart his spirit burned, and it filled me with warmth every time my thoughts turned to him. When Will and I were together, I felt I could be more myself.

David accepted my silence and stared back out at the dark horizon. David was an enigma. I wasn't entirely sure I knew what lay behind the cool mask. He was a man not of deception but of illusion. It was that mystery that had me in its snare, but mystery so quickly fades.

"What is it about me?" I whispered.

He glanced down at his hand on the rail and the signet ring on his finger, but he didn't answer.

I turned and walked away from him, joining Albrecht at the controls.

"Beautiful night for flying," he said. I couldn't see his eyes through his goggles, but I smiled at the way his eyebrows perched above them like the caterpillars of a very large moth. "Very romantic."

I watched the pointer on the map inch slowly north.

"Did you ever marry?" I asked, wondering what type of woman would have taken dear Albrecht as her own.

He let out a sharp bark of a laugh. "Marry? *Nein*, ah, no. No, I have never married."

"I imagine you cut quite the dashing figure in your youth," I said, brushing some condensation off the edge of the navigation machine.

Albrecht lifted the goggles and looked me in the eye. "I had only one passion in my life." He filled his lungs, pushing his chest out as he looked around him with pride. He patted one of the wheels in front of him, then took the vertical wheel at his hip and turned it. The nose of the airship rose toward the clouds, and he smiled. "Some callings demand too much."

I felt like I should have gathered some pity or sorrow for the lonely old man, but as I watched him there at the wheels of his ship, I couldn't see anything to feel sorry for. "But it is worth it?"

He didn't look away from the heavens. "Always."

I stepped into the bow of the gondola and looked up at the envelope above me as it climbed to the clouds. I reached my arm out and grasped one of the ropes tying us to the envelope. It trembled in the still air.

Out on the ocean waters Will was traveling north as well. I couldn't let him die. It would kill a part of me forever. I gave the rope a squeeze. We had to make it in time.

The night stretched on endlessly. David and I took turns manning the firebox and going down into the hold to shovel fuel toward the hopper that fed it into the lift. From there the mechanized engine fueled itself and chugged along merrily, mile after mile.

Every time I checked the needle sliding along the map, it hadn't seemed to have changed at all from the time before, and yet slowly it had crept away from London and steadily north.

Uncle Albrecht had taken to singing opera to pass the time. He had a rough but pleasant voice, but even that couldn't fill the hours upon hours of tedium. It left me too alone with my thoughts. I watched David as he maintained the engine, climbing down into the hold to shovel the dwindling fuel into the hopper.

He came out of the hold with a dark smear across his cheek and forehead as he looked to the lightening sky to the east. In that moment his pretenses were gone. In those moments when he was true and the mask was down, I could understand the potential of us.

As I sat with my back to the rail near the engines, my eyes kept drifting closed. It was warm this close to the firebox, and I had had a very long day. Uncle Albrecht took another swig from his flask of *tonic*, and continued humming to himself.

David adjusted one of the cranks on the engine, then sat down next to me. "Dawn is on the horizon," he said as he rested his forearms on his knees.

"Let's hope so." I tilted my head back and closed my eyes.

I could sleep, but only for a moment.

I woke suddenly with a jolt.

The sky was much brighter. I had to shield my eyes from the glare of it. Lifting my head, I realized I was cuddled up against David's side, his arm slung lightly around my back and resting on my hip. His head had dropped to his chest, and he was snoring slightly. I could feel the warmth of his body lingering on my cheek, and smell the scent of his fine cologne mixed with smoke from the fire surrounding me.

I pushed myself away from him, scrambling to sort out my skirts and find my feet. An unsettling scraping noise trailed along the length of the gondola.

The clouds seemed very high in the sky.

Oh no.

Uncle Albrecht.

I rushed toward the old man slumped in the pilot's chair at the bow. As I reached him, he rumbled out his own loud snore. Large pines loomed on a rising hill. We were heading right for them.

"Uncle Albrecht!" I screeched.

He woke with a start and immediately grasped the wheel, blinking. *"Was, was ist los?"* I grabbed on to the navigation machine as Uncle Albrecht's eyes went wide. Letting out a very explicit turn of phrase in German, he furiously spun his control wheels.

"Stoke the fire!" he yelled.

I ran aft as David was beginning to stir. "David, the bellows!"

He sprang to his feet even as the gondola lurched when it hit the top of one of the trees. I reached the lever attached to the bellows on the left while David spun the dials on the engine, diverting all steam and hot air to the envelope.

I pushed down on the handle with all my strength, but didn't have the power to lift it again until David pushed down on his from the other side. The two levers were connected, and together we pumped life back into the airship.

"Hold fast!" Uncle Albrecht shouted as he turned the wheel at his side and the nose of the gondola tipped straight toward the sky. I clung to the bellows as my feet slipped from beneath me, and I almost crashed into the rail at the stern of the gondola. Finding my feet again, I still managed to work the bellows, my arms and chest burning with the effort.

The airship rose, but it wasn't enough.

The bow of the ship crashed into the tops of the trees. Ropes snapped as the gondola shook violently. The motion threw me from my feet, and I crashed against the back rail.

The force of the blow knocked my breath from me, and I tipped and began rolling over the edge. I hooked the rail in the crook of my arm and closed my eyes as I felt my feet swing over nothingness. I wrapped my other arm tightly on the rail and clung to it with all my strength.

"Meg, hold on!" David grabbed me by the arm, then grasped the back of the long coat.

"We need more lift!" Albrecht shouted. I kicked my feet, trying to find purchase, but it was no use.

The ship leveled off enough for David to haul me back over the rail.

We tumbled together onto the deck, but there was no time to shake off my terror. Another mountain was coming up fast. "Back to the fire," I gasped.

We worked the levers, trying desperately to keep the ship aloft. "Harder!" David screamed as the ship rushed up the slope of the mountain, startling a herd of shaggy brown cows.

A sharp warning whistle cut through the air, and David abandoned the bellows and tended to the gauges.

I ran forward to the navigation machine. Planting my hands on the map, I took in the position of the pointer.

"We've flown too far north," I said, looking up at the broken ropes. The gondola swayed precariously. "Loch Ness is south of us. We have to turn the ship around."

Uncle Albrecht stood from his seat, turning yet another wheel. "How much fuel is in the hold?"

I skittered across the deck and down into the hold. I stared for a moment, as if wishing I could somehow fill the hold with more fuel. We were done for.

"There's none left," I shouted as I climbed the ladder back onto the deck. Another rope snapped with a loud crack, and the gondola swayed as what sounded like a wounded groan filled the air.

"Then we climb as high as we can and hope for the best," Uncle Albrecht said as he pitched the airship higher.

We were hundreds of feet in the air. Hoping for the best didn't sound like much of a plan. I joined David at the engines.

"We'll make it," he said, but his expression was both determined and grim.

Together we worked to pull as much lasting heat as we could out of the engines. Albrecht managed to turn the limping airship around, but we hadn't climbed very far, and the terrain was treacherous at best.

David and I worked the bellows until I feared my arms

would pull from my shoulders. We had to make it, we had to.

The airship continued to sink toward the rugged hills beneath us. I clenched my hands tight on the handle and prayed as we neared another ridge. We weren't going to make it.

"Hold on," David shouted as we swept toward the rocky peak. The bottom of the gondola glanced off the top of the ridge, but then to my relief a long stretch of dark water appeared.

"Aim for the lake!"

We careened over the sweeping mountains and gained speed as we flew toward the ruins of a castle. Albrecht put on his goggles and threw off his coat. "Get ready. We swim."

I struggled to open the heavy coat and threw it off. I ripped at the sleeves of my dress. Then remembered the knife. I grabbed it out of my pocket.

Taking the point of the knife, I stabbed it into my skirts and ripped a wide swath. I brutally freed myself of cloth until I was left with a ragged skirt that barely touched my knees. I had almost drowned once because of my skirts. I wouldn't do it again. When I was done shearing off fabric, I had bare arms and naught but my knickers and stockings covering the lower half of my legs.

David grabbed me by the arm. "When we get close

enough to the water, you jump. If that envelope comes down on top of us, we're dead."

I nodded. "Take care of your uncle."

Uncle Albrecht joined us at the rail. "Don't worry about me. You are young. You must make it to shore."

"*Onkel*, I—"

Two more ropes snapped, and the gondola lurched. A high-pitched whine came from the engines as we rushed closer and closer to the water.

"*Schnell!*" Uncle Albrecht shouted, shoving us both to the rail.

David grabbed me and kissed me so suddenly, I didn't even realize what was happening before he pulled me forward, taking me with him over the rail.

I screamed as I stretched out. The dark water rushed up to meet me, and then I plunged into the icy depths.

CHAPTER THIRTY-ONE

I HIT THE WATER HARD AND FELT THE BLOW DEEP IN MY head and chest as the water crushed me. The force of the fall knocked the air from my lungs, and my nose burned from the lake water that had pushed in. My limbs stung and felt numb as a deep throbbing pounded in my head. It ached with every beat of my heart.

Light shimmered above me, and I reached for it, struggling toward the surface with all the strength I had left. I broke through, and gasped, trying to breathe deeply, but my corset constrained my chest.

I coughed and choked as I heard a loud crash. Turning,

I saw the airship's envelope sinking toward the cold water, a large hole on the side venting steam.

"David!" I screeched, but the wave from the ship's striking the water buffeted me. I swam as hard as I could toward the wreck. The water at the surface was warmer than the water even a few feet down. But I still struggled to keep my teeth from chattering.

"David!" I turned the other way, hoping to see him on the surface. I had to make it to shore. We had landed in the middle of the lake, and it seemed like miles to the water's edge.

One at a time I slapped my arms over the water, dragging myself through the murk toward the castle. I could see the ruined tower jutting up from a prominent rock. If I could climb it, perhaps I could spot David.

He had to be alive.

I hoped for Uncle Albrecht as well, but he was a fragile old man, and the fall into the water had nearly broken me. I couldn't imagine him surviving.

Water washed over my mouth and nose, and I kicked harder. My feet felt as if they weighed twenty stone with my boots pulling them down. I had to make it to the castle.

The rush of a sudden current pulled me down, and my

head sank beneath the water. I kicked back to the surface, and gasped as I looked around. This was a lake. There shouldn't be a current.

A new chill gripped me that had nothing to do with the water. Churning bubbles broke the surface just in front of me, and I paddled backward as fast as I could. The water glowed. Two enormous yellow orbs appeared beneath the surface, moving closer, growing larger.

They look like eyes.

They broke the surface of the water just in front of me. An enormous monstrous head appeared, just like that of the leviathan I had battled before, only not as ornate and almost twice as large. It was like a great smooth snake, with glowing yellow eyes that took up nearly the whole of its face. A shadow moved within them.

The monster stared down at me, then the toothless jaw opened wide, so wide it could easily encompass me.

The head swooped down, gulping water from the surface of the lake the way a pelican would. It was coming straight for me. I turned and tried to swim as fast as I could, but I felt the water around me being pulled toward it, dragging me with it into the mouth.

I was plunged suddenly into a shallow pool as the jaws

closed, encompassing me in darkness. I tried to find my feet and stand, but my feet slipped on smooth metal. It was a machine. Oh, thank the Lord.

Suddenly the head tipped up.

My feet crashed against a grate closing off the depths of the throat. Just because it was a machine didn't mean it couldn't kill me. I stood on the grate, bracing my hands against the roof of the mouth.

The water drained down the gullet. Then a moment later the grate opened up and I fell down the narrow, articulated pipe that formed the throat. The last bit of water carried me down in a swift rush, the joints in the articulation bumping my sore hip the entire way down.

The rushing water deposited me in a wave that washed over a smooth floor. I collapsed onto it, watching the blurred reflection of a pair of lights shine in the large puddle of water.

"That's the lot of them," someone shouted. I coughed, spitting up a lungful of water, my body completely drained.

"Meg, thank the Lord." David appeared at my side, drenched but alive and well. He embraced me, pulling me up to sit. I blinked and saw Uncle Albrecht wrapped in a vivid red tartan in the corner.

"All right, enough," the deep voice grumbled. "She's in a right state. Go tend your uncle."

David scowled, but a Foundry worker bent and wrapped a dark tartan over my shoulders. He tucked it around me even though the bottom of it was soaking up the puddle. I looked up to thank him and recognized his neatly trimmed beard and the wicked gleam in his eye. It was Will's friend, Duncan MacBain. I had never been so glad to see a scoundrel.

"Are you injured, lass?" He patted me on the back as I worked out the last of the water from my lungs. "Ye must've swallowed half the lake."

"I'll be fine," I panted, rubbing my face against the course tartan to dry some of the water.

"Sorry to say, ye don't look it." McBain stood and helped me to my feet. "If you wanted to see William, might I suggest the train next time? It might be a touch safer and less wet."

"We didn't have time." I couldn't forget why we were here. "David and I discovered the identity of the saboteur who has been attacking the Academy. He's here, and he has a bomb." I coughed again, but MacBain didn't leave my side. "Please, Duncan, we have to send a message to MacTavish."

He smoothed his beard. "There's no way to send a message out of the hauler."

"Hauler?"

"This ship. It's used to secretly unload coal or ore from the ships out on the lake. In the cover of night we lift the head onto the deck and use it to scoop material down into this hold. The only reason we're out here at all is because I saw you come over the hill through the spy glass in the operations room. 'Twas a good thing I found Malcolm to pilot her, or we might not have reached you in time."

"How quickly can we get out of this thing?" David asked.

"We can't reach MacTavish until we're settled in the docks. Who is the saboteur, and what is he after?" MacBain answered.

"It's the headmaster. He believes MacTavish and his wife had an affair. He's obsessed with it. He will attempt to destroy something in this Foundry, but I don't know what," I said. The floor shifted, making me feel a bit ill with the motion. Duncan helped me to a handrail along the wall. David and Uncle Albrecht joined us.

"The steamship arrived a few hours ago. He could be anywhere in the Foundry," MacBain said. The floor shifted again, and then I felt a jolt that nearly knocked me from my feet.

"Hold tight. The hauler just came up on the docking

rails. The chains that bring her up into the docks can get a bit rough." MacBain widened his stance as the entire vessel started to shake.

I held on tighter to the handrail. The ship continued to shudder for what must have been fifteen minutes at least. It felt like hours. MacBain didn't seem concerned.

"Get ready," MacBain said. "As soon as the chains pull us all the way up the rails, Malcolm will let us out by opening the belly to dump the cargo. Stay to this side, and when the belly drops, slide down."

I had no idea what he was talking about, until suddenly the floor split in half and dropped down at an angle, creating a steep slide. MacBain let go and slid down the floor, dropping through the crack in the center. David followed, as did Albrecht. I didn't want to let go. I'd had enough of falling, but I had no other choice. I let go of the handrail and slid down the smooth floor. I spread my arms out to try to slow myself, but it did no good, and I dropped through the crack and landed hard on a grate below.

I could smell coal wafting up from beneath the grate as I gazed down into the empty blackness below me. I feared the grate had imprinted itself upon my cheek.

David tried to help me up. My hands stung from my

landing, but I ignored the pain and got to my feet on my own. "Do not take liberties," I warned him. He had taken too many already.

He backed a step, but did not acknowledge what had happened before we jumped off the ship. He looked around. "I knew the Foundry was beneath the ground, but I never imagined anything like this."

MacBain was giving Uncle Albrecht a hand. I ducked under the belly of the dragon-shaped vessel we'd been traveling in and looked around.

We were in a large room easily three times the size of the underground docks at the Academy. Recessed in the arched ceiling was a large fan, spinning furiously as it pushed a cold breeze through the chamber.

The steamship was docked in a rectangular pool behind us, while the vessel we had been traveling in was now beached, pulled up onto thick rails supported by a large interlocking gear system and two heavy chains. From that perch it could dump its cargo through the grate we were now standing on. Its snake-like head rested on a balcony. One of the eyes had been propped open, and a Foundry worker climbed out of the unusual hatch.

He descended a ladder and joined us.

"Where are we?" I asked.

"As of this moment," MacBain replied, "we are directly beneath the ruins of Urquhart. As you can see, we've taken back the castle. Don't worry. We won't let Lawrence destroy it." MacBain motioned to the other Scot. "Malcolm, take them to MacTavish, right away. I have to get back to the operations room. If anything should happen to the fans on my watch, I won't hear the end of it. I'll try to contact MacTavish through the spy glass and warn him. It was good to meet you again, Meg."

"Thank you, Duncan," I said.

David was settling his uncle onto a bench in the corner of the docks. "Will you be all right here?" he asked.

"Go, make me proud," the old man said as he patted David's hand and gave me a confident nod.

David kissed him on the cheek, then turned and ran to me.

"This way," Malcolm said. I followed him up the ramp, with David in step beside me.

The tunnel was very similar to the ones in the catacombs beneath the Academy, save one very distinct feature. At every juncture a large rotating fan turned within a shaft in the ceiling, drawing air through the tunnel and creating a surprisingly cold breeze. Even with the fresh air, I could still catch the scent of fire and burning metal up ahead.

A large hall turned off to the left, and we took it, heading down a set of stairs. Hot air wafted up from the depths. It washed over me like a solid wall of smoke and heat as I entered an enormous room.

Gigantic blast furnaces radiated heat as large buckets glowing with molten iron drifted slowly above, suspended by enormous chains.

The room seemed cast in fire, and the dark shadows of men moved in front of the glowing ironworks. Steam rose off my clothing. I'd never known such heat. Even with three enormous fans in the ceiling of the large room, it was as if I'd just stepped into the fires of hell.

A man strode toward us down the central aisle. Thick black boots had been laced to his knees. A sleek black leather kilt hung around his waist. Instead of a sporran a belt of heavy tools hung at his hip. His hands were clad in large leather gloves, and his chest was strapped in a leather waistcoat that buckled to his neck. He wore no shirtsleeves, and sweat glistened on his bare arms. Soot slashed across his rough cheeks, and a pair of dark goggles hid his eyes.

He walked with purpose. Like some god of the forge, he strode toward me, and I forgot to breathe. Suddenly it was too hot and I needed air.

Lifting his goggles, he looked down on me, and I don't recall how I managed to stay on my feet.

Will.

"What in the name of the Devil are you doing here?" he asked, his normally placid face barely containing his shock. He slowly took in the state of my clothing, and his breathing turned ragged.

I felt exposed to him, every vulnerability laid bare before him.

"And what happened to your dress?" he asked.

David reached my side. "That's hardly a concern."

As fast as a lunging cat, Will grabbed David by the shirtfront and pulled him nearly off his feet. "You have no say in what is and is not a *concern*, especially here."

Dear God, while the state of my dress was worth a lifetime of mortification, we had a man with a bomb to find.

"Will, put him down." My tone left no room for argument.

He reluctantly released David's shirt. David violently straightened his sleeves and said, "The Foundry is in serious danger, MacDonald."

Will crossed his bare arms against the leather waistcoat.

"I'm sure we can handle whatever it is without you."

"Will, please. We have come to stop a terrible disaster." A muscle in Will's cheek twitched as I said the word "we." Now was not the time for jealousy. We had to act fast before disaster struck.

I grabbed Will by his waistcoat and pulled him aside. "I came here to save your life because I *love* you, damn it. Not him, you. If you don't listen to me now, I swear . . ." He had the courtesy to look surprised. I continued, "Headmaster Lawrence discovered MacTavish had an affair with his wife, and he's out for revenge. He repaired the bomb that we found in the toy shop, and he plans to use it here. We have to find MacTavish before it's too late."

Something changed in Will's eyes. They softened, turning as black as the deepest night. I saw once more the man who unfailingly believed in me and fought by my side. "MacTavish was with Lawrence. They went to discuss arrangements for the Automaton Ball in the study."

I believe my heart stopped. "We may be too late. Hurry!"

Will led the way through the ironworks and up a long flight of stairs. At the end of a hall, he turned, then burst in through a door on his left.

I followed so closely behind him, I ran into him as he stopped cold in his tracks.

MacTavish was lying facedown in the center of the floor. A spilled glass of Scotch whisky rested near his head, filling the room with the sharp smell of the drink.

No one moved. No one spoke. It was as if we were all waiting for him to pick himself up off the ground and brush himself off. I regained my senses and stepped past Will into the room. The look on Will's face almost ripped my heart in two. He looked as if he were lost, adrift once again without a father to lead him.

David pushed past into the room as well and gently turned the dead man over. "Dear God, how did it come to this?" he whispered.

I tried to clear my head, but the horror of murder cut too deep. I knelt beside the Foundry master as he stared lifelessly back at me. I had no doubt who had killed him. The question was how. A faint mark marred his neck, nearly covered by his dark beard. I almost didn't notice it.

"He's been strangled," I said. "Headmaster Lawrence must have strangled him." I reached out and gently closed MacTavish's eyes.

We stood as Will came forward and placed his palm over

MacTavish's heart. David tried to gather me in his arms. "What a dreadful sight. Are you feeling faint?" He led me toward a chair. "Come, sit."

"Dammit, David. We're all going to look like him if we don't stop Lawrence," I snapped. "Stop treating me like I'm made of glass."

"Lawrence got what he was after. MacTavish is dead," David argued.

"He's after the truth," I shouted. "And he won't feel he has it until the Amusementists allow him to use that horrible machine on his wife. He still intends to destroy this Foundry, mark my words. And now he has a murder to hide. We're wasting time."

Will muttered a prayer under his breath as he gripped MacTavish's tartan.

One thing didn't make sense. "Why would Lawrence strangle MacTavish? If Lawrence wanted him dead, there are faster and easier methods," I said. MacTavish was a large man, and Lawrence was not. A knife in the back would have been so much simpler.

David considered the dead body. "Lawrence has been taking extreme measures to cover his involvement in the sabotage. Perhaps he wished to make this look like an accident. If we didn't know of his murderous intentions, it would seem MacTavish had choked. Lawrence can hardly use his machine on his wife unless he can return to London free of suspicion."

Choked. I looked up at the ceiling at the fan spinning over my head.

Air.

"Where does this cool air come from?" I asked, even as my mind was working at a furious pace.

"Is this really the time to marvel at the ventilation system, Meg?" David asked.

Will looked up, but then answered my question in a tight voice. "Fresh air is drawn in from hidden vents in the hills and passed through pipes in the lake. The lake water cools it, and the fans keep it flowing through the Foundry."

"What of the exhaust from the blast furnaces?" I asked.

"All dangerous exhaust goes through separate tunnels and vents high on the mountain."

That was it. That was the connection.

"Will, where would you go if you wished to disable the entire fan system?" If a barrier were broken between the two tunnel systems, the poisonous gases from the blast furnaces would circulate through the cool air system, and everyone in the Foundry would die of suffocation.

And then nothing would point to MacTavish as the target, and the headmaster could go back to the Order with his spurious claims of sabotage.

"All the fans are maintained through the operation room," Will answered. "Duncan is watching over them today."

"That's where we'll find the headmaster." I just hoped we would reach him in time.

CHAPTER THIRTY-TWO

AS WE RUSHED THROUGH THE TUNNELS AND CORRIDORS of the Foundry, I prayed to God I was right. Because if we didn't find the headmaster in time, the tunnels would become our crypt.

"This way." Will ran through the twisting passages without error, even though I had lost all sense of direction and it felt to me as if we were running in circles. It was taking too long. Every time we turned a corner, another long corridor awaited us. We would never get there in time.

Finally we reached the operation room.

I burst in through the door, only to step in a pool of blood. I screamed and jumped back.

Duncan lay at my feet, holding a seeping wound in his side and gasping for breath.

No.

I knelt beside him and tried to press against the wound. It bubbled beneath my palm. Will fell to his knees on the other side of his friend.

"Duncan," he urged. "Duncan, you listen to me. You will not die. Do ye hear me?"

Duncan shuddered, then lifted his hand to point at a large open grate in the base of the wall. "Through there?" I asked, as his blood seeped through my fingers.

He nodded. "Repair tunnel, main pit fans," he whispered. Will clasped his hand.

"Duncan, stay here with us," Will demanded.

Duncan drew a labored breath and looked up at Will. "Tell Molly I'm sorry. Tell her I was wrong to doubt her. I should have told her . . . I love . . ." Then the last shuddering breath left his body.

A scalding tear slid over my cheek.

Will pulled his friend close and rocked with him as he choked back his tears. I stared down at the hot blood on my hands, not knowing what to do.

David knelt beside me and pressed his fingers to Duncan's

neck. "He's gone," he pronounced. David looked as if a piece of his neatly ordered world had shattered.

A guttural roar came from Will, like the sound of a wounded animal. He reached to his boot and pulled out a short knife, then charged for the grate.

"Will!" I ran after him and ducked into the grate. A long tunnel stretched out before me, tall enough that I could walk, so long as I hunched over at my waist. It was dark, and I couldn't see, but I followed. David entered the tunnel just behind me.

"Meg, it's too dangerous. Let him go after Lawrence," David called.

"I can't."

With every footfall, I imagined the ticking of the bomb. I could see the little spider striking the flint as it traveled slowly down the line. We were running out of time.

My palms felt sticky as I ran them along the smooth walls of the tunnel. My hair swirled around my face from the cold wind coursing past us.

Suddenly we came to a branch in the tunnels. One led to the right, one to the left, and one straight on.

Will hesitated. In the junction there was slightly more room, and I was able to come up beside him.

"Which way?" I asked, though I realized the question was pointless. Will couldn't know which one Lawrence had chosen.

Will paled. "We have to split up," he said, his voice breaking as he said it. "I'll go left. Meg, take the middle. David, you go right."

David hesitated only a moment. He looked Will in the eye, then nodded and turned down his tunnel. I stepped forward, but Will grabbed my arm.

"If you find him, come back here. I'll confront him."

"Damn it, Will," I said. We didn't have time for this.

"I can't see you hurt, Meg. I can't."

I had opened my mouth to curse his stubbornness, when his fingers laced into the hair at my nape. He dragged me forward and kissed me. I nearly lost my balance as his lips crushed to mine. He poured all the desperate pain of his soul into his kiss.

His lips felt as hot and liquid as the molten iron below us, and I drank it in. I kissed him back with all the love and devotion I felt in my heart. This was not goodbye.

Never.

He broke the kiss, breathing heavily. "Stay safe."

I nodded. "You too."

He pushed forward and kissed me again with searing intensity, then broke the kiss and turned down the tunnel to the left.

Taking a fortifying breath, I tried to ignore my shaking legs as I felt my way down the tunnel. I could see a red light glowing not that far ahead.

I crept toward it as silently as I could. I could hear the noise from the pit and the roar of the fan drawing cold air past me, as if it were pulling me toward it.

The tunnel opened up to a scaffold that reached across a great pit. Down the center of the stone shaft, a wide axle turned, spinning a fan easily twenty feet across. The scaffolding reached out to the main shaft, circled around it, and then continued on to the far side of the shaft, where enormous clockwork gears turned, providing the power for the fan.

Beneath the clockwork gears Lawrence hunched over the bomb. I placed my feet carefully, stepping silently across the scaffolding.

Unfortunately, I made the mistake of looking down. Straight through the grate beneath my feet, the fan spun, looking like a whirling blade. Beyond that the glowing fires of the forge waited. I tiptoed quickly until I reached the circle of scaffolding that surrounded the axle of the fan.

Lawrence rose, his normally slicked and neat hair flying wildly around his face, making him look like the madman he was. I caught my breath and instinctively turned my body sideways so I could conceal myself behind the spinning pipe. The headmaster watched the grate beneath his feet and didn't look up as every step brought him closer. He'd see me. Hell, he'd hear my heartbeat over the fan if he came any nearer. I had to reach the bomb. I edged around the scaffolding, careful to keep the spinning shaft between us. Once I heard him on the straight walkway back to the tunnel, I crept toward the bomb, praying the grate beneath my feet wouldn't creak or rattle.

Finally I reached the bomb and pulled it away from the back wall. My foot slipped, and I fell back against the rail, sending a loud shudder through the entire scaffold.

Lawrence turned, standing at the mouth of the tunnel and blocking my only way out.

"How did you get here?" he shouted, rushing toward me. I ran forward too, afraid of being trapped against the back wall.

As he moved left, I moved right, keeping the axle between us. After taking a large step, he hesitated, then shifted back to protect the scaffolding that led to the tunnel out.

"I won't let you destroy the Foundry," I shouted over the noise of the fan.

Lawrence let out a bitter laugh. "You can't stop the bomb now. I made sure of it."

Just as he'd said, the casing no longer had exposed gears to jam, and I could feel the slight twitch each time the spider struck the flint, but it had been encased in a solid tube. I didn't know how much time we had.

"Now, be a good girl and put the bomb down. If you run fast, you might be able to escape," he coaxed. "But time is running out."

"You won't let me escape. I know what you did." The wind from the fan swirled around me even as I smelled the sulfur from the fires below. "This won't hide murder."

"You always were a clever girl. Genius, really." He gave me a slight smile, but it never reached the murderous intent in his eyes. "I'm not surprised you found me out."

"I don't understand why," I said as I shifted my weight so I could remain light on my feet.

"I loved her!" Lawrence shouted. "I gave her everything—wealth, status—and she never loved me. She gave me a bastard instead of a son." His eyes were wild, his features gaunt and unhinged with pain.

The thought of feeling deep love for someone who didn't return the affection was terrible, lies and deception were terrible, heartbreak was terrible, but there were many things that were far worse. "That's still no cause for murder. What of Duncan? What was his crime against you? And what of the other men you would crush and suffocate with this bomb? What is their great sin?"

He lunged, and I dodged, leaping forward as he crashed into the railing. A bolt popped off and pinged as it fell. Lawrence charged at me again, but this time I lifted up and spun in a perfect pirouette past him.

Grasping for my dress, he barely caught the edge of my hacked-off skirt. It wasn't enough, and the weakened fabric ripped as he pulled. His momentum carried him back and into the rail. He crashed into it, his torso thrown way back. He spun his hands through the air, the bit of red fabric from my skirt waving like a flag.

At that same moment I jumped toward the way out. The scaffolding shifted, and Lawrence tipped backward over the edge.

I watched him fall, his arms out helplessly at his sides, a look of terror on his face. Time seemed to slow as he dropped away, the fan turning like an executioner's blade beneath him.

Shutting my eyes tight, I huddled into a ball, and I heard his body hit the fan. The axle and scaffolding shuddered, and I let go of the breath I'd been holding, even as I heard the shouts of horror from the men below.

My arms cradled the bomb against my chest. Relief flooded through me. I had it at last.

Then I realized exactly what I was holding.

Run!

I felt the ticking like the frantic beat of my heart as I rushed through the tunnels. I ran straight through.

"Meg, what happened?" Will called as we collided half-way down my own passage.

"I have the bomb. Go!" I shouted at him. He wasted no time, and he charged forward. David met us at the junction. He didn't even ask as we all ran toward the speck of light at the end of the very narrow tunnel.

I burst out into the control room and continued on into the halls without stopping.

"Lawrence?" David asked.

"Dead. Fell into the fan. How do we rid ourselves of this thing?"

"We'll disarm it like last time," Will said. "We just need to find wire."

"We can't. He tampered with it." I held the bomb out away from my body, not wanting to touch it any longer but not wanting to put it down, either. "Can we use the hauler to get it into the lake?"

Will shook his head. "We couldn't launch the hauler in time. We need to throw it over the ramparts."

David let out a panicked laugh. "Fine plan. I suppose you keep a catapult lying around."

"We don't have a catapult," Will answered, "but we do have a trebuchet. It's in the storeroom. Hurry."

"They have a trebuchet in the storeroom," David said under his breath as we rushed down a spiral stair.

Will didn't bother to look back as he found his way through the tunnels like a hound on a hare. "We have it for projectile experiments to test the armor on certain Amusements. Cannon fire tends to make the villagers nervous." Will turned a corner.

"Admit it, you like to fling rocks into the lake." David matched Will stride for stride. Will just shrugged.

As we ran through the corridors, other Foundry workers joined ranks. Lawrence's body falling into the pit had stirred them up like wasps from a nest. Will did his best to explain what had happened as a large crowd formed at a set of huge doors. I tried to ignore the blood splattered across some of their faces.

"Get them open," Will called, and the Scots fell upon the doors.

I nearly dropped the bomb.

Inside the enormous storeroom various parts and pieces of Amusements had been carefully organized and stacked from the floor to the ceiling. To the left, in a disturbingly gruesome display, disembodied automaton parts lay in a pile, like a horrid mass grave, while gears and armatures, large curving articulated plates, and even a severed dragon head filled the rest of the room. At first I had wondered why they had a trebuchet. Now I marveled at the fact that they didn't have a catapult. It seemed like every other earthly invention could be found in this room.

"We need the trebuchet!" Will shouted. The Scots descended and removed the piles of other scraps from the large siege weapon. It only took them moments to free it from the rest of the parts and push it out into the hall.

The Foundry men shouted and surged together as they rolled the weapon down the hall and onto a large platform surrounded by moving gears.

"Meg, come on." Will offered me a hand as a crush of

people climbed up onto the trebuchet. I perched on the frame next to the wheel, clinging to the bomb that still ticked steadily in my arms.

It could go off at any moment.

I tried not to think about it, but with each click I imagined the bomb exploding, ripping through my body and destroying everyone around me.

Time was our enemy, as it slipped away.

The platform we were on shuddered and groaned as the gears surrounding us turned, lifting us up toward the ceiling. I looked up, only to see the iron underside of the ceiling split and rise up, exposing the midmorning sun.

We rose out of the ground and came to a stop, perched on a hill in the central bailey of the castle, with the tower to our left and the ruins of the main structures of the castle and great hall ahead of us. Beyond that the placid blue waters of the lake stretched on for miles.

David shielded his eyes as he looked out at the water, but the Scots wasted no time. They climbed onto the trebuchet and quickly extended and locked the arm. Two men scrambled up the length of the arm and then hung off, tipping the lever to the ground as the counterweight bucket rose into the air. They set the trigger.

I handed off the bomb to a man in a green tartan, and he fixed it easily into the sling.

Something was wrong.

"There's no counterweight," I shouted. "It won't fire."

"You there, stones!" one of the Scots shouted, and a group of them charged down the hill toward the ruins of the tower. It would take all day to fill the bucket with rocks. We didn't have the time.

Perfect. We found ourselves atop a hill with a siege weapon that couldn't fire. I glanced around at the men. It didn't matter how strong they were, they'd never carry enough rocks in time.

"Run!" David shouted.

We needed mass.

Mass.

"No!" I screamed. Everyone turned to look at me. "Into the counterweight," I shouted. "All of you. As many as will fit. Hurry!"

"Bloody brilliant," Will said as he scrambled up the framework for the trebuchet and jumped into the counterweight bucket. David followed, and Will offered him a hand in.

Soon the rest of the horde joined them, climbing over the

frame and pulling themselves into the crowded bucket. Several of them who couldn't fit within the bucket clung to the front and back.

"Now, Meg!" Will shouted. I threw myself against the triggering mechanism and then stumbled backward as the counterweight dropped. The men in the counterweight shouted a Highland war cry as they swung down and beneath the belly of the machine, and the long arm flung the bomb high into the air and over the lake.

I held my breath as I lost sight of it over the water.

My heart beat.

Again.

Boom!

I felt the force of the blast like a blow to my chest, and my ears stung from the sound. I covered them but didn't turn away as an enormous plume of water launched into the air.

Tears gathered in my eyes as I listened to the water splattering back down onto the surface of the lake.

The shouts and cheers of the Foundry men drowned out the ringing in my ears. Overwhelmed, I stumbled on the edge of the platform, but Will caught me, held me close to his chest, and swung me around as the Foundry men slapped at us, still cheering.

David remained at the edge of the group, his arms crossed as he gave me a regal nod. I returned the gesture. I never would have made it without him, and for that I'd always be grateful.

"Bloody well done, lass!" Malcolm shouted, slapping me so hard on the back, I lost my breath. "We'll never use stones again."

"Now look what you did," Will admonished, but he smiled at me. All the shadow of doubt had left his eyes. He was safe, and alive. Nothing could have meant more to me.

CHAPTER THIRTY-THREE

SEVERAL WEEKS LATER, AFTER THE CUTS AND BRUISES had healed, even the deep one at the base of my thumb, and some of the endless questions about what had happened had begun to abate, I entered the ballroom of Chadwick manor for the Automaton Ball.

The ballroom glittered with lights and gaiety. Large sprays of flowers adorned the tables and the walls. In the corner musicians played as the Amusementists danced. I walked over to the musicians for a closer look, and they stared back at me in their powdered wigs and eighteenth-century costumes. Of course, "stared" wasn't really the correct word, since every single one of the musicians had a smooth featureless face that reflected my own image back at me.

The first time I had set foot in this house, I had been in rags and in hiding in the servants' quarters below stairs. The entire house had been deserted. Now I looked around at the crowded ballroom filled with light and laughter, and at my own reflection.

I barely recognized myself.

The fabric of my ball gown hardly needed adorning. It was a delicate floral paisley pattern in cream over pale blue that looked like it belonged in a royal tapestry. A frothy collar of glittering glass beads and lace swept across my chest, meeting in lovely blue-and-cream folds of bows that hung off my bare shoulders like the petals of an iris.

Around my neck I wore the clockwork key, polished to a dazzling silver. In that moment I felt like something more than a simple shopkeeper, even more than an apprentice.

I turned around and noticed the Duke of Chadwick coming toward me. His eye patch was gone, and while his injured eye still squinted just slightly, he looked as handsome and well as I had ever seen him.

"Meg, so good to see you." Oliver greeted me with his new bride on his arm. Lucinda smiled warmly.

"You look stunning," she offered, taking my hands.

I turned to Oliver. "Congratulations, Headmaster." It seemed all the wounds that Lawrence had inflicted were slowly healing, and I couldn't be happier for the both of them, though I wondered what had become of Samuel. No one had seen either him or his mother since the incident at the Foundry.

"Have you heard any news on the ship?" I asked. For the last few weeks Oliver had been using his connections to try to help me find the ship that the man in the clockwork mask had escaped upon.

"I'm sorry. My men traced its last known route to France, but there's been no sign of it since." He placed a hand on my arm and gave me a gentle squeeze. "Don't worry, Meg. We'll save your grandfather."

I sighed. I wanted to believe him, but I feared I'd be too late.

"Meg!" Peter trotted up to us, then realized who I was talking to and reverently bowed his head in apology. "Excuse me, Headmaster. We're almost ready for the first dance."

"Of course," Oliver said, laughing at us as Peter dragged me to the center of the ballroom. My friends were standing back in a small group, looking pleased with themselves. I greeted them warmly, kissing each of their cheeks, though Michael blushed so furiously, he looked like he'd suddenly taken fever. Manoj looked particularly fetching in his native clothing as he gave me a short bow of his head in appreciation. Noah stood close to Peter and leaned over to say something near his ear. They were the finest friends I could imagine, and my heart felt full to bursting with pride for what we had done.

Eve was flawless. From her powdered wig to the ornate cream-colored dress trimmed with gold and pearls, she looked like she could have stepped off the top of the music box and into the court of Louis XIV. She had her arms cast perfectly around David's automaton, and the gilded couple waited, frozen in time, for the music to start.

Around the ballroom eight other automaton couples also anticipated the music as they stood in various poses. One pair bowed to one another, the woman's arm and fan extended out elegantly behind her as she held a dainty finger to her chin. Another couple looked as if the man had some work to do to win the heart of the reluctant lady. She seemed poised to walk away from him. Each had an individual personality, and I marveled at how much more my friends and I would be able to do in the future.

The automatons remained still, as if time had stopped for the machines but continued on for the rest of us mortals. The Amusementists danced around them, occasionally pausing to marvel at their craftsmanship.

As the human dancers swirled past, I turned and caught sight of David slowly crossing the ballroom.

He made a fine figure. He looked every bit the cultured aristocrat and perfectly at home among the finery and frivolity of the ball. While his bearing was cool and regal as he approached, his gaze was not, and I knew the mask that he liked to keep would never completely conceal him from me again.

"Attention, attention!" Leader Octavian stood on a box to see over the rail as he called down from the balcony. He had attempted to tame his hair, but it seemed to be rebelling. His face was alight with merriment. "It is time for the challenge to begin."

The crowd broke out in applause as David took his place beside me. We both looked up at the balcony without a word.

"First, a special award of merit goes to Apprentice Margaret and Apprentice David for uncovering a most sinister plot and thwarting inconceivable disaster." He paused as the swell of applause rose. I felt my cheeks grow warm as I stood in shock. He had said my name the way he would any other apprentice.

I blinked, fighting the thrill of emotion. I couldn't afford it now. Only one thing tempered the sheer joy of the moment. No one had believed us until it had been nearly too late. I supposed if they wanted to try to alleviate their guilt in the matter, I could be gracious about it. After all, they had given Uncle Albrecht his key back, and they had given me my name.

"It is with a heavy heart that we mourn the loss of Argus MacTavish and the young Foundry worker Duncan MacBain. Thankfully, Magnus Gordon has agreed to take charge of the Foundry, so our long and prosperous association may continue." Everyone in the ballroom fell appropriately somber, but I had to fight off a chill. I rubbed my hands together. Every so often they still felt as if they held the stain of Duncan's blood. I felt horrible for Duncan's death, and even more horrible that in the aftermath I couldn't stop myself for being very thankful it hadn't been Will's blood on my hands. It so easily could have been.

A murmur rose in the ballroom as a large group of men

in kilts came forward from beneath the balcony. I strained to see if Will was among them.

"It is with our grateful thanks to the Foundry that we present this ball, a celebration of beauty after such dark times. *Ex scientia pulchritudo.*" Octavian clapped his hands, and the crowd backed off the dance floor, leaving David and me alone with our creations.

We took our places at the backs of our automatons, and my hand shook as I rested my finger on the switch. The conductor of the mechanical orchestra tapped his baton on the stand.

"Three and one," David counted, and we flipped our switches in perfect time with the downbeat. Then both of us quickly backed away, allowing our inventions to shine.

The automatons trembled, as if nervous to be in one another's arms, but slowly they took a step, then another. It was working. They danced together flawlessly, spinning around the floor as if they were alive. Soon other automaton couples began to dance, until the ballroom became a mesmerizing swirl of elegance and color.

I listened to the voices of the Amusementists around me. They were filled with wonder and pride. Uncle Albrecht clapped wildly for us in the corner, while Mary Thornby looked as if she'd just swallowed a newt. I smiled sweetly at her, and her mother scowled and ushered her away.

As the song faded, each of the automatons ended the waltz in a bow, then stood, poised to begin again, should the orchestra play their song.

The Amusementists broke out in loud cheers and congratulations. Several of the older members of the Order offered me their praise as the music died away.

I felt humbled by it, and not at all worthy of it. I couldn't have done it without the help of my friends. Working with them and making peace with David had been great achievements, but nothing had been greater than saving Will's life and knowing that one day we would be together.

David met me on the edge of the dance floor and gave me a courtly bow. "Apprentice Margaret, would you do me the honor of this dance?"

I couldn't say no. Instead I placed my hand in his. He led me onto the floor, and as the orchestra began once more, his other hand slid around my waist. The tightness of my corset enhanced the feel of his palm on my side as we began to turn in dizzying circles around our automatons.

David brought his cheek close to mine. "To a job well done," he whispered into my ear.

I leaned back and looked at him. His eyes seemed warmer than they had been. "Indeed."

We danced, and I allowed myself to enjoy the moment. It was only a moment, after all.

As the music began to fade, his gaze dipped to my lips. "I will win you, Meg."

The music stopped, and I pulled away from him. "Oh, David," I sighed. That was just the problem.

When I tried to leave him, he held my hand long enough to place a possessive kiss on the back of it. I turned, leaving him on the glittering dance floor, and retreated to the doors open to the gardens.

Will stood there. The breeze caught in the curling wisps of his hair. His gaze seemed to drink me in, but he didn't say a word. His lips curled in the slightest of smiles.

He looked quite dashing in his black velvet doublet and kilt, like a grand Scottish lord, or at least a brigand dressed as one. It was hard to look at the strength in him, the new confidence, and see the poor stable hand who had hidden with me in the servants' quarters of this very house.

"Care to test your wits against the labyrinth?" he asked, his smile widening as he tilted his head toward the tiny hedge maze that didn't reach higher than one's knee.

I laughed. "I'm so glad you're here."

"I wouldn't be if it weren't for you." He looked down at his feet, then back up to meet my eyes. "You're beautiful."

I knew I blushed. I could feel the tingling in my cheeks as I reached into the new pocket I had sewn into the billowing folds of my skirt.

"You sewed a pocket into a ball gown?" I could hear the laughter in Will's voice and feel the warmth in his eyes.

"Of course. They're frightfully useful. I made you this." I opened my hands and revealed the little frog I had finally perfected.

Will shook his head in mirth as he reached for it. At the last moment it sprang to him, and he caught it against his chest. He touched it gently on the head, then tucked it lovingly into his sporran. "I'll treasure it."

A heady thrumming began in my body, a visceral awareness of who he was and all that we'd done together. I placed my hand gently on his shoulder, and he tenderly gathered my other hand in his.

We swayed together to the music, our foreheads touching like the sweetest kiss. It was all the dance I needed.

"I don't understand why you would choose this, when

you could have all that that world offers," he whispered.

"You don't need to understand." I lifted my chin to look at him. "Just trust in me."

"I love you, Meg. To the end of my days, I swear it." He gathered my hand and placed it over his heart.

"That is all I need," I said as we danced.

ACKNOWLEDGMENTS

WRITING BOOKS MIGHT BE A SOLITARY EFFORT, BUT I could not do this as a career without the help and support of so many wonderful people. I'd like to thank my agent, Laura Bradford, for always having a cool and level head no matter what. I give all my heartfelt thanks and good wishes to Anica Mrose Rissi and Courtney Sanks, who helped me so much along the way but now have moved on to new and exciting paths in their careers. I am so glad to have met and worked with my new editor, Liesa Abrams, and I'm very thankful she has taken up the reins and shown such support and enthusiasm for this series. I'd also like to thank Michael Strother for being the lynchpin that seems to hold it all together. Special thanks also go out to my critique partner, Angie Fox, and my beta readers, Julie and Katie Wallace, for their constant encouragement and support.

The covers of these books have been amazing, and I'm so proud and honored to have the talent of Angela Goddard, Regina Flath, and the rest of the Simon & Schuster art department working so hard on such remarkable works of art, especially the sculptor who has created the mechanical creatures, Matthew Lentini.

More than anything, I'd like to thank my new fans and all the bloggers and reviewers who have taken time to read my books and spread the word about them. I'm so grateful to all of you. I couldn't do this without you.

And finally, I'd like to thank my family. Thank you for your patience. Thank you for your love. And thank you for making my life so joyful.